Eye of the Beholder

Nebraska Series, Volume 4

Ruth Ann Nordin

Published by Ruth Ann Nordin, 2023.

Chapter One

Maine
April 1874

Mary Peters reread the ad in the newspaper. Ads asking for a wife were fairly common, but this particular ad caught her eye for a variety of reasons. One, the man who wrote it seemed straightforward, a quality she admired because she didn't trust people who uttered flowery language which could be deceptive. Two, the man was realistic about his expectations. A farmer would benefit most from a woman who could handle the harsher elements of living on a farm. Three, the part boldly stating he expected her to bear him children told her that this was not a man who minced words. He knew exactly what he wanted and sought it. Such a man might not be overly concerned with how a woman looked.

She glanced at her reflection in the store window. She often passed the dress shop on her way to the restaurant where she helped Mrs. Jones cook meals for her hungry patrons. Her plain face with an unusually big nose that made her eyes and thin lips look smaller than they actually were didn't draw any interest from men. Her pale smooth skin would have been her best feature had it not been for the freckles that dotted her cheeks and nose. Her frizzy mousy brown long hair that she unsuccessfully tried to tame with her brush was mercifully forced under a bonnet.

Plain Mary Peters. She heard the term used often enough by her family and friends. Certain that they meant no harm in the adjective used to describe her, she didn't take offense to it. Besides, she was plain. Considering that they could call her ugly, plain was actually a kind word.

Biting her lower lip, she turned her attention back to the ad. Unlike other men requesting women who were pretty, this one simply required hard work, dependability and willingness to bear him children. She wasn't afraid of any of those things. Pretty, she couldn't give him, but the others she easily could. Though she never spent a single day on a farm, she was willing to learn what she needed to do to help him. Her mother had borne her father twelve children, so she was sure that she wouldn't have any problems with getting in the family way.

She'd send him a letter, and if he wished to marry her, she'd go to him. Fear of the unknown did not hold her back. She welcomed the adventure of leaving her old world behind for a new one. A fresh start might even be a welcome relief after living in her sisters' shadows all of her life. Her sisters were beautiful. They found husbands well before they turned eighteen. She recalled the wedding of her closest sister who was only two years her senior:

Grace had just turned sixteen, and she was thrilled to marry her childhood sweetheart. Before the wedding, Mary decorated Grace's silky brown hair with pink rose petals. Her sister wore a long flowing white gown trimmed with lace, which was a labor of love that Mary spent the past two months creating. Mary wanted her favorite sister to look her best during the ceremony, for it was a day Grace had eagerly planned with her from the moment Calvin proposed.

While their other sisters decorated the church, they had the moment to themselves in the small church room to the side of the sanctuary.

"You are beautiful," Mary smiled as she glanced at her older sister.

"I feel beautiful," she confessed as she looked at her reflection in the mirror. "That's what love does to a woman, Mary. When Calvin looks at me, it's as if I can see myself through his eyes, and I know when he sees me, he sees the most beautiful woman he ever laid eyes on."

That's because you are pleasing to gaze upon. Grace wasn't plain. She didn't have to deal with the snickers from the young men when they thought she was out of hearing range. Men practically worshiped the ground Grace walked on.

"Someday, you'll know what I'm talking about," Grace told her. She reached out and took Mary's hand just as Mary was ready to put another petal in her hair. "Love is the most wonderful feeling in the world. Your time will come."

Mary smiled, gently pulled her hand away and returned to her work. She knew better than to hope to be beautiful in the eyes of a man. She caught sight of the contrast between her and her sister and the difference was like looking at night and day. If she married at all, it would be a miracle.

The memory ebbed from her consciousness as Mary contemplated her situation. Grace and Calvin moved to New Jersey where he got a good paying job, and the departure of her closest sibling left a hole in her heart. As much as she loved her other sisters and brothers, Grace's presence had been the one reason she lingered on in Maine as long as she did. She heard of men out west seeking wives and had been tempted to go to one, but she couldn't bear to be apart from her sister. It seemed that fate dictated the separation anyway, leaving her free to pursue her own dreams for the first time in her life.

Slipping the ad into her pocket, she hastened to the restaurant so she could start her work on time.

AS SOON AS MARY ARRIVED home from work, she hung her hat on the hat rack in the entryway and noted that her parents occupied the parlor. Her father sat in his favorite blue chair, reading another book, while her mother worked on her knitting. She often knitted clothes for her thirty-one grandchildren. The house remained silent, as was often the case since her siblings left to marry and have families of their own.

Taking a deep breath, she stepped into the room, her shoes seeming to echo on the hardwood floors, though the pounding in her heart distracted her from the sound.

They looked at her as she shifted from one foot to the other in front of them.

"Mary, is something on your mind?" Her father closed his book and waited for her to speak.

It was now or never. After handing him the ad, she braced herself so she could speak before she lost her nerve. "Today I made an important decision. I am going to answer one of those ads asking for a wife. I found one that is of particular interest from a farmer in Nebraska, and from the sound of it, I believe he and I will make a good match."

Her father read the ad, handed it to her mother, and stared at Mary as if she suddenly grew a second head. "You intend to marry a stranger?"

She sat on the edge of the wooden chair, close to the open window. Since she broke into a sweat under their intense stares, she was grateful for the breeze drifting into the small room.

Her mother loudly sighed and patted her graying brown hair that was neatly tied back into a bun. "Honey," she began, "are you sure this is a wise idea?"

Her father nodded his approval at her mother's question. His frown deepened the wrinkles around his gray eyebrows.

Mary licked her lips nervously. "I thought you might be relieved," she softly admitted, her heart racing with a sense of urgency she wasn't familiar with. All of her life, she never displeased them.

"As it is, none of the men here will marry me, and I know you worry about what will happen to me once you die."

"Mary, this man could be older than your father," her mother said.

"I plan to write him a letter asking him his age. If he responds, then I'll know if he's worth marrying. Besides, I would like to see the prairie. I heard it's beautiful."

Her father made a shooing motion with his hand. "We have beautiful days in Maine. Every fall is witness to that fact when the leaves change into spectacular colors. I defy Nebraska to hold a candle to this state."

"I'm nineteen. No man has come by to court me, nor do I perceive that one will if I stay here. I don't want to be a spinster. I want to get married and have children."

"But what about love?" her mother asked.

"Love is for beautiful women, Mother. I understand why men ignore me. The man posting this ad needs a wife. This is my best chance. I don't expect him to love me. I just want someone who can provide for me and my children."

"Still, an arrangement to marry someone you never met may not be the best avenue to pursue," her mother countered as she gave the ad back to her daughter.

Taking a deep breath, she stood up, clutching the ad in her hand. "I'm sorry but I am old enough to make these decisions without your approval." The knot in her stomach tightened.

"Let your mother and I discuss it and then we'll talk to you."

Her father's dismissal angered her but she kept silent as she strode out of the room. Her hands trembled as she climbed the narrow wooden staircase to her small bedroom that had once belonged to her and Grace. The room happened to be above the parlor and since the window was open, she could hear her parents as they talked. She sat on her springy thin mattress and stared at the bare white wall so she could detect their voices over the chatter from people as they walked past the house.

"What if the man who wrote that ad is unsavory?" her mother asked her father. "He could be a criminal or abusive."

A long pause followed before her father spoke. "Or he could be a young man who wants a wife to help him with his farm."

"But how can we know?"

"We can't, but we do know Mary. She has always been a practical and smart girl. Though she has a heart of gold, men rarely look beyond appearances. You know how hard we've tried to find her someone, but no one will talk to her long enough to get to know her."

"Surely, they'll grow out of that," her mother said. "As men mature, they learn the value of a good woman. Looks do fade."

"And how old do these men have to be when they realize this? Would you have her marry someone as old as I am?"

"Nebraska is far from here. We'll probably never see her again. We'll be lucky if she writes."

"Men out west who are in need of wives might be the answer to our prayers. We need to think of what's best for her. Once this man gets to know her, he will be glad she went to him."

"First we lose Grace and now Mary." Mary could tell by the way her mother's voice choked that she was crying.

"Now Abby, do you really want the poor girl to spend her life alone because we were too selfish to let her go?"

Her mother's sobs increased. "She may be nineteen but she'll always be a baby to me."

"The youngest child is usually the hardest to let go." His footsteps echoed on the floor as he approached his wife. He most likely knelt in front of her and rested his hand on her knee, as Mary had often seen him do when he wished to comfort her. "She wants to have babies of her own. Her brothers and sisters have their families. Isn't it her turn?"

Seconds spanned to minutes that seemed to drag for what seemed like an hour before her mother finally relented.

MARY EXPERIENCED A mixture of feelings as she wrote her response to the ad. Anticipation, hope and curiosity. Surprisingly, doubt was not a part of her swirling emotions. Deep down, she felt that this was the best course of action for her to pursue.

She didn't know the best approach to answering a man she never met, so she decided to stick with the basics.

Dear Neil Craftsman,

My name is Mary Peters, and I am a nineteen year old woman who has never married. Though I grew up in town, I am willing to adapt to farm living. I am competent in cooking and sewing, so I can make you good meals and clothes. I have helped the midwife deliver babies, so I can assist you with the birth of your animals. I am not afraid of hard work, and you will find me most dependable. I also come from a family of six brothers and five sisters, so I am confident your request for children will be fulfilled as well. May I ask your age? If you wish to respond, please write to PO Box 54.

Sincerely,

Mary Peters

The next day, she left the house to send the letter. Her heart raced with a sudden wave of fear that he would tell her not to come. The walk to the post office seemed to be quicker than usual, and she stood in front of the small building, wondering if it might be better to not answer the ad. Rejection from men who saw her happened often, but what if he didn't like something in her personality? But how much could he learn from her in a short letter?

And what if he asked her to marry him? Her family would miss her. She wouldn't share Christmas with them anymore. She glanced at the envelope in her shaking hands. A raindrop fell on the white paper. Wiping the wet spot off the envelope, she glanced at the cloudy sky. She should have brought an umbrella. Apparently, she wasn't thinking straight if she neglected to note the threatening storm.

Her mother had offered to go with her, but she wanted to do this by herself in case she chickened out at the last minute. She could easily tell her parents she sent the letter and never got a response. No one would be the wiser and she could continue to live her life as she had up to that point. Wouldn't it be better to dream that he said yes if she sent it rather than find a letter telling her not to come?

Behind her, a child called out to her mother. She recognized Bertha Lindsey with her two-year-old daughter. Bertha stopped in front of the bakery a couple of buildings down from the post office. Looking up and seeing Mary, she waved. The daughter waved as well.

Mary smiled, nodded and watched them as they entered the store. Taking a deep breath, she turned her attention back to the letter. If she didn't send this, she might never be like Bertha. She had a husband, a child and another child on the way. Mary knew she didn't need to fool herself into thinking Neil Craftsman would take one look at her and fall in love with her the way the men had fallen in love with her sisters and Bertha. But he might be happy to have her assistance on the farm, and perhaps, given time, he might be content with her.

I won't know unless I try.

The decision made, she went inside the post office to send her letter.

A MONTH PASSED AND Mary fluctuated between running to the post office and dragging her feet. What if he accepted? What if he declined? Her stomach was a tangled mess, though she managed to hide this fact from her family and friends. Then, on a Tuesday, his response came.

She didn't dare open the letter in public. Instead, she hurried home, raced up the stairs and shut her bedroom door behind her so she could have some privacy. Standing in the middle of the room, she took a deep breath to settle her nerves. This was it. Her future hinged on the contents in a single envelope. *No, that's not true. If he says no, I can answer another ad. If only other men weren't so concerned with a woman's looks.*

She carefully opened the envelope and unfolded the paper. Some money and a train ticket fell to the floor. Startled, she bent to pick the items up. As she did so, it occurred to her that his answer was yes. Her heart thumped loudly in her ears while she eagerly read the letter's contents.

Mary,

I am thirty and grow wheat. I also manage a sizeable number of cattle. You sound like a woman who will suit me. Enclosed are the ticket for your trip to Nebraska and some money for anything you may need to buy for living here.

Neil Craftsman

Thrilled, she turned toward her bedroom door. The dollar bill stuck to her shoe reminded her that she needed to put the ticket and money in a safe place. She shoved them under her mattress before she flew down the steps.

"Mary, what's gotten into you?" her mother called from the kitchen. The woman looked startled as Mary entered the room, her face flushed. "Why, I've never seen you so worked up over anything before. From the way you're smiling, I take that it's good news?"

"It is!" Mary thrust the letter in her direction. "He said yes. I'll be leaving in a week."

Her mother accepted the piece of paper and read it.

Mary gathered the ingredients to help her mother with the pot roast she planned to make for dinner. "He even sent me a train ticket and some money for anything I may need to buy before I leave." She set the armful of potatoes, celery and carrots on the counter before she reached for the seasonings. "I can't think of anything to buy. I already have everything I need. I'm not even sure what farm wives need." She washed the vegetables. "I wonder what life will be like out there. I'll have to do some research so I know what to expect."

Realizing that she was rambling, which she rarely did, she stopped so her mother could speak if she wished. Her smile faltered when she saw that her mother kept her eyes on the letter, her mouth in a firm line.

Feeling awkward, she put on her apron. She adjusted her bun and wiped her hands on the apron when she noticed they were clammy. Afraid to speak, for she suddenly realized that she didn't want to know what her mother thought, she began cutting the vegetables.

The early afternoon sunlight poured through the window, giving her adequate lighting for her task, but the heat coming from the oven caused sweat to cover her brow. The lack of a breeze blowing into the kitchen didn't help matters nor did the heat rising in her face from the knowledge that her mother wasn't pleased.

"So, you will leave next Thursday." Her mother's words sounded distant.

Unsure of what to say, Mary spent the next five minutes adding slices of vegetables to the roast her mother settled into the deep baking dish.

Mary licked her lips before asking, "Is there anything you wish to advise me on? I do wish to be a good wife for him."

The older woman sighed as she seasoned the meat. "Mary, are you sure you want to do this?"

"Yes. Father's right. I do want to get married and have children."

After what seemed like an eternity, she said, "It's natural that you should feel that way. Nevertheless, since this arrangement is done without you having met him first, we should buy you a return ticket." She covered the pot roast and vegetables with a lid and placed the dish into the oven. Taking a deep breath, she asked, "May I see the ticket? I will buy a return ticket for you on the day you will arrive in Omaha. Then you won't have to spend the night there."

Timidly fingering the string on her apron, she forced her eyes on the woman staring expectantly at her. "You don't think this will work?" The question barely came out as a whisper.

"We must be practical about this, Mary." The woman's words were firm, her posture resolute and imposing in the small room.

Her joy deflated, she stiffly nodded and went to get the ticket.

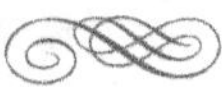

ON THE DAY SHE LEFT, her family gathered to see her off. She hesitated in knowing how to say good-bye. Shifting from one foot to the other, she waited for the conductor to call for passengers to board the train.

"Well, this is it," her father said in a solemn tone. "Be careful when you're on the train. Don't talk to men you don't know unless it's the conductor. As for Mr. Craftsman, trust your instinct."

"Your father is right," her mother quickly inserted. "If he seems like a bad man, you come right back."

Not wishing to argue, she nodded her agreement. However, she made up her mind, and she decided that should Neil look at her and find her unsuitable for him, she would remain in Omaha and find employment. Women could work as teachers or governesses, and she did have experience cooking in a restaurant. Options were available should marriage fail to be in her future.

"All aboard!" The conductor's voice boomed through the small one room station.

"It's time for me to go." She forced a smile, quickly blinking back her tears. Her family didn't like it when she cried.

"You will write, won't you?" her mother asked.

"Yes. I promise." She clenched her hands together, suddenly aware that she was nervous.

Clearing his throat, her father held out his hand to her.

Surprised, since he didn't make it a habit of touching her, she shook it.

Her mother also shook her hand. "Take care of yourself."

"I will. And thank you both, for everything." Her voice shook so she refrained from saying anything else.

"All aboard! We depart in two minutes," the conductor called.

"Have a good trip," her brother said.

The others voiced their well wishes before she got on the train.

Showing the conductor her ticket, she wiped her tears on her crisp handkerchief. She found her seat, noting the one next to hers was empty. A new life. She could do this. Looking out the window, she gave one last smile to her parents who had followed her to the platform. The train pulled out of the station, and despite the sorrow of leaving her family, her heart leapt with a sense of adventure.

Chapter Two

Omaha, Nebraska
June 1874

Dave Larson pulled the brake on his wagon and tied the two geldings' reins to his seat. He hopped down to the ground, his brown boots hitting the dirt road that served as one of the main streets in Omaha. Taking off his brown hat, he used his sleeve to wipe the sweat from his forehead. He ruffled his dark blond hair and set the hat back on his head. The sun beat down on him, causing his gray eyes to squint. His light blue shirt and brown pants felt sticky as sweat clung to his body.

He debated entering the mercantile but decided to check the post office first. After verifying nothing important came, he made his way past several people, exchanging the usual pleasantries on the way to the mercantile. He didn't care to waste time dealing with anything but purchasing the food that would give him something doable to eat for the next month. Though he didn't live far from town, he preferred to keep his visits to at least once a month. He had a farm to manage and didn't like missing his work.

He stepped into the mercantile and nodded at Ralph Lindon who owned the place.

"Good to see you, Larson." The fifty-year-old thin man with a head full of shaggy white hair and glasses smiled. "What brings you into town today?"

"I have a minor emergency. I ran out of food."

"Again?"

He grinned ruefully. "I know. When will I ever get organized?"

"Should I gather your usual items for you?"

"No. I'll just run through the store and throw whatever I see into the basket."

He chuckled. "You're a hopeless cause, Larson."

Dave shrugged and began his haphazard quest for food.

Neil Craftsman entered the store. "I have to buy a ring for my bride!"

Dave dumbly stared at his neighbor who nodded a quick greeting in his direction as he strode over to the counter next to the cash register where Ralph stood.

"Is she the woman who answered your ad?" Ralph asked.

"Yes. She comes from Maine," Neil replied.

Dave still couldn't believe it. Neil posted an ad for a wife? Dave didn't realize he wanted to settle down since most of the town knew he was busy trying to sow his wild oats. Dave shook his head. Perhaps the man realized that running around a whore house wasn't the most productive use of his time. It made sense that he had to send away for a wife since no self-respecting woman would marry him if she knew his past.

"So, you're going to settle down and be a family man?" Ralph inquired as he accepted the money for the ring, looking as shocked as Dave felt.

"There comes a time in a man's life when he has to take responsibility for his future," Neil replied. "I'm already thirty."

"I hope you plan to honor those wedding vows when you make them." He handed Neil the change.

"Oh, I intend to. After my father died, I realized it was time to get serious about having kids. Someone has to take over my farm when I die."

Dave watched as the grinning groom exited the store. Glancing at Ralph, he raised an eyebrow. "Do we trust him?"

"Stranger things have happened. I'll know soon enough when people bring in their news. Being a store owner, I can't help but hear what goes on in town."

"Of course, you don't add to the gossip," he teased.

Ralph's eyes widened. "I might straighten out some wrong thinking. If it's true, then it's news. If it's false, then it's gossip."

"Sure." He didn't hide his sarcasm. "I don't think I'm any more of a loss cause than you are." Chuckling under his breath, he turned back to the items on the shelves. To his dismay, he realized that he had selected the same items he usually bought. He wasn't the only one who noticed it.

"It looks like you got the usual," Ralph stated when Dave brought the basket to the counter.

Two other customers entered the store, preventing Dave from defending himself. After all, a single man could only manage so many recipes. Since Ralph quickly rung up his order so he could assist the old women with the sewing supplies, Dave was spared the older man's ribbing.

Exiting the place, he carried the two boxes full of food and settled them into the back of his wagon. With any luck, it would get him through a month, though it was due to be bland. A wife who knew how to cook would be a blessing, he thought as he recalled his mother's tasty pot roasts with fresh vegetables and fruit salad.

His stomach growled at the memory. He lost ten pounds in the seven months he spent by himself on the farm. He occasionally made it out to his parents' place to eat a good meal but not as often as he wished.

Though Neil was the last person Dave looked to for advice on anything to do to improve his life, he had to admit that a wife was probably the smartest thing a man could do for himself. He did need another set of hands at the farm so someone could share the burden with him. Not that he considered farming to be a burden, but it would be easier to get the chores done if he had a wife. He knew his next trip to Omaha would involve posting an ad in the papers back east asking for a wife. Plenty of men did it. He supposed he should too, especially since he didn't know any available women who were old enough to get married.

As he got ready to jump onto his wagon, he looked toward the station of the Union Pacific Railroad. The train was sitting on the tracks, waiting for people to either hop off or get on. He wondered briefly which of the few women disembarking could be Neil's intended from Maine.

He hesitated, his body turned to the wagon, wondering if he should satisfy his curiosity and see what type of woman answered an ad in a newspaper. Would it give him an idea of what to expect when one responded to his ad? Drumming his fingers on the side of the wagon, he happened to spot Neil who left the saloon, quickly tucking in his shirt.

He felt a rush of sorrow for the person Neil went to meet. For all his talk about a wife and settling down, Neil didn't seem willing to give up the pleasures of the flesh. Disgusted, Dave decided that she needed to be warned about who she would be marrying. He couldn't stand idly by and watch another man mistreat a woman the way Clyde had mistreated his sister.

Dave crossed the boardwalk and entered the airy room of the train station. People milled about, stretching their legs and asking directions to the nearest restaurant.

He bypassed the old women and a plump brunette with child in tow as well as a pretty woman in the striking yellow dress. None were Neil's type. For a moment, he thought the pretty blond searching the crowd would be Neil's woman, but an elderly gentleman snatched her away.

He inched his way through the crowd. He was tall enough to look over the heads of most of the men and women, but still short enough not to call too much attention to himself.

He searched the crowd, finally spotting Neil and a woman in a hunter green dress over by the newspaper stand in the corner of the room. Dave's eyes rested upon her plain appearance. He knew she didn't match up to Neil's standards, though she did have an ample bosom and nice hips.

The man running the newspaper stand looked uncomfortable, standing as far away from the couple as the stand would allow him. Trying to be as unobtrusive as possible, Dave wove through the crowd, determined to rescue her.

When he realized that Neil was unhappy, he halted by the stack of newspapers to his right. The man at the stand seemed relieved to have someone nearby. Glancing at the man, he saw the man shake his head.

"There's a fight brewing," he whispered to Dave. "I'd stay out of it if I were you."

Interested, Dave turned his attention back to the unlikely couple.

"Miss Peters," Neil began, a smile plastered on his face, "you are not what I expected."

The woman paused for a moment as if considering her words with great care. "Your ad asked for a hardworking and dependable woman who can provide you with children. I assure you that I'm not afraid of work, and I will prove myself loyal. As for children, my mother has borne my father twelve of them, myself included. I am able to do what you ask. I have in no way misled you."

"When I wrote that ad, I did not expect...I wanted...I don't doubt that you can work hard and provide me with many children. But..."

Dave knew Neil well enough to realize the man was flabbergasted. His hands waved about him and his mouth moved but no sound came out. The woman looked no more pleased than Neil, although she remained composed. There was a certain dignity in the straightness of her back and the tilt of her head. She had inner strength that saw her through the toughest of circumstances. The thought impressed Dave.

"But?" She waited for Neil to finish his sentence. When he didn't speak, she said, "But you had a different kind of woman in mind?"

Neil blinked and shook his head. "I couldn't get drunk enough to get you with child!"

Dave winced at the cruelty of the remark. Even if Miss Peters was the ugliest woman alive, no one deserved that. He expected the woman to burst into tears, but she did not.

She stood before Neil and in a very calm voice said, "Then I surmise that this arrangement won't work."

"You're right it won't," Neil snapped.

Dave knew it irked the man to no end that she declared it before he did.

"Very well. I won't trouble you any further, and you may have your money back." She handed him the bills that had been neatly folded in her purse. "I don't wish to have anything from you. The trip here is enough. Thank you, Mr. Craftsman."

Neil grabbed the money with a huff and stomped away, cussing under his breath about women. "Next time I'll request a pretty wife," he grumbled as he passed Dave, not seeming to notice him. He plopped his hat onto his head and stormed out of the building.

Dave found this particular woman to be intriguing. She maintained a quiet dignity in the midst of adversity. Such a woman should not be overlooked. He stepped around the stand and got his first good look at her. She didn't possess the classic beauty most men sought, but she wasn't ugly like Neil claimed.

She sat on the bench, hands folded in her lap, head slightly bowed. She looked as if she waited for someone to pick her up, instead of enduring a torrid rejection. The only indication that Neil had disturbed her was the fingernails digging into the palms of her hands. He detected freckles on the bridge of her big nose and her rosy cheeks, which he found charming. As he neared, she glanced up at him, her aqua colored eyes wet with unshed tears. She blinked a few times, clearing them.

He liked her eyes. They were a lovely color.

Her fingers relaxed, her palms marked by tiny red crescents. "Am I in your way?"

He smiled and shook his head. "No, ma'am. Considering the fact that you're sitting on a bench that's stuck in a corner, you aren't in anyone's way."

She looked surprised and he wondered if she had ever received a kind word from the world of men. He suspected she was eighteen or maybe a little older, and upon further inspection, he noted a sweet look about her.

"Oh. Then you wish to sit?" She quickly stood and moved away from the bench. "I can find somewhere else to go. I should get a newspaper anyway."

"I can buy one for you and bring it here."

"Why would you do that?"

"Why not? You're a stranger in this community and it would only be fitting if someone welcomed you to town. I notice that Neil Craftsman did a lousy job of it."

She sighed and smoothed her hands on her dark green dress which matched her bonnet. "Oh. You overheard?" Her cheeks grew red as she stared at the beige travel bag by her feet.

"I overheard Neil giving up a decent woman. You know, I couldn't help but be impressed with how well you handled yourself."

She shrugged. "I figured, in the long run, he did me a favor."

"He did you a bigger favor than you realize. I guarantee you're much better off without him." Now that marrying the man wouldn't happen, he no longer felt the need to warn her about his loose morals.

Shifting from one foot to the other, she returned his gaze and said, "I should get a paper."

"May I buy it for you?" he asked.

She hesitated for a moment before digging a coin out of her purse. "This should cover the cost."

She was generous. He held up his hand in protest. "That's not necessary. After what you went through, it would be my pleasure to show you that one person in Omaha knows how to welcome a lady. I'll be back faster than you can say Dave Larson."

Her eyebrows furrowed but he left before she could say anything. He nodded a greeting to several people who strolled through the station until he reached the man selling papers at the stand.

"Felt sorry for her too?" the man asked as he took the coin.

Dave raised an eyebrow. "I was thinking more along the lines of respect and admiration. It's not every woman who can hold her own against the likes of Neil Craftsman."

Once he purchased a copy, he returned to her and handed it to her, surprised that she was still standing.

"Thank you, sir." She accepted the paper. "I should allow you the space on the bench."

"Please stay. I wish to speak to you and it'd be easier to do that if I'm sitting next to you instead of yelling at you from across the room."

A small smile turned the corners of her lips up. "I can't argue with that logic."

So she had a sense of humor. That was nice to know. She sat down and he sat beside her, careful to keep a respectful distance between them in case people talked.

"What is it you wish to discuss, Mr...?"

"My name is Dave Larson."

"Oh. I'm afraid I missed that when you told me the first time. I must be having one of those days."

In more ways than one, he thought as he recalled her conversation with Neil. When he realized she was waiting for him to continue, he cleared his throat. "I'm not graceful at this sort of thing, Miss...?"

Her eyes grew wide. "I'm sorry, Mr. Larson. My name is Mary Peters."

"Miss Peters, the truth of the matter is that while I overheard you and Neil talking, it occurred to me that you're the kind of woman who would make a man a good wife. Now, I know it's strange that we just met this way and you're likely to think I'm crazy, but you're the kind of woman I've been looking for. You're kind, strong, and generous. You told Neil you were hardworking and dependable. I'm sure you have other admirable qualities as well."

She stared at him, as if not believing her ears. Finally, she shook her head. "Surely, there are other women in town that are more to your liking."

"You'd be wrong to assume that. The women I know who are of childbearing age are already taken, too young, or a relative. I need a wife. It can be tough to keep up a farm without help. In fact, I was trying to come up with an ad asking for one."

She glanced at the paper resting in her lap. "I don't know, Mr. Larson. I really am not what you are looking for."

He realized he needed to find another way to convince her to marry him. "I'm forced to write an ad since you said no. Would you help me figure out what to say? I want to make sure I have the right woman. There's no sense in sending for her if she can't handle what I need on the farm."

"Alright. I can do that."

He searched his pockets. His cheeks grew warm. "I didn't bring anything to write with or to write on."

She picked up the paper and sorted through it. Finding a blank space on the paper, she tore it and handed it to him. "I do have a pencil you can use." She opened her purse and took it out. Giving it to him, she waited for him to begin.

He grinned at her. "You're the kind of person who'd take the shirt off her back for a fellow in need."

She blushed.

"I beg your pardon, ma'am. I didn't mean that the way it sounded. I was quoting an expression my father uses. It means that you help others out without a thought to yourself." Wishing to ease her embarrassment, he motioned to the paper in his hand. "What words do you figure will best attract a woman who won't shy away from life on a farm?"

"I've never lived on a farm. What would she have to do?"

"Obviously, I need someone to keep up my house. I don't have much time to clean, do laundry or cook. As it is, I don't eat much besides jerky."

She frowned. "A man needs a better diet than that."

"Exactly. I may be twenty-two but I burn everything I attempt to make. It's rather sad. Do I write that I want someone who can cook and clean?"

She nodded. "If you work outside all day, you'll need your energy, and you'll need a variety of foods for that."

"I do need some help with the few animals I have. Sometimes, I don't get around to milking my cow until mid-day and again past sundown. Can you imagine how uncomfortable the poor animal is during the day? It would be a big help if she'd do it for me. I don't mind showing her how to do it. I just hope she's willing to learn."

"What type of farm do you own?"

"I grow corn and beans. Besides a cow, I have a stallion, two geld-ings and a mare. The mare is due to foal in a week or two. I would like help in the delivery in case something goes wrong. Most of the time, mares deliver without assistance but you never know until the birth is done. Do you think a woman would be willing to do that?"

She shrugged. "I don't see why not. Women throughout history have helped deliver human babies into the world. I don't think an an-imal would be much different."

He appreciated her agreeability to learn new skills, even when it was clear that she had no farming experience. "Where did you come from?"

"From a small town in Maine. My father owned the grocery store, and my brothers helped him with it. My sisters married as soon as they turned sixteen or seventeen. I worked at a restaurant."

"How old are you?"

"Nineteen."

As he took another moment to examine her, he noted that her eyes had the most amazing color. At times they looked green but at the moment, he swore they were blue. She certainly had a lovely smile and straight, white teeth. Her hair was braided under her bon-net but several strands broke free, which he found charming. Her frame was certainly pleasing to behold. She had curves everywhere a woman ought to have them. He couldn't understand why someone else hadn't married her yet, but their loss was his gain, if he could get her to go with him to the judge.

"You'd really help me out if you save me the time in placing this ad and marry me."

"You may want someone who is more acceptable to look at."

"There's nothing wrong with the way you look."

She seemed stunned by his announcement. "Well, I'm not thin."

"Considering the intensity of the Nebraska winds on some days, a thin woman could easily get blown away. At least I wouldn't have to run after you to keep you safely on the property."

She laughed.

He chuckled. She had a nice laugh. "I'd like to get back to my farm and make sure everything is fine out there. If you're willing to be my wife, I'd like to marry you right away."

"Is there no one to help you?"

"No. I'm all by myself."

She glanced at the travel bag sitting at her feet. "You are serious, aren't you?"

"Of course. However, if you'd rather return to Maine, I'll post the ad and hope you'll answer it. Then you can come back out here. I'd prefer to skip that and just marry you now."

She nodded. "Alright. I'll help you in any way I can on the farm."

She definitely impressed him. He stood up and took her luggage. "The courthouse is on the way home. I know Judge Johnson. He's my brother-in-law, so he'll see us right away."

He led her to the wagon and placed her bag in it. He looked over at her and found her missing. A quick scan of the area notified him that she picked up a bonnet that had blown off a little girl's head. The mother thanked her and tied the bonnet back onto her daughter's head. He shook his head. What was Neil thinking when he let her go?

He stepped to the side of the wagon. "If you're still willing to marry me, we can do it over there." He pointed to the courthouse down the street.

She looked startled by his words.

"I'll take the fact that you aren't protesting as a yes. May I walk you to the building?" He held his arm out to her.

After a moment, she nodded and gave a slight grin. "I can't get married alone."

"Neither can I. It's a good thing we're together." His smile widened as she put her arm around his and walked with him on the boardwalk. "How long did it take for you to get here?"

"Nearly a week."

"What do you think of Omaha so far?"

"It's big, and there are a lot of people."

"Overwhelming?"

"A little. The town I came from was smaller."

"Well, it'll be just us at the farm so you might miss the crowd. Of course, I have a handful of relatives you'll get along great with, so you won't be confined to my presence all the time."

"It hardly seems like being alone with you will be a bad thing. You strike me as an honest and good man." She looked away from him as she said it.

"I reckon that we'll get along just fine."

They reached the front entrance to the courthouse so he opened the door for her. She thanked him and went into the building. The thought flashed through his mind that her hips would serve nicely to put his hands on during lovemaking. He hadn't considered that part of the equation until that moment, and he found that he couldn't wait to enjoy this aspect of marriage.

Chapter Three

Mary didn't know what to think as she walked with this stranger. The old and faded blue shirt and brown pants didn't detract from his strong masculine appeal. His dark blond wavy hair reached down to his collar, evidence that he didn't visit the barber often. His new beard was rough and short, so he apparently took time to shave at least once a week. His easygoing and friendly demeanor drew her to him, so obviously, she wanted to marry him.

But why would he want to marry her? Surely, the qualities he mentioned that he liked about her weren't enough to grab his attention. After all, didn't most women, prettier ones, have the same characteristics? They didn't belong together. While she was plain, he was handsome. Why hadn't he found a wife yet?

The courthouse was filled with activity. People scurried around, doing whatever it was they came there to do. Some appeared happier than others, and a fat man who huffed by them looked annoyed. Apparently, he wasn't having a good day. They passed a young couple, the tired woman holding a newborn. The man said a polite greeting which they reciprocated. Mary's head spun as much as it had in the train station from all the unfamiliar faces. She knew more people lived in Omaha than in her small Maine town, but being swarmed by them unnerved her.

She sighed with relief when Dave held her arm to keep her safe by his side. He led her to the front desk where a middle-aged skinny man with glasses read a book.

"Good afternoon, sir. How may I help you?" The man folded the page in his book before closing it and looked expectantly at Dave.

"Good afternoon. Miss Peters and I wish to be married," Dave replied. "Is Judge Johnson available? He's my brother-in-law."

The man grinned. "I'm sure the judge has time for kin." He dug out several pieces of paper from a drawer under the counter and handed them to Dave. "Let me check and see what he's doing. Go ahead and fill this out."

Dave turned to her and winked as the man left. "We'll be hitched soon enough."

She anxiously wet her lower lip with the tip of her tongue. "Mr. Larson, are you hiding a deep, dark secret I should know about? Did you kill someone?"

He stopped writing on the paper in front of him and looked at her. "Did you just ask me if I committed murder?"

"Perhaps that didn't come out quite right. It's just that you are an eligible bachelor. You could easily find a woman."

"I did. You're standing in front of me. I think it took all of ten minutes. Of course, if I had gotten you to agree to my proposal the first time I asked, then it would have been done in two."

She softly laughed. "You do have a way with words."

"You have a great laugh. I think being married to you will be lots of fun."

He had a way of unnerving her. No man had ever seemed sincere about even talking to her unless he wanted to find out about other women. She half-expected that he would tell her he was joking and leave but he returned his attention to the papers. She felt self-conscious, standing next to him and not knowing what to say.

She examined her surroundings with closer scrutiny than necessary. She counted the stars on the American flag, studied the picture of the president, and counted the number of people passing by the front door until she got bored of that. She turned her attention back to the counter, noting the title of the book the man had been read-ing. It seemed odd that such details should be of such interest to her when her entire life was about to change.

I came here for a change. I expected to get married today. I shouldn't be surprised to be here. But I thought I'd be with Mr. Craftsman, not Mr. Larson.

The man returned with a smile on his face. "The judge said he'd be delighted to marry you, Mr. Larson."

Dave smiled. "He probably wants to get a look at who I'm mar-rying." He handed her the paperwork and pencil.

She gingerly held them in her hands. Glancing at him, she asked, "Are you saying that there aren't any single women in town?"

"None that suit me. You're doing me a tremendous favor. There are plenty of men who know a good thing when they see it. I'm just glad I got you before someone else did."

He had no idea how wrong he was, but she realized, with sur-prise, he honestly believed it. Neil's blatant rejection had been soothed by Dave's kindness. She vowed that she would be the best wife she could possibly be for the wonderful man standing next to her. She turned to the papers and filled them out.

Dave gently took her hand and led her to the judge's chamber where they would marry. She tried to swallow the nervous lump in her throat, but her mouth was too dry to obey her command. His hand felt warm and strong in her smaller, shaking one. When they were in the room, he turned to her and smiled.

"I hope this is as good as a church wedding," he told her.

She struggled to respond but a wave of dizziness came over her. Giving up on a normal voice, she simply nodded, aware that he was still holding her hand. She'd marry him anywhere. No man as kind and sincere as Dave Larson ever crossed her path before.

Judge Johnson, a tall, slender man with neatly trimmed brown hair and a mustache, brought in two witnesses. "Dave, you sly devil, you." He grinned as he reached to shake his brother-in-law's hand.

Dave let go of her hand so he could oblige the older man. "Hello, Rick. This is Mary Peters. Well, she won't be Peters for long."

She marveled that he could be so casual about getting married. Her stomach flipped and flopped like crazy.

"Good afternoon, ma'am," Rick warmly greeted. "These are Danny and Richard Smith. They'll be here to witness the event in case you decide to run off and leave poor Dave high and dry out there on the farm."

She realized he was joking since the other men chuckled. She wondered if they laughed because they knew there was no way she would leave Dave, though he might leave her. After all, he was too good looking for her.

"Now Rick," Dave began, "Mary and I are going to spend the rest of our lives together. We're going to be very happy."

How Dave could know that, she didn't understand. They barely knew each other.

"How did you two meet?" Danny asked him.

"I posted an ad for a bride and she was the best of the three replies I got," Dave responded.

Her jaw dropped at his lie.

"Why didn't you tell us you posted an ad for a wife?" Rick wondered.

He shrugged. "If she didn't come, then it would be embarrassing. This way, it's a joyous event with good news all around."

His brother-in-law nodded and turned his attention to the vows.

She should thank Dave since he had just saved her from humiliation. Though no one knew Neil had been the one who sent for her, she was fortunate Dave happened to pass by, needing a wife to help him at the farm. She wouldn't have been offered a marriage any other way, and she understood their marriage would be a partnership. In exchange for his protection and home, she would keep the house clean, care for him, and give him children. Love, at least on his end, would not factor into the equation, and she was content with that.

The judge's words interrupted her thoughts. "Do you, Dave Larson, take Mary Peters to be your lawfully wedded wife from this day forward, for richer or poorer, in sickness and in health, for better or worse, forsaking all others, as long as you both shall live?"

Dave, who held her hand, widely grinned and said, "You bet I do," which earned a couple of chuckles from their audience.

She realized that optimism and cheerfulness were his key personality strengths. Whether or not he would enjoy her company, she didn't know, but she already enjoyed his. Being near him was akin to stepping out into the warm sun after a long, cold winter's night.

Rick Johnson turned to her. "And do you, Mary Peters, take Dave Larson to be your lawfully wedded husband from this day forward, for richer or poorer, in sickness and in health, for better or worse, forsaking all others, as long as you both shall live?"

"I do," she said.

The judge asked for the ring.

Dave glanced at her sheepishly. "I knew I forgot to buy something."

Rick shook his head. "You'll have to forgive him," he told her. "Dave has a tendency to forget things."

"It's true. I forgot to mention that fact about myself."

She shyly smiled. "It's lucky for you that I have an excellent memory."

"This is why I chose her," he told Rick. "Can we still get married even though we don't have a ring?"

"Here, Dave." Danny handed him a piece of string that was tied in a circle large enough to slip on a finger. "My daughter handed me this today. It's a ring she made for herself that she wanted to give me.

You can widen it so it can fit her finger. It'll do until you buy a real one."

"It's perfect," she assured him, touched.

Dave slid the pink string on her finger and warmly pressed his lips to hers for a simple kiss. No man kissed her before. Her stomach fluttered and her lips tingled from the action. She reminded herself that this was not a love relationship.

"You are now man and wife," Judge Johnson concluded. "Congratulations!" He patted Dave on the back. "I have to admit that your family will be upset you didn't wait until they were all gathered together so they could witness the wedding."

"Nonsense. Mary came in on the train today, and I won't take her out to the farm without being legally wedded to her."

"Sally will insist on meeting your bride."

"Sally's my big sister and his wife," Dave informed her. Looking back at Rick, he thanked him and took the marriage certificate. "We'll see you all another day."

"It was nice meeting you, ma'am," Rick smiled.

She returned his smile and accepted Dave's arm so she could walk next to him on their way back to the wagon. Once he helped her onto her seat, he untied the reins. She clutched her purse. Suddenly, she didn't know what she was going to say to him. Deep in her heart, she knew she was safe with him, but he was still a stranger and she had never been good at making conversation with men.

"Are you ready to go home, Mrs. Larson?"

The way he said her new name, as if he always called her that, shocked her. She cleared her throat and shifted as he urged the horses forward. She took a deep breath. "May I ask why you lied to the judge about how we met?"

"I thought that version was more romantic. It'll make for better storytelling when the women in my family get together to talk."

"Thank you for not telling them about Mr. Craftsman. I promise that I will be a good wife for you."

"I have no doubt about that. You impressed me back there."

She had no idea how she impressed him but she figured it didn't matter. She straightened her back. "You need help delivering a baby horse?"

"Well, my mare is due to foal soon. The mare's name is Susannah. I bought her at an auction a year ago. She is three years old and already proving to be an excellent riding horse, though the original owner didn't think she'd amount to much when he sold her. It was the best deal I ever made. She's worth triple the price I paid for her. It just goes to show you that you can't judge a book by its cover. Fortunately, my stallion took a liking to her right off the back, and now she's ready to give me another horse." By the gleam in his eye, she knew he was proud of Susannah.

"Have you delivered a foal before?"

"A couple but none of my own."

She nodded and, unable to think of anything else to say for the moment, she turned her attention to the remaining buildings as they left town. She noted that several people stopped to watch her and Dave as they passed by. Most likely, they were wondering what he was doing with her. She pushed the thought aside. Whatever his reason, he married her knowing full well what she looked like, so he already knew what he was getting himself into.

As the last house out of town slipped from view, she noted her surroundings. The afternoon would soon give way to evening, but the sun was brilliant in the sky, casting a warm yellow glow over the gentle rolling hills that splashed an assortment of greens that intrigued her. A peace settled in her heart as she contemplated her future, and that peace was all she needed to know that coming here was the best thing she ever did for herself.

Dave's words interrupted her thoughts. "I came out here with my family on a wagon train when I was twelve. My father received 160 acres free and clear for establishing a home and working the land. It was ten years ago when I left New York, but I do recall that life was easier back east. It's not always easy out here."

"Are you trying to scare me?" She offered him a slight smile.

"No. I meant what I said back there. You're doing me a favor by coming with me. I don't want to disappoint you. I have very little money to my name and a humble home. I reckon it's not what you're used to, and it's not like the ones you saw in town. Mine is made of sod."

"I'll be frank with you, Mr. Larson. I'm a simple woman, and I don't frighten or dissuade easily. If you hope I'll take to running for the next train ride out of here, you've got another thing coming." Desire to be with Dave had already lodged itself in her heart, so if sleeping in a dirt house for the rest of her life meant she could stay with him, then she'd readily pick that option.

When they arrived on his property, she discovered that his house wasn't the only building made of sod.

"Before I came here, I read about these types of buildings, but I've never seen one," she commented as he pulled his horses to a stop in front of the rectangular barn that was larger than the house.

He hopped down from the wagon, went to her side and helped her down.

She approached the barn and touched it. She recalled what she learned about sod buildings. The prairie grass and dirt had been mixed together to form neatly stacked bricks that were two feet high, one foot wide and six inches high. A fine plaster made of lime, sand and water covered the outer walls.

"It's sturdy," she commented.

"The plaster is called stucco and it protects the sod from the rain and snow. Otherwise, it would turn into one muddy mess. I do have to deal with a leaking roof if it rains enough, but I try to keep the roof in good shape so that doesn't happen too much. Some farmers carve out dwellings in the sides of the hill, but the section of land I bought is flat." He stood next to her, watching her.

"I suspect that this building is practical out here on the prairie. It's not like you have a lot of trees or clay bricks to build houses with."

She turned to examine her surroundings. To the north and east stood tall grass though several trees dotted the landscape.

He followed her gaze. "The river cuts through the land in that direction. I made a pathway to it so it's easy to get back and forth. The river is about a mile away and there's a slope that dips down so you can't see it from here. I get drinking water and bathe there." As an afterthought, he slowly added, "Cow chips provide fuel for the fire when I cook." He waited for her reaction.

She nodded. She expected life out here to be drastically different from Maine, so this news didn't startle her. "Do you have a place where you store the cow chips?"

"In the bucket in the corner of the barn. I just take what I need, but I don't cook often. Most of the time I eat raw food or jerky. I collect drinking water and put a barrel of it in here for the animals and one next to the house. I'll bring a fresh supply of water to the house every day for you to use, and if you need more, say the word and I'll bring it to you."

"I'll do what I can to help you." She turned her attention to the corn that grew to the south and west. "Your crop seems to be flourishing. You manage this all by yourself?"

"I do the best I can. My family helped me build the house and barn."

She smiled. "It's amazing that you manage so well. You take good care of your things."

He seemed pleased by her analysis. "It's all in a day's work."

"This is a great place you have. Are you hungry? I could fix something for you to eat if you want to check on the mare."

His eyes grew wide. "Susannah! I forgot all about her. I have some food in the wagon. I'll take it into the house after I check on her."

"Can I come along?"

"Of course." He grinned and nodded to the entrance of the barn.

She returned his smile. "Back in Maine, I helped the midwife deliver a couple of babies, but I've never watched a horse give birth." Mary felt a mixture of apprehension and excitement by the prospect of witnessing a new life entering the world in the next two weeks.

The first thing she noticed when she entered the barn was the potent smell of manure. She subconsciously held her breath, so she wouldn't cringe. Realizing that Dave didn't seem to notice the stench, she hoped that she would get used to it.

He opened the stall door and entered so he could check the horse. "Hi there, Susannah." He patted the horse on the back.

Susannah neighed a greeting but kept her eyes trained on Mary.

"It seems that she's aware of me," Mary commented, her mind shifting from the stink to the pregnant mare.

"Animals are pretty smart. They pick up on things real quick. Don't worry though. In a matter of days, they'll know you well enough."

"How many animals do you have?" she asked.

He led Susannah out of the stall. "I have two geldings, one cow, a stallion and a mare."

She subconsciously backed up as Susannah approached her. She detected a hint of amusement in his eyes from her timid reaction to the large beast. "I didn't grow up around animals. It'll probably take me longer to adjust to them than it will for them to adjust to me."

"Susannah's a gentle mare. She wouldn't harm anyone. Do you want to touch her?"

No, she didn't, but she knew that the sooner she got used to the animals, the easier the transition from city to farm living would be, so she took a deep breath and braced herself for anything the horse with the bulging belly might do. She reached out and tapped the mare's neck.

Susannah snorted, as if humored by her shaky fingers.

"We'll get you more comfortable as time passes," Dave assured her. "We should get your things into the house. I'm going to take Susannah to the field so she can walk around."

She followed him to the field and watched as he opened the fence. Susannah, apparently used to the process, obediently went in and didn't look back as he closed it. Mary saw the stallion glance in her direction, and despite the fact that this was an animal instead of a person, she turned away, feeling self-conscious. Her eyes drifted along the open field and she caught sight of a cow chewing the grass in another gated area.

Dave returned to her. "I'll get the geldings in the fields after I show you the house. It's not much but when it rains, it keeps dry. My parents warned me that plaster would keep the place from getting dirty, but I thought I knew better and didn't worry about it until the dirt started turning into mud. Plaster's on the walls now." He chuckled. "Some lessons have to be learned the hard way, I suppose."

She followed him to the wagon and reached for her travel bag.

"I can get that for you," he offered.

"It's not heavy. I can manage."

"I know but I'd like to do it. It makes me feel useful."

Startled because no man, besides her father, had ever carried anything for her, she didn't know what to say.

He took the travel bag and said, "I'll get the boxes next. Are you ready to see your new home?"

"Yes."

As he walked beside her, he asked, "Why didn't you bring a trunk? This bag doesn't seem large enough to carry many clothes."

"Oh, I wasn't sure what to expect so I only packed the necessities and a dress. I figured that I should wait and see what it was like on a farm so I would know what type of dresses I need out here." She shrugged. "I like to sew anyway, so it gives me a good excuse to do that."

"Then I'll take you back to the mercantile tomorrow so you can get supplies for that. If I had thought about it, I would have taken you there after we left the courthouse."

She paused, her feet three steps from the front wooden door of the sod house. "Have I inconvenienced you?"

He stopped and shook his head. "No. I'm the one who didn't think to ask if you needed anything before we left town. If anything, I'm the one who's inconvenienced you." He smiled and opened the door. "Well, this is it."

How did she luck out in marrying him? He was the most caring man she'd ever met. Realizing that he waited for her to enter, she quickly went over the threshold, aware that he followed her into the dwelling.

She wasn't sure what to expect from the house. The first thing she noticed was the smell of dry earth. Sunlight poured through two small windows, lighting the interior of the structure. One window faced the barn and the other faced the grassy fields that led to the river. The home consisted of a large room and a small room. The large room served as a kitchen and a bedroom. The small room, to the side of the bedroom, seemed to be a storage room. The complete structure could fit in her parents' dining room and parlor, but the lack of space didn't bother her.

He set her bag on the bed.

"The mattress is made of straw," he explained. "My brother made the wardrobe. I don't have a lot of clothes, so you have plenty of room on this side." He took a good look at the bed. "I don't have an extra pillow yet. For the time being, you can have mine."

"If you have some old clothes or towels, I can probably sew a pillow for you."

"Actually, I do have a couple of old shirts that I've been meaning to use as rags or burn." He looked at her. "I burn my trash."

She began to nod but stilled the motion to give him a good look. "Are you trying to scare me again?"

Perhaps he changed his mind about being married to her since he got a chance to look at her inside his home and near the marital bed. Neil's words returned to her consciousness as if he'd slapped her in the face.

"No," he softly replied. "The truth is that I keep expecting you to say you'll have no part of this because it's not exactly a setup for a woman. I do want you to stay."

Relief flooded through her. "I'm happy with the place." Just hearing him say that he wanted her to stay brought a newfound sense of devotion to the wonderful man who stood next to her.

"My old shirts are over in this pile." He pointed to the bottom of the wardrobe. "I haven't gotten a chance to deal with them yet."

She knelt down and examined the soft cotton material. Two of the three shirts needed to be mended and could easily be worn again. The one that was beyond repair would do well for the beginning of a pillow. The flour sack she spied next to the shirts would help complete the task. "I can take care of these."

"I'll bring the boxes in while you put your things away."

She went to perform the task, glad that he wouldn't see her undergarments. It was silly to want to hide such things from him since they were married, but she had just met him. He returned as soon as she placed her bag in the bottom of the wardrobe.

"I have to warn you that these boxes don't contain much for two people." He set them on the table in the kitchen.

She strolled to the kitchen and looked out the window that gave her a view of the barn and cornfield. "It is a lovely view," she noted.

"I'm glad you think so. My mother told me to put a window in the kitchen so my future wife could look outside while she cooked. I'm glad I followed her advice."

She turned to the boxes and opened them up so she could examine the contents. It seemed to contain little else but jerky, though she noted a couple other items. At least she spied a bag of flour and baking soda on the kitchen shelf next to the window. Above it was another shelf which held two well-used pots, a pan, a coffee pot, dishes, and utensils.

"The cookstove is over here." He motioned to it.

Next to it was another table to lay things on.

"I do have some hand towels for washing dishes." He picked up two flour sack towels. "The bar of soap and towels for bathing are in the center of the wardrobe. Also, a wash copper, washtub and mangle for laundry are in the storage room. I don't have much else in there. I suspect that will be the baby's room."

She didn't know why talk of children should cause her to be nervous, but she couldn't manage to look at him. Of course, it was natural that they would have children. There was more to being married than sharing in the tasks of maintaining the farm.

"Do you want to see the storage room?" he asked.

"I'll check it out later. I thought I would get supper started."

"I can't wait to eat whatever you make. It's bound to be better than what I usually put on my plate."

"I'll do my best." She started taking out the jerky, vegetables, and fruits from the box in front of her. "Do you have a fruit and vegetable garden?"

"No. I started one but didn't want to mess with keeping it up."

"I used to have one back in Maine. I'd like to get one going here."

To her surprise, he rested his hand on the small of her back. His touch was gentle but firm. Warmth flooded through her. The gesture spoke of familiarity and intimacy that came naturally to a husband and wife. She swallowed the nervous lump in her throat. She couldn't help but be keenly aware of his soft lips as he kissed her cheek. His scent reminded her of the outdoors.

"I'm glad you're here," he whispered. Before she could respond, he said, "I should take care of a few chores. Just yell for me when supper is ready. I'll be in the barn."

Struggling to clear her head, she watched as he ran out the door and to the barn. Her trembling hands indicated her apprehension over losing her virginity. She knew it was a threshold that married women crossed, but she didn't know what to expect. Part of her was curious while another part of her wished to flee. She took a deep breath and focused on making the meal.

Chapter Four

After dinner, Dave showed Mary the weed infested garden next to the house. "I know it needs a lot of work. Are you sure you want to plant vegetables here?"

"Yes. I enjoy gardening." She bent down to pull out a weed. "It won't take long before I have it ready to go. I know how to can vegetables too so we can eat them in the winter." She examined the property with a close eye, noting the lack of trees in the immediate area surrounding the house. "You don't have any fruit trees?"

"I have an apple tree over in that direction. I can collect some apples for you."

"No. I can do that when I need them. I notice you bought some from the mercantile."

He raised an eyebrow in her direction and wryly grinned. "I bought them because they don't require any cooking to prepare. I'm still amazed you can take the mediocre ingredients I had in the house and make a great tasting meal out of it."

Blushing at his compliment, she shrugged and focused on straightening her dress. He had a way of unnerving her. No man had ever talked to her in such a kind manner before. "It was a simple dish."

"And it tasted better than anything I make." He leaned towards her and kissed her on the cheek. "I have to milk the cow before she starts complaining, so I'd better get back to the barn."

"Will you teach me how to do that?" She wanted to prove to him that she could be useful on his farm so he wouldn't regret marrying her.

"You had a long day. You should go back into the house and rest."

"I'm not tired. I spent the whole time on the train sitting down. It actually feels nice to get out and do something, and I've been curious about what farmers do."

He reached for her hand and gently squeezed it. "I won't tell you no, but if you find that you need to lay down and rest, I hope you do. I don't want to wear you out."

Pleased by his concern, she shyly smiled at him. Her heart fluttered when he turned to the barn, still holding her hand, and walked close to her. The wind rustled the growing corn stalks, masking the sound of their feet as they crunched the grass. The clear evening sky showed her a quarter moon and stars ready to emerge for the night. The remaining sunlight cast an orangish tint on the buildings and land, reminding her of her walks home after a day's work at the restaurant. A brief wave of homesickness washed over her, but one glance in Dave's direction replaced her reminiscence with the joy of finding a man who seemed to genuinely like being with her.

They arrived at the barn, and she noted that he had returned the cow and horses to the barn before supper, for they all stood at attention as soon as they strolled through the open door. The unfamiliar odor of manure still assaulted her senses, but she hardly noticed it since Dave was so close to her that their shoulders touched. Letting go of her hand, he went to grab a pail and stool.

"Would you like to try milking her?" he asked as he approached the cow.

Clearing her throat, she nodded. "Yes." Determined to overcome her fear of the task, she marched to the stall and sat on the stool he offered her.

The cow didn't seem to mind her presence, though it continued to eye her, as if it were studying her. She offered the cow a hesitant smile, suddenly wondering how much animals could decipher in what went on around them.

Kneeling beside her on the straw, he shoved the pail under the cow's udder. Aware that the horses also stared at her, she forced her attention to her husband.

"I'll go first so you can see what to do." He tipped his hat back and leaned towards the cow. "These are teats." He pointed to the long nipples hanging from the udder.

She watched, half-repulsed and half-fascinated as he squeezed the milk out of the cow. The sound of the liquid squirted into the metal pail. His hands were quick and sure, demonstrating that he had done this many times before.

He stopped and asked, "Are you ready?"

She wiped her clammy hands on her apron and lightly wrapped them around the teats. The cow mooed, making her wonder if the animal found her efforts amusing.

"You can use more pressure." Dave's low voice caressed her ear.

She jerked back out of habit since she wasn't used to being so close to another person.

"I promise I won't bite," he joked.

Relaxing, the corners of her mouth turned up. "I've never been this close to a cow before." Or a man, for that matter.

"I'll help you."

With their arms touching and his hands enclosing hers, she could hardly concentrate on the matter at hand. He felt wonderful. Her heart fluttered in her chest. He applied pressure on her hands and the teats expelled more milk.

She laughed. "That's the oddest thing I've ever felt."

He chuckled. "I don't even notice it anymore, though I recall my sister Jenny hated this chore so much that she exchanged chores with the rest of us to get out of doing it."

As he continued to work with her, she asked, "How many siblings do you have?"

"I have three brothers and two sisters. You'll get to meet them soon enough. They'll be curious about you once Rick tells them I married you today. Try not to worry about meeting them. They're great people."

"I have eleven siblings, six brothers and five sisters."

"That must be a busy house."

"I'm the youngest, so my parents are living by themselves again. I think they like the quiet."

"Probably."

When she realized that he was staring at her, she blinked. "What?" Did she say something wrong?

"You're milking her on your own." He held up his hands.

Surprised, she looked down at her hands which had just squirted more milk from the teats.

"It looks like you're more of a farmer's wife than you thought." He rubbed her back, her skin tingling from the action.

Understanding that he found her pleasing, her spirits soared.

NIGHTFALL CHASED AWAY the shades of pinks and purples that streaked the sky. As tired as Dave was from the day's events, he realized that Mary must be exhausted. She journeyed on a train, made him the first tasty meal he had in two months before doing light cleaning and milked a cow, and put her things neatly away. She amazed him.

He bathed in the river to get the four days' worth of sweat and grime off of his body. He wished to be clean when he approached her.

Had he known that he was going to marry her when he woke up that morning, he would have bathed and dressed in his better clothes. He shrugged as he rubbed the lather all over his chest and arms. The point was he struck gold when he married her. He proceeded to wash his hair and finished rinsing the rest of his body.

He didn't understand what Neil found upsetting about her. He realized that, compared to the women Neil usually associated with, she was unimpressive, but she possessed qualities that were endearing. She had curves where a woman ought to have curves. He suspected her flesh was soft and warm. He wondered what she looked like under her clothes. The knowledge that he would soon find out excited his imagination. His pulse raced with anticipation as he stepped onto the sandy riverbank.

The night air felt cool against his wet skin as he dabbed it with the towel. The lantern sitting on the smooth large rock gave him enough light so he could shave. With the soap worked up to a decent lather, he rubbed it over his jaw. Holding a small mirror in one hand, he knelt by the river and washed the sharp blade before he carefully shaved the blond whiskers from his face. He went slowly so he could avoid cutting his tan skin, but he nicked himself in a couple of places. He waited until the small cuts stopped bleeding, washed them with the water and dried his face.

As eager as he was to consummate his marriage, he wanted to look his best, so he took his time in getting dressed in his black trousers and green shirt which he only wore for special occasions. To his recollection, he hadn't worn them more than three times, not including Sundays at church. The fact that they were loose on him served as another reminder that getting married was the smartest thing he ever did. He picked up the mirror again and combed his wavy locks which were drying off nicely in the cool breeze. When he couldn't think of another thing to do to get ready to meet his bride, he collected his things and headed for the house.

MARY ANXIOUSLY SAT on the bed, wearing nothing but a white nightshirt. The candle resting on the kitchen table cast a soft glow over the house which remained cool despite the warm air outside. Though she struggled to concentrate on sewing the new pillow together so Dave would have something to rest his head on, every sound caused her to jerk straight up. He told her that he would be back after taking a bath in the river, but she had no idea how long that would be. If she knew what to expect, her nerves wouldn't be on edge. Why didn't her mother ever tell her about the wedding night? The answer flashed itself in her mind like a bolt of lightning. Her mother didn't expect her to marry. That's why her mother bought her a ticket returning to Maine and refused to give her any insights into being a good wife.

If there was something Mary wasn't, it was stupid. She knew that her parents feared that Neil would take one look at her and tell her to go home. And hadn't he? Their assumption had been correct, even if her father remained hopeful. She blinked back the tears in her eyes as she pulled the black thread through the flour sack that covered some cotton she found in one of the storage boxes. Maybe she worried over nothing. Perhaps Dave would return and go to sleep without a single thought to lovemaking. But how could he expect her to have a child if he didn't have relations with her?

The door opened and she blushed as if he knew what she had been thinking. *My goodness*, she thought as her eyes greedily drank in the sight of him. He was the best looking man she'd ever seen. He had been handsome before, but when he dressed up and shaved, he looked spectacular. She guiltily returned her attention to her sewing.

"You're making a pillow already?" he asked as he closed the door.

Speech failed her so she settled for nodding. Her heart raced as he sauntered across the room to set his dirty clothes and towel in a basket by the wardrobe. He stood three feet from her with his back turned to her while he put his shaving kit and lantern on the small table. She detected the smell of soap emanating from his body.

She dared a glance at his broad back, narrow hips, and long legs. Pricking her finger with the needle, she returned her attention back to her work. If she was thinking straight, she'd have taken her thimble out of her sewing kit. But how could a woman think straight when she was about to consummate her marriage?

"I thought you might be too tired to work," he said, turning around to face her.

She couldn't bring herself to look at him so she stared at the needle as she pulled it through the fabric. "I was earlier, after we milked the cow, but after I washed up in the river, I got my second wind."

She unsuccessfully willed her racing heart to slow down. Her feet shifted on the worn brown rug next to the bed. The silence hanging in the room was almost unbearable. She didn't know what to say, nor did she have any idea as to what he was thinking. When he sat next to her, she poked her finger again. Her hand reflexively pulled away from the source of the pain. She rubbed her thumb and finger together to ease the discomfort.

"I can do without a pillow for tonight." His words were barely a whisper which only intensified his meaning.

Slightly shaking, she obediently laid the pillow in her lap. She took a deep breath.

"Mary," he began, placing his tanned hand over her pale one, "since this marriage happened suddenly, do you need some time before we..." He paused as he searched for the right word. Finally, he finished, "Before we consummate it?"

She dug her nails into the material in her free hand. Did he dread the thought of making love to her like every other man did? She wasn't sure how to answer his question and the sting of rejection prevented her from being able to vocalize any words.

He cleared his throat. "I don't want to rush you. We could just sleep in each other's arms tonight."

Looking cautiously at him, she managed to ask, "What do you want?"

He offered a shy grin. "I reckon I'm like other men. I'm ready on a moment's notice. But I won't take liberties without your go ahead."

An overwhelming feeling of relief coursed through her. At least he could make love to her without getting drunk. That right there was a major improvement over the man she thought she was going to spend tonight with.

"I've never done this before," she slowly confessed. "I'm a bit nervous."

He softly chuckled. "That makes two of us, sweetheart."

"You're nervous too?"

"Well, I'm more eager than nervous."

Her face grew hot when he took the items out of her hands and set them on the table next to his shaving kit. She quickly wiped her sweaty palms on her nightshirt. This was it. Soon she wouldn't be a virgin. She swiped her lips with her tongue again. It seemed that her lips and mouth dried up whenever he was near.

"Will it ease your nerves if I blow out the candle?" he asked.

"Yes."

While he went to perform the task, she slipped under the blanket on the bed, her body stiff. As soon as the small house was dark, she tensed. She closed her eyes and willed her trembling to cease. Soon it would be over and then she would know what to expect next time. She heard him shuffling around but couldn't tell what he was doing. Taking a deep breath, she willed herself to calm down. Only, her body refused to obey her silent command.

He took longer to get into bed than she thought he would, and when he put his arms around her, she knew what had delayed him. His bare flesh felt warm. She hadn't expected him to be naked.

"I want to please you," he murmured, his breath caressing her ear. His hand found the nape of her neck and massaged it.

To her surprise, the simple action soothed her. "Whatever you do will be fine." Since she didn't have a clue as to what to do, then he had to be the one to do it...whatever it was.

"Well, then I'll just play it by ear. You let me know if you don't like anything and I'll stop."

Gulping, she nodded.

His full lips pressed lightly against hers, as if asking for her permission to continue. She tentatively returned the kiss, finding the kiss exciting and terrifying at the same time, for it was just a prelude to the impending event that somehow seemed more monumental than anything she had ever done in her entire life. He kissed her again, this time using more pressure while he pulled her closer to him. Even through the nightshirt, her breasts tingled against his chest. The intimate embrace relaxed her and more of her tension subsided.

His mouth parted and, surprised, she also parted her mouth. The invasion of his tongue as it found its way into her waiting mouth pleased her. She could taste him and marveled that a kiss could be so potent. A low groan, barely audible to her ears, came from deep in his throat as he pressed his arousal firmly against her hip. Still holding her against him, his hand slid from her neck to her shoulder and lower, traveling over her nightshirt until it covered her right breast.

She gasped with desire as he cupped her breast in his palm. No one had touched her so intimately until that moment, and an unexpected thrill raced through her.

His mouth departed from hers. She was ready to squeak in protest when she felt his lips leave a trail of hot and wet kisses from her cheek to her ear and down her neck. Her body softened as his hand glided over the curve of her hip until it settled at her thigh where her nightshirt ended. He found her bare leg and slid his hand under the shirt. His hand was calloused from years of working on the farm, but he stroked her with care.

He nudged her until she rolled onto her back and he knelt over her. Instinctively, her legs parted for him as he brought his hand between her thighs so he could feel her tender flesh. Excitement coursed through her body as she eagerly waited for what he would do next. The sensations he drew out of her were new and delightful. His fingers played with the soft opening before he tentatively inserted a finger into her. She moaned and lifted her hips to deepen his entrance.

"Oh Mary," he whispered against her neck. "I never imagined you could feel so wonderful."

Aware of an aching sensation spreading through her, she shifted against him. She knew she needed something to ease her sudden pleasurable discomfort but she didn't know what. All she knew was that when he withdrew his finger, she was slippery and easily accepted two fingers that sought to explore her.

She moved against him in response. Her body, steadily increasing in the intensity of her newfound pleasure, was demanding something happen, though she didn't know what that something could possibly be. All she did know was that she wanted to prolong the moment.

When he withdrew his fingers, her eyes fluttered open to see what stopped him. The feel of his thick arousal against her opening alerted her to what he was going to do next and instinctively, she tensed back up, so when he penetrated her virginal barrier, she wasn't ready for it. Her hands clenched his arms and her legs tightened around him.

It stings, she realized.

"Are you alright?" He stopped and waited for her response.

His muscles were stiff from the effort he employed to halt his movements, notifying her that it wasn't easy for him to pause on her behalf. Her heart warmed at the realization that he cared for her well-being. Though she was tempted to ask him to get out of her, he was her husband and he had every right to come upon her person this way. They couldn't have a child if he didn't finish.

Taking a deep breath to settle her nerves, she replied, "I'm fine." Forcing herself to stay still, she allowed him access to whatever he wanted.

His tongue swept across her lips until they parted for him. Despite her anxiety, a wave of sweetness washed over her as his tongue found hers. She realized that, even while his arousal urged him to rush things, he slowed down to ease her into the consummation of their marriage. Wanting to give him pleasure for his thoughtfulness, she urged him to continue.

As he moved inside her, the stinging sensation ebbed from her. Relief flooded through her, sending an instant message for her anxious body to relax. A pleasant sensation gradually spread through her as he increased the momentum of his thrusting. His hands drifted down to her hips and held her firmly against him.

Wrapping her legs around his waist, she sighed, glad that her initial reaction had been replaced by this satisfying experience. Her hands traced the muscles in his arms, intrigued that he could be gentle and strong at the same time. Closing her eyes, she concentrated on the new sensations he produced inside of her.

She could enjoy this. Lovemaking didn't have to be something to dread after all. Overjoyed, she eagerly returned his kisses when he brought his mouth from her neck to her lips. His body shuddered above her when he found his release. He pulled her tightly to him as if doing so intensified his gratification. His breathing was heavy and his body covered in sweat as he collapsed on top of her.

She snuggled against him, aware that the male part of him had softened but enjoying the feel of him still inside her, where she felt an intimate connection with him.

After a few moments passed, he lifted himself on his elbows so he could softly kiss her. "Did I hurt you?"

Opening her eyes, she said, "No. It was a little uncomfortable but that didn't last long. I liked it." She felt grateful for the darkness which hid her blushing at her confession.

He eased off of her and rolled to his side. "I liked it too. I find great joy in you."

His voice, barely audible, sent a shiver of delight through her as he held her in his arms. She pleased him. Feeling sheltered and warm, she smiled. Her husband was a gentle man, she realized. She closed her eyes and listened to the soothing rhythm of his deep breathing.

Chapter Five

Sunlight struck Dave's eyes and he tried to roll onto his side to avoid it, but the soft body next to him stirred in protest. Squinting, he opened his eyes and smiled at Mary's sleeping form. She was curled up next to him. Nothing he experienced prepared him for the ecstasy he found in bed with her. Ignoring the sun, he studied her face, noting how peaceful she looked. He wondered what dreams could entice a faint smile on her rosy lips. He blinked in surprise. Wasn't her nose bigger the day before? He shook his head. Obviously, his poor attention to detail misled him on that observation. Her nose really wasn't that big after all. It seemed better proportioned to her face. Her thick eyelashes fluttered, and he suspected she might wake up but he was wrong.

Reaching up to her head, his fingers played with her frizzy hair which reached the middle of her back. The tight curls sprang back as soon as he released them. He chuckled. Given how quickly she seemed to adjust to the sod house and milking a cow, he wasn't surprised that her hair displayed the same characteristic to remain unmoved by something new. She had a strong constitution and he admired her for that. Living on the prairie without the comforts of her home back east, she would need it.

He reluctantly turned his attention to the window. He couldn't recall the last time he slept so late but knew he better check on the mare and milk the cow before it got too late in the morning. As he sat up, she murmured and wiggled closer to him. After waking her up to make love to her again during the night, he was shocked that his body responded with an urgency for more. Reminding himself that he had that night to satisfy his desires, he stood up, quickly dressed and combed his hair.

He quietly left the house to feed the animals. One look at the expectant cow notified him that she needed milking, so he picked up his pail and obliged the animal who seemed relieved that he didn't make her wait this time. When he was done, he took the barrel he used for clean water, emptied it to get rid of the bugs that landed in it and placed it on a cart so he could wheel it to the river.

The morning seemed brighter than usual as he examined the green hills in the distance. The view greeted him every morning on his way to the river that snaked through his land. Dave chose this particular section because of the view of the hills. There was something calming about it, as if no matter how complicated life got, everything worked out well in the end.

Though the day had just begun, the lack of wind and shining sun revealed that the day would be a hot one. He wondered if a storm was brewing. Sticky hot days seemed to be accompanied by nighttime thunderstorms. Looking up, he didn't see a cloud in sight. That, however, didn't mean the sky would stay clear through the rest of the day or evening. The Nebraska weather could change with little warning.

He filled the barrel with the cool water and wheeled it to the house where he dutifully filled a couple of buckets in the kitchen as he did every morning. He smiled when he saw Mary open her eyes.

"Good morning," he warmly greeted.

She gasped and sat up. The sudden movement caused her nightshirt to fall off her shoulder, revealing a glimpse of her cleavage. Mesmerized by the sight, he paused as he dipped a clean cup into one of the buckets.

"I didn't realize I slept as late as I did." She hopped out of bed and turned her back to him so she could tuck the sheet and blanket neatly into place. The shirt barely concealed her cute bottom as she leaned over the mattress.

He debated flinging her back onto the bed and having his way with her but recalled the day's chores that needed his attention. He muttered under his breath and forced his eyes off of her curvy figure so his erection would go away. Night couldn't come soon enough. He gulped the cup of water and set it on the counter.

"What time is it?" She walked over to him.

His eyes fell to her bare feet. She seemed unconcerned about walking on the dirt floor. He decided it was time to put something on the floor to protect her feet. The small rug by the bed wasn't enough.

"Dave?" She stood in front of him, her eyes a clear blue sky color with hints of green spread throughout them. Her expression was one of concern.

He took in the intoxicating aroma of their scents mixed together that lingered on her skin. There was something primitive and satisfying in knowing he claimed her as his own. He reached for her arms and gently pulled her to him. He lowered his head and kissed her. He noted her hesitation. He pulled away from her, trying to judge her reaction.

As if she understood his quizzical expression, she said, "You surprised me."

He relaxed and smiled. "Get used to it, sweetheart. I plan to kiss you often."

This time when he bent to kiss her, she closed her eyes and waited for him. He held her tightly to him and brought his lips to hers. She sighed and brought her hands to his shoulders. When their kiss ended, he continued to hug her.

"You must be hungry," she whispered. "I'll make you breakfast."

He released her. "I was thinking of returning to town today so you can pick up better foods to cook. I'm guessing that jerky isn't your first choice."

"You guessed right. Will it inconvenience you to go back?"

"No. I got the necessary stuff out of the way. Corn and beans don't require me to watch them all day to grow, and Susannah won't foal for at least another week. Besides, you might want to pick up some material to make dresses or even some pants."

"Pants?"

"Some farm work may be easier if you don't have to worry about a dress. And I could teach you to ride a horse, unless you're familiar with that already."

"No. I've never ridden one before."

"I don't have a side saddle, so you'll need to learn to ride like a man. The pants will do well for that. Also, if there's anything you want to buy for this place, feel free. It could use a woman's touch now that one lives here."

She turned her attention to the fruits stored in a bowl. "I didn't mean to sleep so late. I'll try to wake up earlier tomorrow."

"You needed to rest after taking the train all the way out here." He kissed the top of her head. "You're too hard on yourself. It's alright to be human." He glanced out the window. The sunlight poured across the grass and over the barn. "I'll get Lewis and Clark hitched up to the wagon."

She shot him a questioning look.

"Those are the two geldings," he informed her. "My nephew named them after he learned about the explorers who traveled out west."

She seemed amused. "At least you know he pays attention in school."

Grinning, he turned to the front door. "I won't be long. I can't wait to taste what else you can make."

He noticed her blush as she grabbed a skillet from the shelf. His heart warmed at the sight of her cooking in their kitchen. Before, the house had been a place to sleep. Now it felt like an actual home. Happy, he opened the door to go to the barn.

TWO HOURS LATER, THEY arrived at the mercantile in town. Mary's white bonnet protected her from the hot sun, but her blue dress was made of thick material that made her break into a sweat. She figured a thinner fabric would be better for this weather. The two dresses she brought with her were better suited for winter.

He helped her down from the wagon. She blushed as he led her to the entrance of the store with his hand placed on her elbow. It would take some time before she got used to his closeness and affection. A quick view of the store revealed that she could buy all the items she needed from this place.

"Good morning, Larson," the middle-aged man smiled from behind the counter.

"Good morning!" Gently urging her to walk beside him, they closed the gap to the owner, their shoes clicking on the wood floor. "Yesterday, I got hitched to Mary over here. I posted an ad and she answered it, so I went to meet her when she hopped off the train. Mary, this is Ralph Lindon."

"Nice to meet you, ma'am," he said, his eyebrows raised in interest.

"Hello," she replied.

"I thought Craftsman was the only one getting married yesterday," Ralph stated, leaning forward on the counter.

She shifted awkwardly as he glanced back at her.

"I forgot to mention that I was expecting my bride to come in on the train as well," Dave lied.

Ralph gave him a startled look. "How could you forget to mention something like that?"

He sheepishly shrugged. "I was distracted, what with running out of food and all."

"It's amazing you managed to get to the train station." The man shook his head before grinning her way. "I hope you can help him remember things. This boy needs all the help he can get."

Relaxing, she smiled. "I'll do what I can."

"Oh, I should buy you a wedding ring." Pointing to the display case featuring jewelry, he asked, "Which one do you like best?"

Pleased that he wished to do that, she scanned the selection of necklaces, bracelets and rings. Focusing on the gold bands with various sizes of diamonds on them, she pointed to the one with a simple gold band. She couldn't see the practicality of buying one with a diamond, though women in Maine seemed especially impressed with them. If she had learned nothing else from her short time on the farm, she understood that a diamond that stuck out of the ring could snag onto other things and prevent her from getting her work done. Besides, she wanted to be with Dave, whether she had a ring or not.

"It looks like you got yourself a winner," Ralph told Dave as he took the ring from the display case and handed it to him. "You'd be surprised at the spendthrifts I see in here."

"You would be surprised at her other attributes." Dave smiled at her as he slipped the ring on her finger. "It looks just right." Turning to Ralph, he paid for it.

She examined the lovely piece of jewelry, aware of its solid cool presence on her finger.

The small bell rang as the door opened. Three women, a petite redhead and two blonds entered the store, their heads bowed together as if sharing a secret. As the door closed, the group erupted into a fit of giggles.

"Good day, ladies," Ralph called out. "May I help you?"

The curvaceous redhead looked over at him. "Not now, Mr. Lindon. We'll take a look around first." Returning to her friends, she whispered something that caused them to engage in another bout of laughter. They made their way to the window by the store and bent over the figurines.

"What did I tell you?" Ralph spoke to Dave, his voice low so the women wouldn't overhear him. "Spendthrifts. However, they do make me money, so I won't complain."

Dave groaned. "I swear, you're worse than all of my sisters put together."

"Well, while you're here, I got a price chart of what I expect to pay for so many bushels of your corn come harvest time. Care to check it out?"

"It's good to be prepared for how much you'll rip me off," Dave joked. Turning to her he said, "Throw whatever you want in this. Alright?" He picked up one of the baskets that was on the floor by the counter and handed it to her.

She accepted it and began her search of the items on the shelves, realizing the three women watched her. Her cheeks grew hot but she struggled to ignore them as she grabbed flour, cornmeal, and salt. She managed to find a section in the store with a protruding wall that she could hide behind. She wished they would go back to talking about whatever they found humorous when they entered the place.

As she spied other food items of interest, she realized that shopping for her husband was a fun venture. She couldn't wait to present him with a homemade apple pie that people back in Maine often complimented her on. With all the apples he bought and the apple trees on their property, she could make many of them. She wanted to do what she could to please him since he had shown her great kindness.

When the bell rang again, she peered around the corner of the wall. She couldn't see the front door, but she witnessed the three chatty women strolling past the window, so she knew they left the store. Why they found her interesting enough to examine, she didn't know. A couple of women in her past had laughed at the sight of her. Returning to the shelf in front of her, she decided that she didn't want to know. She'd rather believe it was because they didn't recognize her. She wanted to get back to enjoying her newfound relationship with her husband.

She paused as she considered sending a letter to her parents and Grace so they knew that she made it safely to her destination and did, in fact, marry after all. She decided to ask Dave if he would take her to the post office before leaving town.

Making her way to the back of the store, her eyes rested on two tables that held an assortment of colored fabrics that she could sew into clothes. She touched them to determine their quality and texture. Grace once told her that wearing blues and greens brought out the colors in her eyes. Furrowing her eyebrows, she tried to decide if she should stick with her usual solid colors or choose a pattern. She wondered what Dave liked. Did men even notice the designs on a dress? Probably not. She'd wear what she wanted. She mentally summed up the cost for two dresses, a pair of pants and a shirt.

"You're still here?"

The man who spoke caused her spine to stiffen. She didn't have to look at Neil to know it was him. Determined she wouldn't show her hurt over being rejected by him, her eyes met his. "Of course, I'm still here. I came to Nebraska to start a new life."

He stood before her, five inches taller than her. His trimmed brown hair, neatly combed under his black hat, complimented his blue eyes, and he dressed in a new blue shirt and black pants. Though he appeared attractive, she remained unaffected by his looks. In fact, she hadn't found him appealing when she first met him. He seemed too imposing, though she wouldn't let him detect her hesitation around him. He bothered her and it had nothing to do with the way he talked to her.

He shook his head and shrugged. "I admit that I'm surprised. I expected you to hightail it out of town."

"You expected wrong."

"Whatever will you do to support yourself?"

Naturally, he couldn't imagine that a man would be willing to marry her. She understood the insult for what it was but refused to let it upset her. "Mr. Craftsman, I am not a child. I'm fully capable of taking care of myself."

"So it would seem." He motioned to the basket full of food. Sighing, as if the weight of the world rested on his shoulders, he continued. "I am responsible for your predicament. It's only fair that I offer you some money to get you by until you find a job."

Biting back a sarcastic reply, she coolly answered, "I am fine. There is no need for your charity."

Relief washed over his face.

Disgusted, she picked up the basket and turned to leave.

To her shock, he held up his hand to stop her. "Miss Peters," he quickly began, "in light of the fact that you are staying, I would ask one small favor."

The last thing she felt like doing was granting this rude man a favor. However, she detected a weakness in him that prompted her mercy. Taking a deep breath, she nodded and waited for him to speak.

"People may not look well on me for deciding not to marry you. Will you simply tell them that you came here seeking employment?"

Had he not criticized her at the train station and in this store, a bitter knot wouldn't have twisted in her gut.

"There's no need to lie, Neil." Dave appeared from the corner of the aisle. He wrapped an arm around her waist and pulled her close to his side.

She gladly leaned against him for support.

"She came for me," Dave continued. "I placed an ad in the paper asking for a wife and she was the best reply I got from the three women who responded. If you ask me, I lucked out."

Clearly taken off guard, Neil's blue eyes darted from one to the other. "So, you're married?"

"Judge Johnson married us as soon as we left the train station yesterday."

A light of understanding lit up his eyes. "I see. Then congratulations are in order."

Ralph appeared and smiled widely at his three unsettled customers. "I thought I heard an extra customer in here. Craftsman, did you know Larson placed an ad for a wife too? What a coincidence that she came on the same day your woman was due to come in! Speaking of which, are you a responsible married man now?"

Neil offered Ralph a regretful look. "As it turns out, she never showed up."

The owner shook his head. "I'm sorry to hear that. Maybe the next one will work out."

"Yes. I should head over to the newspaper office."

"Aren't you going to buy anything?"

"Right. Yes. I'll come back for it later. Good day." He didn't glance in her or Dave's direction. He just tipped his black hat to Ralph and rushed out the front door.

She exhaled. Her encounter with him unnerved her. Dave magically appeared out of nowhere and rescued her once again. She had heard tales of knights in shining armor coming to the aid of a damsel in distress, and this man standing solidly next to her fulfilled all of her dreams of such a nobleman. She felt like a wilted flower next to him. A pair couldn't be more mismatched.

Dave turned to Ralph and motioned to the fabric. "Mary will be buying some of these." Looking in her direction, he asked, "Did you pick out the ones you wanted?"

Breaking out of her thoughts, she selected the cloths that appealed to her. When she was done, she asked if she could send her parents and sister a letter so they wouldn't worry about her. He agreed, and once they purchased the items, he took her to the post office.

ON THEIR WAY OUT OF the post office, a woman in her late twenties, holding a young boy's hand, waved to them.

"I should have expected this," Dave muttered. His encounter with Neil left him in a sour mood and this didn't help. Turning to his new wife, he warned, "My family's going to hover around you now that they know I got married."

"Shame on you, David, for not telling anyone you were expecting a bride," the blond with long hair pulled back into a braid said as she rushed over to them. A four-year-old blond-haired boy struggled to keep up with her. The woman smiled warmly at Mary. "I'm David's older sister, Sally. I'm married to Judge Johnson."

"Guess how she found out about you?" he wryly asked Mary.

"It's a pleasure to meet my new sister." She turned to Mary and widely smiled at her.

"It's nice to meet you too," Mary shyly replied.

"This is Greg." Sally nudged the boy in the shoulder.

"Good day, ma'am," the boy greeted.

She smiled and said hello in return.

Dave stepped aside so an elderly couple could pass them. Mary backed up to the wall of the post office building, and the rest of the group followed suit so they could be out of the other pedestrians' way.

"Well, you could have knocked me over with a feather when Rick told me what happened," Sally continued. "Really, it's a good thing my husband keeps me informed about what's going on or else David would have forgotten to tell us he married you."

"I'm sure waking up next to her every morning would refresh my memory," he inserted, recognizing her joke for what it was so he didn't take offense to it.

"Perhaps," she consented. "I'm sorry that he didn't bring you by my house yesterday before you left town. I only live two blocks from the courthouse. We could have drunk coffee or had a snack."

"She just got through a long train ride. She needed to rest," he replied.

"Did you grow up on a farm?" Sally asked her, ignoring him.

"No. I grew up in a small Maine town near the ocean. I worked at a restaurant."

"Wonderful!" She clapped her hands together. "We have to get together for the cooking contest. Maureen Brown and her friends win every year, and Jenny and I need some help."

"I'll be happy to do what I can."

He groaned loud enough so his sister would hear him. He knew he'd have to share his wife eventually but hoped the matter would be delayed as long as possible. That, unfortunately, was looking to be an impossible task.

Sally waved her hand at him and looked at a bewildered Mary. "Anyway, I am so excited to meet you! Jenny will be sorry she didn't come for a walk with me since I happened to run into you. We'll all be like sisters." She giggled and put her hand to her chest. "How silly of me. We are sisters." She took Mary's hands and nearly jumped up and down. "I can't wait to learn all about you. If David married you, then you must be pretty special."

Mary blushed. "I am looking forward to getting to know you and Jenny."

"Did he tell you about his brothers and sisters yet?"

"A little bit."

"Well, there are six of us all together. Four boys and two girls. From oldest to youngest there's Richard, me, Tom, David, Jenny and Joel. Richard, Tom, and I are married. You should see some pictures so you can place our faces with our names."

He slid his arm around Mary's waist and instinctively pulled her closer to him, as if doing so would prevent his sister from hauling her off to her home. "We have to give Mary time to settle into her life here first. She just got here yesterday."

"Of course." The blond nodded understandingly. "And you two are newlyweds. Surely, you'll want time to yourselves."

He breathed a sigh of relief.

"So, when will you bring her out to meet everyone at Ma and Pa's farm?"

He glanced at Mary who peered questioningly at him. His breath caught in his throat at the alluring sight she presented.

"David?"

Sally's voice brought his focus back to the conversation at hand. "Oh, uh...A month ought to do it. What do you think, Mary?"

"That is fine," she agreed.

"A whole month?" Sally groaned. "David, you will drive everyone mad with curiosity about her."

"You'll get to see her at church on Sundays," he reminded her.

She reluctantly nodded. "I suppose it can't be helped. Who knew you could be selfish?"

"Well, I married her."

"The baking contest is in two weeks. Will you at least spare her for one day so she can help me and Jenny win it?"

He glanced at Mary. Sally was right. It was selfish of him to keep Mary all to myself the entire time. Besides, the sooner Mary got acquainted with her new life, the happier she'd be. "Do you want to help out?"

"I do enjoy cooking, but if you need me at the farm, then I should be there."

"I'm sure I can survive one day by myself."

"Wonderful!" Sally cheered. "I'll let you two get back to the farm." She pulled Mary away from him and gave her a big, warm hug. "I can't wait to tell Jenny I met you! The contest is on Tuesday. I'll be by to pick you up at eight."

Mary nodded and they said good-bye to his sister who took Greg's hand and led him to the mercantile.

Dave looked at his wife and smiled. "I reckon you'll be close with my sisters."

"She seems nice."

"Do you need to get anything else while we're in town?"

"No. I'm ready to go home."

He nodded and waited for two men to pass them before leading her to the wagon.

Chapter Six

On Sunday, Dave noticed that Mary wore her best dress which happened to be the same one she arrived to Omaha in. He also wore his best clothes. Understanding that she was nervous on their way to town, he pulled her close to him to reassure her that he would be with her.

As they arrived in town, he gave her a brief description of his family so she wouldn't be at a total loss when she saw them.

"My oldest brother, Richard, is thirty. He works in construction and lives in town. He is married to Amanda, and they have three children, eight-year-old twin boys and a five-year-old girl. Then there's Sally. You met her already. She's twenty-seven and is married to Rick Johnson, the judge. They have Greg, the four-year-old. Tom is twenty-five and is married to Jessica. They have two girls, ages four and two, and a baby on the way. They work the farm right next to ours. Of course, you know me." He winked at her. "My younger sister, Jenny, is twenty. She has two-year-old Jeremy. Then there's Joel, the seventeen year old."

"I hope I can remember all of these details." She shifted against him and adjusted her bonnet.

"Oh, after we get together with everyone a couple of times, it'll come together. I hope that seeing them at church first will be less intimidating. At least, this will ease you into it. Then, when we go to build my parents the barn, you'll know their names and faces." He glanced at her. "I usually head home within minutes of the final hymn so I can get back to work, but would you like to stick around longer?"

"No. I'd rather go home shortly after the service is over. I doubt that I'll be what they expect."

"Probably not. You'll be even better." He kissed her cheek. Before she could respond, he parked the wagon in the large churchyard. Most of the people stood outside the brick building, talking and laughing. "Be prepared for the bombardment of my family who'll want to meet you."

She took a deep breath and nodded.

He did admire her ability to confront new situations with surprising ease since she didn't show her anxiety on the surface. After he helped her down from the wagon, he smiled at her. "As excited as I am to show you off to my relatives, I confess that I like having you all to myself. I can't be affectionate with you in public like I can be when we're alone."

Her eyes grew wide. "You want to show me off?"

His eyebrows furrowed. That was an odd question. "Sure. You're my wife and I'm proud of you. Why wouldn't I want to show you off?"

She blushed, stared at the ground and shrugged.

Giving her a quick kiss on the cheek, he whispered, "I'll be with you, Mary."

She slipped her hand through the crook of his arm.

Sally ran over to them, nearly dragging her husband and son with her. "I'm glad you brought her here," she told him.

"We are going to go home when the service is over. After my month with her to myself, I'll stay longer," he promised. "How are you doing, squirt?" he asked the boy who waved at him.

"You won't stay for the potluck?" Sally asked.

"Sally," Rick gently inserted over the chatter around them, "don't you remember what it was like to be a newlywed? Give them time so they can enjoy being alone for awhile." He shook Dave's hand and grinned at the couple. "It's nice to see you two again." He nodded to Mary.

Sally glanced over her shoulder. "Jenny!" She bolted across the lawn, swerving around two groups of people who mingled before the service.

Rick chuckled. "You'll have to forgive her. She's a little excited about you, Mary."

"A little?" Dave rolled his eyes.

Sally and Jenny made their way over to them. Jenny held the hand of her two-year-old son.

Dave sourly noted that several people stepped away from Jenny, as if being in her presence would pollute them. He suddenly wondered if he should have warned Mary about Jenny's lack of a husband.

"Good morning, Mary," Jenny greeted, obviously glad to meet her sister-in-law. "Hello, Dave."

He smiled. "Good morning, Jenny. Hey there, Jeremy."

"You have a new aunt," Jenny told her son. "Her name is Mary."

"I see Richard and Amanda over there!" Sally took Mary's hand and urged her away from Dave.

"What are you doing?" Dave asked, annoyed that he had to fight his sister to hold onto his wife. He knew Sally could be pushy but this was ridiculous!

"Richard and Amanda are entering the church," she argued, not letting go of Mary's hand while he held Mary's other hand. "I want to introduce her to them before the service is over and you haul her home."

Mary, who looked overwhelmed, assured Dave that it was alright with her, so he let her go. Jenny and Jeremy followed them.

He sighed.

Rick laughed. "I'll retrieve your wife for you before the service begins."

"From the way Sally's acting, it'll take both of us to pry her off of her." He examined his surroundings. "Are Tom and Jessica here?"

"No. I haven't seen them. Oh, there's your parents."

They waved the middle-aged couple over.

"Where's Joel?" Dave asked his father while his mother picked Greg up and hugged him.

"He stayed on the farm to kill the rat stuck in the walls of our house," his father replied. "Your mother refuses to return until it's gone, so I told him to skip church today so he can take care of it."

His mother shivered. "A rodent doesn't belong in a house. The Lord will understand that this is an emergency." She set a giggling Greg down and looked at Dave. "I heard you got married on Wednesday. Where's your wife?"

"Sally went all the way to the farm to tell you about Mary?" Dave asked.

"No. I paid her a visit this week and found out when I saw her."

"Sally took her into the church to meet Richard and Amanda."

"Well, I think I'll introduce myself. It's only right that I welcome her to the family." Smiling, she skipped to the church, holding Greg's hand.

His father grinned. "I have to confess that your ma was excited to hear you married. She's hoping for more grandchildren."

"Well, Mary's a fine woman."

"I'll have to give the women time to talk to her before I make my introductions. I don't want to overwhelm the poor girl."

"Where are Tom and Jessica?" Dave wondered.

"Oh, their daughters got sick so they had to stay home today." his father replied.

The church bell rang, announcing that the service would soon begin so they entered the church. Once Dave spotted Mary surrounded by Sally, Jenny, Amanda and more women and children, he shoved his way through the group, took her hand and led her to his usual spot which was, thankfully, away from his siblings.

"What do you think of my family?" he asked as they sat in the wooden pew.

"They are very nice," Mary said, her face blushing from all their attention.

"I have to admit that I'm jealous. I was hoping to be the one to introduce you but Sally beat me to it."

"You have nothing to be jealous of, Dave."

That's what she thought. He knew his family would be interested in getting to know her, but he didn't imagine for a minute that they would hog all of her attention.

They stood up to sing a couple of hymns before Minister Greene stood up to give his sermon. Dave was secretly relieved that after the service, he could take Mary back out to his home and be alone with her.

THREE DAYS LATER AFTER supper, Susannah was ready to foal. Dave had set the other animals in the pasture so he could concentrate on the mare. He inspected her in the stall with a strange feeling of apprehension. Her water broke as she laid down on the clean straw, but the birth slowed once a hoof poked through. Twenty agonizing minutes passed without further progress. He shook his head and examined the irritated mare that grunted and snorted while she struggled to push her foal from her belly. He took off his shirt so he could wash his arms up to his elbows with the soap and clean water in a bucket waiting for him by the stall.

Mary ran into the barn, her expression controlled in the midst of the stressful situation. "I brought the clean towels for you."

"Hold onto them until I ask for them."

She nodded and stayed back while he rushed to the mare and knelt before her. His attempt to walk Susannah around so the foal would slide back into the womb and reposition itself failed, so he needed to intervene. Thankfully, he went through this with his father's mares, so he knew what to do.

"Easy, Susannah," he softly said as he stroked her belly. "I'm going to help you."

The horse snorted her reply.

His hand followed the foal's hoof up into the birth canal, making his arm slippery as he kept his other hand on the mare's belly and braced his knees on the ground so he stayed in place. At least the hoof out of the womb was a front hoof. He sought out the other front hoof which was bent to its chest. He grabbed it, the muscles in his arm and back straining as he pulled the hoof towards the mare's hind hooves so he could rotate the foal's head to the birth canal.

Susannah neighed and jerked her head to look at him.

"Your babe will be out soon," he assured her.

Turning to Mary, who silently watched them, he asked for one of the towels which she handed to him. The two slippery hooves were safely out of the birth canal, so he took the towel and grabbed them. He pulled them towards Susannah's hind hooves, straining against the weight of the animal that struggled to get out of the womb. When the shoulders and head appeared, he decided to see if the foal would progress without further help. He backed up and stood next to Mary so he could give the two animals space.

To his relief, the foal's upper body emerged on its own. It stopped when its hips were at the threshold of entering the world.

"Do you need to pull it out again?" Mary whispered.

He glanced at her. "I don't know yet. The foal could be resting for a moment. Birthing can be a lengthy process."

She nodded and waited expectantly beside him, her hands clenching the second clean towel as she stared at the mare and foal.

Before long, the foal's hind hooves left the womb and the animal rested against its mother's belly. Satisfied, he returned to the bucket of water and dipped the soap into it.

"They'll lay like that for about fifteen minutes," he said as he rubbed the soap in his hands.

"I must admit that it was thrilling to watch the birth." She smiled at the two horses.

"Would you like to name the foal?"

"Really?" Her eyes turned in his direction.

He nodded.

"I'd have to think of a good name. How did you decide on Susannah?"

"Jenny named her. I'm no good with picking out names." After working up a good lather, he spread it on his arms and chest.

"I'll have to think of one." Shooting another look at the stall, she smiled. "It's not all that different from a human giving birth. Every birth I've been to has been like this."

"You have to stick your arm up the woman's birth canal?"

She shook her head, seeming amused at his joke. "You know, I have seen the midwife stick her hand up there to help rotate the baby so it comes out easier."

He cringed, not wishing to imagine an entire hand in that area of a woman's body. He quickly rinsed his upper body. "I'm sorry I jested."

She laughed and rubbed a towel over his arms and chest to dry him off. "What I meant was that Susannah is already bonding with her foal. It's the same way with human mothers. Despite all the pain and length of the labor, they can't wait to hold their babies."

Smiling, he enjoyed the way she fussed over him, making sure she wiped all of the water off of him before she put his shirt on. "You'll have your turn," he promised.

She paused, her fingers on his buttons.

By the pretty shade of pink that rose in her cheeks, he realized he caught her off guard. His hand cupped the side of her face, his thumb caressing her cheek. "You'll make a wonderful mother, Mary."

Her eyes met his and he detected the unshed tears there.

"Did I say something wrong?"

She blinked and shook her head. "It's just that I never thought I'd be a mother. I mean, I hoped but..." She shrugged. "It's hard to explain." When she looked at him, the tears were gone. "I'm happy here, Dave."

Glad to hear that, he wrapped his arms around her and pressed his lips firmly against hers. He could feel her heart beating with his. He now fully understood the meaning of two lives becoming one when a couple married.

The mare neighed, and they turned their attention back to the animals. Susannah stood up. The foal stumbled but followed suit. The umbilical cord broke easily under the mare's hoof.

"They got it from here," he announced, touched that Mary buttoned his shirt for him.

"I'm glad I was here to watch it."

His arms felt empty when she went to pick up the bucket and dumped the dirty water in the grass outside the barn.

He retrieved the used towels from the ground and gave them to her. She plopped both into the bucket and picked up the bar of soap

"I would like to wash these in the river."

"Alright," he said. "I'll finish cleaning up in here."

She paused in the entryway of the barn. "I left you a cup of fresh water and some cut up apples and oranges on the kitchen table. I thought you might want a snack after all the work you did."

An unexpected emotion that he didn't understand tugged at his heart. "Thank you, Mary."

She nodded before turning back to the river.

TWO DAYS LATER, MARY lifted the lacy curtain that framed the kitchen window so she could watch her husband take the mare and foal out to the gated field where they could be free from the confines of the barn. Dave's broad shoulders made him appear larger than life. His clothes were loose, though his belt held his pants up so they didn't fall down. She blushed as she recalled how his naked body felt as it pressed against hers. That he made love to her as willingly as he did meant everything to her since it meant that he found her acceptable to touch. She found becoming one flesh to be very pleasing, especially since during the act, she actually felt beautiful. She forgot how she really looked when it was just the two of them in the dark.

He called out to his stallion but the horse shook its head and neighed in protest. She chuckled as he made a pleading motion to the animal which took a moment to consider its options before it trotted over to him. She caught sight of his profile as he turned to lead the animal to the saddle resting on the ground. His handsome features intrigued her, making her eager to stare at him.

He had shaved each day, saying that he didn't want his beard to scratch her face. Her heart had raced with excitement when he kissed her afterwards. "You see, isn't that better than having to rub your face against a stubbly bush?" She didn't care whether he shaved or not. She would gladly kiss him anytime he wished. She owed him because he saved her from a spinster's life. Truth be told, she doubted any other man would have been willing to marry her. She determined to be the kind of wife who would bless him. She hoped the apple pie she was making would be a start.

Glancing back from the crust she was rolling out on the table, she spied him saddling the horse. He had a big smile on his face. He was happy out here. His own joy spread outward until it affected her. She couldn't recall a time in her life when she had been as content as she was at this moment.

As soon as he rode the stallion out of her view, she focused on making the pie. Once she set it in the oven to bake, she decided to mend his shirts. The process didn't take long. She already finished sewing a pair of brown britches for herself. She hesitated to wear the pants, but Dave wished to teach her to ride Susannah. "She's a gentle mare. You have nothing to worry about," he had assured her. She could only hope he was right. The thought of riding a horse terrified her. What if she fell off?

She directed her attention back to the beige shirt in her hands and noticed another bug walking along the floor by her foot. She stomped on it, immediately killing it. Living with bugs in the house seemed to be a given, but she barely noticed their invasions. She was a woman in love, and love made everything wonderful.

She finished with the mending, placed his shirts in the wardrobe and returned to the pie which was done. The smell of apples and cinnamon filled the house. She couldn't wait to surprise him with it. By the time she set the table, she happened to glance out the window and saw him. He returned and let Jack go into the field.

Pouring the coffee into their cups, she looked up and smiled when he entered the house. "Hello, Dave. I made johnnycakes, a salad, bean soup and apple pie." She placed the cups next to their bowls and plates.

Striding to her, he returned her smile, took her in his arms and kissed her. "Coming home to you is my favorite part of the day." She laughed as he spun her around before letting her feet settle on the ground.

"You might change your mind about that when you taste the pie. Then coming home to dessert will be your favorite thing. In Maine, the customers at the restaurant used to order more than one slice."

He gave her another kiss. "They must miss you." He released her from his embrace and went to his seat.

They missed the meals she made. As for her, she knew her family missed her, but they would most likely be relieved when they learned that she had married after all. They did worry about her. She did miss them too, but living in Nebraska was turning into more of an adventure than she hoped it would be when she got on the train. She turned her attention to her husband and sat across from him.

"I see that your pants are ready," he noted. He bit into his jonny-cake.

"Yes. I suppose I can't talk you out of teaching me to ride Susannah?" She picked up a spoon and twirled it in her hand instead of putting it into her bowl of soup.

"I didn't think anything scared you. If I had told you that I wanted you to ride her right after we married, would you have bolted for town?" His eyes twinkled as a grin spread across his face, so she knew he was joking with her.

Deciding to ignore his question, she asked, "Would you like to try a slice of pie?"

"Not until I'm done eating the main course. I love your pies too much. If I start in on one slice, I'll eat another and another until I'm too full to eat anything else. You make the best pies I've ever tasted. Of course, everything you make tastes like a feast fit for a king. I reckon you'll give my sisters the satisfaction of winning the baking contest next week."

She blushed at his compliment. "Your mother and sisters seem nice."

He took another bite of his food and swallowed it before he thoughtfully studied her. "A woman should have some female friends. I've been selfish in keeping you all to myself."

"I enjoy being with you, Dave."

"I hope so. It would be a shame if we didn't get along."

Placing her spoon in the bowl, she stirred the beans.

He took a drink from his coffee cup. "After dinner, I'm going to repair a part of the wall in the barn that is deteriorating."

She paused, her spoon, full of bean soup, halfway to her mouth. "I thought you already did that."

"Oh, this is another section of the wall. Sod barns need constant repairs. The family is planning on getting together in three weeks to build a wooden barn on my parents' property. The lumber is due to arrive at that time. It would be a good chance for you to get to know everyone better. You'll have to spend most of the day with the women since I'll be helping the men with the barn. Do you feel up to going?"

She nodded. "Yes." She took a bite of the soup. She hoped her nervousness didn't show. She knew that sooner or later she would attend a family gathering.

"You have nothing to worry about. You'll get along with everyone just fine. Why, the women couldn't get enough of you at church. And who knows? With any luck, we'll announce that you're expecting. Wouldn't that be fun?"

She almost spit out her mouth full of soup. She quickly swallowed it so she could say, "Dave, it's too soon to know." Her cheeks grew hot, though why they should when it was just the two of them, she didn't know. Perhaps it was the fact that making love to him was still new.

"We have three weeks to find out. If you don't menstruate in that time, we'll know. I wonder if we'll have a boy or a girl."

She stared at him in disbelief. "Really, Dave, with the way you talk, it would seem like a done deal."

He shrugged and continued to eat. "Will you be going to the river to bathe this evening?"

"No. I did that earlier today."

He looked disappointed but didn't say anything.

Her eyes grew wide. Surely, he didn't want to see her naked. Deciding he couldn't possibly want such a thing, she turned her attention back to her meal.

After they ate and he congratulated her on another delicious meal, he left to repair the barn wall. She cleaned the dishes and set them out to dry. The humidity made the heat feel thick, so she reasoned he might be thirsty. She grabbed a cup and filled it with water. Upon her arrival in the barn, he sat on a stool and whistled a happy tune while he mixed the sand and water in a well-used bucket.

She frowned. "Doesn't plaster include lime?"

He immediately stopped stirring the mixture and smacked his forehead with his hand. "I can't believe I forgot that." He jumped up to get the lime from the shelf in the corner of the barn.

She chuckled. She inspected the hole he had filled in with dirt. The hole wasn't big but it could increase in size and cause damage if it wasn't taken care of in a timely manner. Dave might be forgetful, but he did well in maintaining his things.

He returned with the lime and dumped it into the bucket. "Thanks for saying something. I don't know what I'd do without you."

"You'd probably do the same things you did before we met."

"I remember that I did a lot of running around because I'd forget stuff, like adding lime to the plaster. You save me from having to redo my tasks."

She shrugged. "Anyway, I thought you might be thirsty, so I brought you some water. I can see that you have your hands full so I'll set the cup over on this bench. I'll come back for it later."

He thanked her again.

Smiling, she returned to the house.

THE NEXT MORNING, DAVE saddled two of his horses in the barn. There was nothing quite like the smell of leather and a horse together. He thought that Mary's adventurous spirit would endear her to riding a horse once she got over her fears. Noting the sound of footsteps, he peered over Susannah's back and saw his wife making her way over to him. The sight of her in trousers intrigued him. He let her borrow one of his shirts, which he surprisingly noted she mended without saying anything to him about it, and the green shirt with dark brown pants and her new boots accentuated her curves. He smiled as he approached her. Since she didn't have a hat, she wore her blue bonnet, which made her eyes appear bluer than her usual hue. The wind played with the braid dangling to the middle of her back.

"I'll have to make my own shirt," she stated as she unsuccessfully tried to expand his shirt's width around her bosom. Giving up, she sighed, her arms dropping in defeat at her sides.

He hid his amusement. He rather enjoyed the way her breasts strained against his shirt. He had yet to see them, and any attempts to see her without clothes on had been met in vain. For some reason, she didn't take a liking to the idea.

"Maybe you should undo the top two buttons," he suggested.

"That might work." She did so, and fortunately, her undergarment was low enough so he got a generous view of her cleavage. "Yes. That is better."

He couldn't agree more. Dragging his attention from her chest, he led her over to Susannah who was patiently waiting for them. "Now, Susannah is a draft horse. Actually, Jack, Lewis and Clark are too."

She blankly stared at him.

He blinked. "Oh, right. You aren't familiar with horses. A draft horse is gentle. Susannah likes to go slow, so you don't have to worry about her running off with you. She knows to stay near me and Jack, and once she gets used to you, she'll know to stay with you as well. I admit, it was difficult to pull her away from her foal, but here we are and everything is ready for you. I can help you get on if you'd like."

She nodded and went to the mare. She closed her eyes for a moment, as if bracing herself for a dreaded task that loomed before her. When she opened them, he smiled reassuringly at her. He realized she was shaking the moment he touched her hand. Knowing that touch could soothe a horse, he figured it might soothe her as well. He applied enough pressure on her shoulders to be firm without hurting her. He kneaded the knots in her muscles until he felt her relax.

"I think I'm ready," she said.

He held her by the waist and guided her up on the animal. After she settled into the saddle, he stroked her thigh. "You did it on the first try. You're a natural. You just don't know it yet."

Susannah shifted impatiently under her. Mary gasped and grabbed the reins. Deciding it was a bad idea to laugh, he turned his back to her, chuckled under his breath and tipped his hat lower so she wouldn't detect the mirth in his eyes when he faced her again. He hopped up on Jack, the saddle conforming to him.

"You make it look easy," she remarked, a hint of envy in her tone.

"It is easy, once you get the hang of it, which you will. Give Susannah a gentle nudge, like this." He tapped Jack in his sides with the heels of his boots.

Jack started off at a leisurely pace. Dave glanced next to him and tried to appear nonchalant as he watched her on the moving mare. She gripped the reins, her knuckles whiter than the puffy clouds overhead. Her expression reminded him of someone who struggled to be brave while inwardly panicking.

"Susannah will pick up on your..." He paused, not wishing to embarrass her. "That is to say that horses are sensitive to people's emotions. Now, she's a great horse. She won't buck you off."

"Buck me off?" Though he wouldn't have thought it possible, her face paled even more. "What does that mean?"

He reasoned that telling her that it meant 'to throw her off' might serve to increase her anxiety, so he pointed to the land that went along the river. "That area over there is nice and flat. It'll be a good starting place."

She looked as if she was going to insist he tell her the meaning, hesitated, and gave a slight nod of her head.

Relieved she didn't pursue the topic, he led the way to the river, making sure he took it slow. Mary didn't speak, which wasn't surprising. She most likely needed all her energy to maintain her balance. His eyes drank in the rolling green hills in the distance while his ears tuned into the soothing babble of the river and tweeting of the birds. This path was one of his favorites on the property. It not only gave him a good view of the land surrounding his farm but he could monitor any activity that went on around him. Once in awhile, a stray bull, cow, pig, or horse would venture onto his property, so he'd have to return it to its rightful owner.

Most of the time, it was one of Neil's animals that broke loose since he didn't do a very good job of watching them. On occasion, Dave caught a tear in Neil's fence when he returned one of the animals. Rather than wait for Neil to fix it since Neil didn't rush on any of his chores, he repaired it himself. Tom's cows rarely ventured onto his land. Fortunately, the branding on the cattle told him their correct owner, and since Tom didn't raise pigs, he knew right away that those particular animals belonged to Neil. Fortunately, his property contained one hundred and fifty acres, so he rarely had any dealings with Neil.

"All of this land is yours?" Mary asked.

Surprised that she spoke, he waited for her to catch up to him before riding next to her. "Beyond this river is my father's land. Tom owns the land in that direction." He pointed behind them. "And

Neil's farm is that way." He motioned in front of them. "His boundary is farther up ahead where that wooden post is. Can you see it from here?"

She squinted. "I think so."

"Over on this side is the corn." He glanced at the land to the other side of them. "Come harvest time, most of the neighbors get together to help with gathering the crops. It's a good way for women to come together and gossip. I reckon you'll have a good time, though cooking for us men might be exhausting. We can be worse than locusts when it comes to eating the goodies you women make."

"Are you trying to scare me again?" She grinned at him.

She's pretty when she smiles. Why didn't I notice that before? He shook the thought aside. "Just a warning. I hope you'll save a slice of your pie for me when no one's looking. I'd hate to miss that special treat."

"I'll be sure to do that."

He studied her as she sat on Susannah. Her shoulders dropped from their rigid position. Her thighs no longer clenched the sides of the animal. The reins rested loosely in her hands. The worried wrinkles on her forehead disappeared, and the firm line of her lips turned up in slight amusement.

"Well, just look at you," he said.

She frowned. "What?"

"You're riding a horse and your posture isn't so stiff. You're already graceful on the beast."

She looked relieved and smiled. "I guess you were right. Riding a horse may not be so bad after all."

He chuckled. She was a natural rider, alright.

Chapter Seven

A week later, Sally arrived right after Mary cleaned the breakfast dishes. Dave put the plate he finished drying on the shelf, took one look out the window, and sighed. "She doesn't waste any time in stealing you from me, does she?"

"She's not stealing me." She grinned at him and shook her head, secretly pleased that he didn't want her to leave him for the day. Done with the dishes, she pushed the chairs back to their proper position around the table.

He shrugged. "I reckon it depends on how you look at it."

To her surprise, he crossed the short distance between them. He held her to him and gave her a passionate kiss, his tongue brushing hers. The action sent a thrilling spark through her.

"I hope you win," he whispered, his lips lingering against hers.

Lightheaded, she nearly stumbled against him as he pulled away from her.

"I better greet her before she barges in on us," he said.

She took a moment to regain her composure before removing her apron and folding it. Then she set it on the table. Following him outside, she breathed in the sweet scent of clover. The July air felt refreshingly cool that morning, a strong contrast to the oppressive heat they endured for the past week and a half. The thunderstorm from the previous night helped to cool things off. She wondered if she would ever get used to the nighttime storms. The thunder crashed so loudly, she bolted upright in bed, her pulse racing, as if a gun just went off. Her action stirred Dave out of his slumber, and he held her to calm her. Of course, holding soon led to lovemaking.

Shaking her head to clear it, she turned her attention to Sally who pulled on the reins of her horse so her buggy came to a stop. "Why, David, I believe you put on a little weight," Sally greeted. "Married life is treating you well."

He grinned and winked at Mary. "I can't complain."

Mary blushed. She tied her green bonnet over her hair which she had pulled back into a bun. The breeze rustled the lower half of her green dress. "I made you a sandwich and a salad for lunch."

He placed a hand on the small of her back and kissed her cheek. "I'll miss you."

"I'll miss you too." She still felt shy when he showed her affection, especially when they were in front of other people.

Sally shook her head. "Honestly, David, I'll have her back at six. With the way you're acting, you'd think I'm taking her away for a year."

He helped Mary get into the buggy. Her cheeks flushed a wild shade of red when he patted her behind. She glanced at him, shocked but oddly pleased. To her relief, Sally didn't notice it.

He chuckled and waved to them. "Go and show that Maureen Brown there's a better cook in town."

Sally clicked her reins so her horse trotted away from the house. "I've never seen my brother so happy. I guess placing an ad in the paper asking for a wife does work out. Though why he didn't bother telling us about it, I'll never understand. We would have been thrilled to come meet you at the station and see that you had a church wedding. Every bride deserves a memorable wedding."

"I did have a memorable wedding. Dave was very romantic."

"It's obvious he wants you all to himself. That's to be expected for a man in love. And your face is glowing as well. I'm glad you two found each other."

"He is a wonderful man." Mary glanced back and saw him enter the barn. The horses neighing at the sight of him brought a low chuckle to her throat. Most likely, they were glad to see him because he fed them.

Sally's horse turned down the well-worn grassy road and the house and barn slipped from view. Mary held onto the seat, bracing herself for the bumpy ride. Turning back to Sally, she couldn't help but note the resemblance between the two siblings. Sally shared her brother's wavy blond hair, gray eyes and high cheekbones.

Mary cleared her throat. "Dave said that we will all get together when your parents get the lumber for the new barn."

"I should hope so. Church isn't enough time to learn about you or to have you learn about us, and poor Tom's kids have been sick so they had to stay home for the past two weeks. And you haven't even met Joel. He got stuck in the ditch on the way to church last Sunday, though how that happened, I don't know. I suspect there's a brother among us who'd rather not go to church."

Sally smiled and continued, "Just wait until harvest time. You'll get to meet your neighbors. Do you know who your neighbors are?" Without waiting for Mary's reply, she laughed and shook her head. "Probably not. David barely mentioned his family. I'm sure he didn't give you details on the people who live around you. Well, there's Tom and Jessica Larson. Then there's Jimmy and Doris Parson, Zachary and Mildred Phillips, Roger Sloane and Neil Craftsman. They're good, hardworking people. Of course, they'll bring their kids. Poor Roger's wife died two years ago. He has a couple of teenage sons. Neil's still single and has no children, though rumor is he posted an ad for a wife."

Mary quickly glanced away from her, not wishing Sally to take a good look at her and detect the truth. She didn't wish to think of Neil. Though she wouldn't trade Dave for anyone, the rejection was still fresh.

Sally grinned at her. "You must be overwhelmed by the idea of meeting everyone at once. I know I'd be shaking if it were me. I don't know how you gathered the courage to leave your home to come here."

Relieved to be off the subject of Neil, Mary turned back to her new friend. It seemed to Mary that Sally loved to talk, and as they continued their ride to Omaha, she discovered that she was right. Sally spent the entire time telling her stories about how her family left New York because their father got tired of living in the confines of a crowded city with little pay from his job.

"So when he learned of the Homestead Act passed by Congress, he decided it was time to head out. Richard was old enough to stay back there since he was twenty at the time. However his wife's parents had just died and we all thought of her as one of our own, so she insisted that she and my brother come with us. We went with a wagon train and have been here ever since."

As more buildings and houses popped up around them, Mary knew they were in the city. A handful of people lingered about and talked to each other, their laughter carrying on the wind to greet her ears. Most of the people strode to their destination, some entering or leaving the shops that lined the street. The other horses pulling buggies or wagons kicked up dust in the air. The noisy activity in the town seemed like a drastic change from the quiet and stillness of the farm.

"I should tell you ahead of time about Jenny."

Noting the uncertainty in Sally's voice, she turned to her. "What is it? Is she sick?"

"No. Jenny has a two-year-old son, and she's not married."

"Did her husband die?" That's what she assumed since she hadn't seen him at church.

"Clyde didn't marry her. In fact, when he found out she was expecting, he ran out of town. Our brothers spent a month trying to track him down, but they couldn't find him. She sews clothes for a living so she can be home with her son."

"That must be hard for her."

"She doesn't complain, but you're right. I suspect she spends a lot of time wishing she had done things differently."

By the time they arrived at the boarding house, Jenny was waiting for them on the porch while her son ran back and forth collecting rocks and throwing them. When she saw them, she smiled and picked the boy up in her arms.

"I'll help you," Mary called out to her.

"If you'll take Jeremy, I can get myself in," Jenny said.

Mary nodded and leaned forward to take the blond-haired boy who looked startled.

"Don't you remember your Aunt Mary?" Jenny asked him. She sat next to Mary and brought him to her lap where he watched Mary with intense interest. "You saw her at church for the past two Sundays. She married your uncle Dave."

"It looks like he got his Uncle David's memory," Sally teased.

"I'm sure he'll warm up to me soon enough." Mary smiled at him. "I have lots of nieces and nephews back in Maine, so I'm used to children. He needs time to get used to me. Hi, Jeremy."

He briefly curled his lips upward before sucking his thumb and resting his head against his mother's breast. Sally clicked on the reins as soon as two men on their horses passed them.

"He's a cute boy," she told Jenny, hoping the woman heard her over the shrill laughter of a woman who talked with her friend in front of the beauty salon.

"If you look close, you'll notice he has David's chin," Sally said.

Mary glanced at the woman sitting on her left. "Do you mind if I ask why you call him David?"

Sally chuckled. "I like the name David more than Dave, but he prefers Dave. We agreed I could call him David after I won the race."

Jenny peered across Mary to look at Sally. "To be honest, that wasn't a fair race since you're five years older than him and you were fifteen at the time."

Sally shrugged. "He insisted that he could beat me because I was a girl. I don't think he's ever claimed to be better than a woman ever since that day. I did Mary a favor."

Mary turned to Jenny. "Sally told me that you're twenty. I'm nineteen."

"I wondered how old you were. Sally guessed that you were my age. I don't get a chance to talk to women my age, so I'm glad you're here. No offense, Sally, but sometimes it's nice to have someone who's as old as me."

"That's why I was excited that we're doing this baking contest together," Sally replied.

Mary couldn't recall a time when anyone, except for Grace, seemed to be as interested in her as these women apparently were, and their attention made her feel special. Dave made her feel special too, but it felt different with his sisters.

Sally led the horse to turn left on another street where houses stood close together. They stopped in front of a modest yellow home. Mary followed the women and Jeremy out of the buggy and followed them inside the house which was as sunny and bright as Sally's personality. Mary had grown up in a home similar to this one, and strangely enough, she didn't miss a home made of wood. The simple sod house appealed to her for the simple reason that Dave came with it. She glanced at her sisters-in-law when they stopped to stare at her in amusement.

Jenny grinned. "I told you she was thinking of Dave."

Ignoring their knowing looks as they stood by the counter in front of the window overlooking the small backyard, Mary took off her bonnet and placed it on the table in the corner of the room. "Where's Greg?"

"I just told you that he's at Rick's parents' house." Sally burst out laughing. "You've got it bad. I hope you can concentrate on baking."

"I'm sorry. I'll focus."

Sally took a box of toys from the counter and placed it on the floor so Jeremy could play. The excited youth didn't need any prompting as he knelt before the box and sorted through the colorful trains and blocks.

Mary joined the sisters who walked to the kitchen table and sat down.

"Alright," Sally began. "We need to decide what we're going to make. There are three categories we can join: cookies, pies and breads. Every year we enter all the categories, but Maureen Brown's group manages to snag first place for each category. Should we enter each one again this year?"

"We might as well," Jenny replied.

They looked at Mary who shrugged, surprised they wanted her opinion. "It can't hurt."

"Great!" Sally nodded, satisfied. "I figure we can each pick a category and enter it. Who wants to make what?"

"When I worked at a restaurant in Maine, people complimented my pies," Mary said, her shoe tapping the wooden floor. "I'll make an apple pie."

"Good. Jenny?"

"I'm not as good at cooking as you are, so I'll take the cookies." Jenny glanced at Jeremy.

"Then I'll make the bread. I hope it turns out better this year." She glanced at Mary. "Last year, the wheat loaf we made turned out soggy. I never saw the judges spit food out as fast as they did. It was quite embarrassing."

Jenny chuckled. "Maybe. But looking back on it, it was funny."

Sally joined in the laughter. "How did it get soggy anyway? I mean, it was like a damp sponge."

"I think we're better off not knowing."

"I think I'll make banana bread since last year's fiasco made me realize that I have trouble with the wheat."

Aware of her anxious foot tapping the floor, Mary shifted in the chair and crossed her ankles to stop the irritating sound.

"I'll make walnut sugar cookies," Jenny offered.

"Great! Now that we have everything planned, let's get started."

After sorting through Sally's food pantry, Mary realized they needed more sugar, yeast, and apples. "I'll go to the mercantile and pick up the things we need."

Sally laid down the flour, bananas, walnuts and baking soda on the counter. "I'm sorry. I thought I had enough for whatever we planned to make."

Jenny stopped setting aside the bowls and spoons on the table. "Mary, I can show you how to get to the mercantile from here, and it would be nice to take a walk. Sally, do you mind watching Jeremy?"

Sally shot a smile at the boy who was too wrapped up in stacking the wooden blocks to concern himself with their conversation. "I think I can manage. Without Greg here, he behaves very well."

Jenny nodded as she took off her apron and set it next to the bowl. "Ralph Lindon will probably have his hands full with women buying last minute supplies." She handed Mary her bonnet and put her own on. Glancing at Sally, she said, "We won't be long."

The walk to the mercantile should have been pleasant since the sun shone brightly and the air refreshed Mary's lungs. People went about their business, going from one building to another, depending on the tasks they needed to do. Horses pulled buggies down the streets. People passing by talked and laughed. The smell of steak cooking drifted from the restaurant, bringing back a sense of nostalgia as Mary briefly recalled working for Mrs. Jones. Next to her, Jenny pointed out the businesses they walked by. On the surface, everything was normal. But try as she might, Mary couldn't shake off the strange sense that something remained amiss.

As they rounded the corner of the street where the mercantile stood, it occurred to her what was wrong. The women who went by them seemed to purposely avoid eye contact with them. Though Mary's trips to town had been limited, she understood that common courtesy dictated that people acknowledge one another as they strolled past each other. She glanced at Jenny who didn't notice it. Or did she notice it and chose to ignore it?

When they entered the store, the bell above the door rang, causing two women standing by the baskets full of fruit to turn to them.

The rail thin, middle-aged woman took a moment to look Jenny up and down as if determining whether or not she was worth the polite greeting. Finally, she said, "Good morning, Miss Larson." The woman wore a flashy blue dress and had so many feathers in her hat that Mary unwittingly recalled an image of a male peacock strutting about in front of the female of his species.

"Good morning, Mrs. Brown." Jenny stiffly smiled. Turning to Mary, she said, "This is Maureen Brown. Mrs. Brown, this is Mary Larson."

"Oh really?" The woman now turned her attention to Mary and inspected her from head to toe. "I don't recall seeing you before."

Mary shifted uncomfortably. "I arrived two weeks ago." Her voice sounded weak to her ears.

"Are you the girl who married David Larson? The one who answered his ad asking for a wife?"

Mary blushed. How could this woman know that? She didn't go to the church that Dave did, and Mary didn't recall seeing her before. "Yes, ma'am."

Her eyes made another sweep of her frame. "Well, I guess you never know what you'll get when you ask for something."

Shocked at her words, Mary failed to respond. Shooting Ralph a quick look, she prayed that the man wouldn't be too much longer in dealing with the male customer. She could use a distraction right about now.

"My, my though," Mrs. Brown continued as she motioned to the young woman standing next to her. "Isn't this a neat little coincidence? Cassandra Tyler answered a similar ad that Neil Craftsman posted asking for a wife. She arrived two days ago. They will wed in church this Sunday after the service. Isn't that romantic? Did you and David marry in church?"

"Uh...no. We married at the courthouse."

"Oh." Her disapproval showed. Then she shrugged. "Well, at least he did right by you. In the meantime, I am taking Cassie in since I am good friends with Neil's mother. We can't have unmarried couples fornicating now, can we?" She looked pointedly at Jenny.

It was then that Mary understood what was wrong. Most of the people had shunned Jenny for having a baby out of wedlock.

"Everyone calls me Cassie," Cassandra offered with a courteous smile. "It's nice to meet you both."

"It's nice to meet you too," Jenny softly answered.

Mary nodded and did what she could to smile. Cassie fit the very definition of beauty. Her raven curls framed her flawless pale skin. Her clear blue eyes, perfectly constructed nose and full pink lips went very well with her slender, hourglass figure.

"Mr. Craftsman must have been pleased when he saw you," Mary commented as she recalled the look of revulsion on his face when he saw her. He had looked as if he just sucked on a lemon.

"I dare say he was," Mrs. Brown enthusiastically agreed. "He couldn't stop grinning. Why, he was like a little boy who just received a new toy. He's one lucky man. And Cassie is as sweet as she looks." She patted the woman's arm affectionately. "We get along as if we've known each other our whole lives."

"Of course we do," Cassie sweetly responded.

To Mary's relief, the male customer purchased the watch and turned to leave the store, leaving Ralph free to help them. "Good morning, ladies," he jovially said as he made his way to them.

The customer passed them, offering an obligatory greeting before exiting the building.

"How may I help you?" Ralph looked at each woman, his hands behind his back.

"Mr. Lindon, I am not particularly fond of the selection of cherries you have here." Mrs. Brown motioned to the basket full of ripe cherries on the shelf behind her. "Surely, you have ones that are fresh. I can't make one of my infamous pies with wilting fruits."

"Mrs. Brown, I assure you that those are fresh. The farmer brought them in first thing this morning."

"Hmm..." She wrinkled her nose and inspected them. "I don't know, Mr. Lindon. I can't see paying this price for cherries that look as if they've been sitting here for a week."

By the gleam in Ralph's eyes and subtle smile on Mrs. Brown's lips, Mary realized that this bargaining appealed to them. The bell rang behind her, but she didn't dare look away from the intriguing exchange taking place in front of her.

Ralph puffed his chest and said, "Now you know that I pride myself on my word. When I say that I got those cherries today, I mean I got them today."

She crossed her arms and tilted her head to the side, the feathers on her hat ruffling by the action. "Be that as it may, I am suggesting that the farmer who brought them in misled you into believing that these are fresh."

He rubbed his chin. "You have another price in mind for those cherries?"

Nodding, she said, "I'll give you half of what you're asking."

"I'll give you ten percent off."

She gasped. "That's robbery."

"I believe you need those cherries to make that pie for the baking contest today."

With a loud sigh and a pained expression, she replied, "I want forty percent off."

"Twenty-five percent off and you got a deal."

"Very well." Glancing at Cassie, she said, "Sometimes you have to give in. I have won every baking contest for the past five years. I'm not superstitious by nature, but I think fresh cherries have something to do with it." Returning her eyes to him, she rummaged through her purse. "Have them delivered to my home. I have a few other errands to do before I start cooking. I can't be trudging these all through town." She handed him the money for the cherries. "And I don't want a single one crushed. I don't get famous for my pies by using inferior fruits."

"It's nice doing business with you." He took the coin and slipped it into his pocket.

Mary thought the big smile on his face stemmed more from the haggling process than from making money.

"Come along, Cassie. We have many things to do before we win the contest. We'll see you later, Mr. Lindon." As they strolled past the two women, she nodded at them. "Miss Larson, Sherry."

Jenny offered a half-hearted greeting while Mary stared after the two women, not surprised that Mrs. Brown forgot her name. It happened several times in Maine. Though the woman's manners came off as snobby, Mary couldn't help but be impressed with her ability to get a lesser price on the cherries.

Looking at Jenny and Mary, Ralph asked, "What can I do for you two ladies today?" He put his fists on his hips and waited for their order.

Once they gathered the ingredients they came for, they returned to Sally's residence where they made their assigned dishes.

THE CONTEST TOOK PLACE in the flat, lush green church yard. Mary noticed the afternoon sun shining brightly on the ten tables by the time they arrived with their food. Jenny took Jeremy to Sally's in-laws so they could watch him for the two hour event. They set up their table among the other contestants so that the tables formed a circle. Each table had a selection of breads, pies or cakes, and cookies on it, and the teams varying from two to four women arranged their entries.

The breeze cooled things off enough so that Mary hardly noticed the heat. The sound of chatter and laughter filled the air as Mary helped Jenny set out the red and white striped cloth over their table. Sally took the apple pie, cookies, and sliced banana bread out of her son's wagon and placed them neatly on the table. Jenny added a stack of saucers and a pitcher of water while Mary laid out the utensils and cups.

"I think we have everything," Sally said, straightening a wrinkled section of the cloth.

Jenny shook her head. "You are too particular about things."

"I'm not particular. I'm thorough. Besides, presentation is important."

"To male judges? I don't think so. Men hardly notice little details like where you place a flower."

Sally arranged the daisy in the porcelain vase and smiled as she put it between the pie and the bread. Then she took out another daisy and vase and set that one between the pie and cookies. She sighed and clapped her hands. "Perfect!"

Jenny rolled her eyes, causing Mary to chuckle.

The minister stood in the center of the lawn, surrounded by the tables. He held up his hands and asked for their attention. "Good afternoon, ladies. I am glad you could all make it to our annual bake off. Your judges will include Ralph Lindon, Sheriff Meyer, and yours truly. We will begin sampling your goodies in five minutes."

Sally squealed. "This is so exciting! I just know we're going to win." She began cutting sections of the pie and putting them on three saucers and adding a fork to each one.

"Don't forget the red napkins." Jenny handed them to her. Turning to Mary, she whispered, "I'd set them on the table, but she'll just pick them up and put them somewhere else. Once she gets started on something, there's no stopping her."

When Sally was satisfied that she put everything where it belonged, she chose the chair next to Mary so that Mary sat between her and Jenny. She smiled. "I think I got it just right."

"It looks terrific," Mary assured her.

A fly landed in the pie. Leaning forward, she shooed it away, knocking over one of the vases in the process. Gasping, she jumped up and set the daisy and vase back in its proper place. Then she returned to her seat, fidgeting.

"Relax," Jenny said.

Sally glanced at them. "I really want to win this year. With Mary's help, we have a good chance." She reached forward and squeezed Mary's hand and told her, "Of course, we like spending time with you too, but the fact that you're an excellent cook is a bonus."

Ralph approached them, a big smile on his face. "Good afternoon, ladies." He tipped his hat. "Mrs. Larson, I have to admit that the dress you made holds up well to the wind. It didn't seem long strong material when you bought it."

"You made this dress?" Jenny inspected Mary's dress while Sally directed him to the food in front of him. Jenny's eyes widened. "You did some fine stitching."

"Thank you. I learned to sew when I was eight. I find it soothing," Mary replied.

"Can I come out to your place so you can teach me how to do this? Of course, I would like to see Dave too."

"You better wait for two weeks before making the trip," Sally good-naturedly warned while Ralph ate. "I had to pry him off of her in order to get him to agree to let her enter this contest."

"It wasn't like that," Mary argued.

"Right." She rolled her eyes. "Anyway, she'll get to come out to Ma and Pa's place when the men get together to build the barn. I'm sure anytime after that will be fine for you to intrude on David's alone time with her." She grinned knowingly at Mary who blushed.

"I see that Dave is eating better these days," Ralph commented.

They turned their attention to him.

He pulled a writing pad out of his vest pocket and wrote his score on it. "Sally and Jenny, your foods have improved as well."

"Oh, we can't take full credit for that. Mary gave us some pointers." Sally glanced at Mary. "I told you that you would be a big help to us."

"Well, it's much better than last year. I'll talk to you later." He winked and headed for the next table.

Minister Greene nodded a greeting to them as he arrived at their table. He lifted his fork to sample the pie before he ate a cookie and slice of bread. Though Mary tried to pay attention to him, her eyes kept drifting to Mrs. Brown's hat because the breeze caused the crazy peacock feathers to flutter. For a reason she couldn't explain, the effect seemed hypnotizing.

"This is good!" The minister's statement brought her eyes back to him. His eyebrows raised and head nodding, he wrote their score on his pad. Holding the pad and pencil at his side, he told Jenny, "My wife was impressed with the banner you sewed for the church."

Jenny smiled. "I enjoyed making it."

"Are you sure you don't want to join the choir? We could use a lead vocalist and my wife says have the sweetest soprano voice she's ever heard."

"I appreciate the offer, but I don't think someone of my reputation would be appropriate for the choir."

He frowned. Glancing over at Mrs. Brown, whom Mary guessed was the real reason behind Jenny's hesitation, he sighed. Looking back at Jenny, he said, "The Lord is forgiving, even when people aren't."

Mary thought that was nice of him to say.

The sheriff hurried over to them. Without waiting for Sally to hand him a plate, he grabbed the saucer and shoved a fork full of pie into his mouth. The sunlight bouncing off of his shiny gold badge caused Mary to avert her attention back to Mrs. Brown.

She peered around his large, imposing frame when Mrs. Brown bolted out of her chair to stop a child from pulling the tablecloth off of the table next to hers. The plump matron at the table put her hand over her heart while Mrs. Brown returned the pie to its rightful position. The woman appeared grateful for Mrs. Brown's assistance. Mary expected Mrs. Brown to scold the young boy, but she patted him on the shoulder and knelt by him so she could talk to him. When the child turned away, he joined his apologetic mother with a smile on his face, so whatever Mrs. Brown said to him, she displayed a kindness that Mary wouldn't have anticipated from her. Perhaps there was more to Mrs. Brown than met the eye.

The sheriff's huff directed Mary's attention back to him. His face, void of emotion, unsettled her, for she had no clue as to what he thought of their food. He scribbled something in his pad and made a beeline for the next table.

"Don't mind him," Sally said with a wave of her hand. "He's not very friendly, though he does a great job of enforcing the law."

Once the judges were done, Minister Greene stood in the middle of the lawn. "I want to thank you wonderful ladies for coming out here today. As difficult as this decision is, there can only be one team that is declared the winner. We take the total of all three categories and the team with the highest score wins. This year, the award and five cent gift certificate to the mercantile for each member on the team goes to Sally Johnson and Mary and Jenny Larson. Congratulations, ladies."

Sally gasped and hugged Mary.

Jenny laughed. "Let her go. You're squeezing her to death!"

Mary didn't mind. She was glad that Sally finally got to win. The women around them applauded.

"Ladies, now you can sit back and eat," Minister Greene concluded.

After they ate their meals and were cleaning up, Mrs. Brown and Cassie strolled over to Mary. "We want to congratulate you," Mrs. Brown announced. "Obviously, we have a worthy opponent."

"Thank you," Mary replied uncertainly as Sally and Jenny continued collecting the dirty dishes.

"I got a chance to sample your apple pie. You are an excellent cook." Mrs. Brown smiled at her.

Surprised by the woman's warmth, she wasn't sure of how to respond.

"We must get together some time. You married one of the Larson boys. His name is David?"

"Yes," she hesitated. Didn't the woman remember their conversation earlier that day?

"He's a fine boy. His farm is next to Neil Craftsman's. I think they help each other when it's time for the harvest. Cassie, you two will be neighbors. What a wonderful chance for you to get together and talk or come into town and shop with her."

"Yes, Mrs. Brown. You're right." Cassie barely looked in Mary's direction.

Mary had no such inclination to visit Cassie since she didn't want to associate with Neil.

"There's my fiancée," came a familiar voice.

Mary braced herself for Neil's arrival.

"Speak of the devil," Mrs. Brown warmly greeted. "We were just talking about you."

He kissed Cassie's cheek before he noticed Mary. He suddenly stood up straight and glanced uneasily at her.

"Apparently, your farm is next to David Larson's," Cassie demurely told him, batting her eyelashes at him.

"We must all get together sometime," Mrs. Brown stated.

From the looks on Neil's and Cassie's faces, Mary realized that Mrs. Brown was the only one who was enthused by that notion.

"Well, Mary has a real talent for cooking," the woman insisted. "Of course, Cassie is wonderful at the task as well, though perhaps Mary might teach her a thing or two. It never hurts to improve your skills."

Cassie slightly frowned in Mary's direction.

It didn't occur to Mary, until that moment, that as beautiful as Cassie was, she felt inferior to her. Mary couldn't recall a time when anyone felt inadequate next to her. After all, Mary didn't have much to offer. She was nothing compared to Cassie. Cassie had beauty, charm, and grace. She was the very definition of what a lady should be.

Feeling uneasy, Mary spoke up. "I had some of your bread, Cassie, and I thought it was delicious."

Cassie relaxed.

"We should gather our dishes, Cassie dear," Mrs. Brown said.

Mary turned back to her table, figuring that the discussion was over. Behind her, Neil cleared his throat. Sally and Jenny had stopped to talk to Minister Greene and his wife, so she had no option but to talk to him. Stifling a groan, she turned to him.

"You didn't tell them about…" He shifted from one foot to the other. "Well, that is to say…" He faltered.

"No, Neil. They don't know that I originally answered your ad," she whispered. Like she wanted them to know he rejected her!

He appeared relieved.

"Don't worry about it, Neil. No one will ever find out."

He paused for a brief moment before asking, "Is Dave good to you?"

She blinked, taken aback. "Yes, as a matter of fact, he is."

"I'm glad to hear that." He glanced back at Cassie who smiled sweetly at him. "It looks like things have worked out."

She sighed. He apparently wanted affirmation. "She's lovely, Neil. You make a good couple."

He nodded. "Thank you, Mary." Then he walked away.

She took a deep breath to settle her nerves. She didn't enjoy these confrontations and could only hope that they wouldn't have another reason to talk.

Sally approached her. "Are you ready to go home? I better return you before David comes riding into town searching for you."

Mary laughed at her joke, immediately feeling better. "I'm ready."

Chapter Eight

Five days later, Dave was ready to clean the stalls after breakfast when someone called out to him, "Dave? Are you in there?"

Recognizing his brother's anxious voice, Dave set the rake down and came out of the building, lowering the top part of his hat so the sun wouldn't get in his eyes. "What's wrong, Tom?" He set his hands on his hips and waited for the twenty-five-year-old blond to answer his question.

His older brother looked relieved to see him. "Neil's cattle escaped sometime early this morning and are headed to town. We need to get them rounded up and back home. Can you help?" The black stallion shifted under him.

"Sure. I'll be there soon."

"Alright. The cattle were last spotted on the corner of Zachary Phillips' and Jimmy Parson's properties."

"I'll be there."

As Tom rode off, Dave went to the house where Mary cut up apples to set in the freshly made crust for another one of her delicious pies. His mouth watered just thinking about it. She paused, her knife halfway down a red apple, and glanced at him.

"Is everything alright?" she asked, her expression immediately concerned.

"Neil's cattle broke free of his fence sometime early this morning. I have to go help bring them back. I don't know how long I'll be. It sounds like a group of us farmers will be there. Hopefully, I'll be back by mid-afternoon." He placed his hand on the small of her back and gave her cheek a warm kiss, noting the sweet smell of lilac soap in her hair.

"I'll clean the stalls after I milk the cow. I want to get this pie in the oven first." She finished cutting the apple in front of her.

"Isn't it just like you to pitch in and help at a moment's notice?" His heart swelled with pride. "You're really a special woman, Mary. I'm lucky that I found you when I did."

She prettily blushed at his words.

Giving her another kiss, he headed for the barn where he gathered the necessary items to saddle Jack. He was ready to get on the horse when he remembered to get the lasso.

It didn't take him long to catch up to the other men who were rounding up the cattle to turn them back to the Craftsman farm. Neil, Tom, and Jimmy chased after their respective cattle.

Joel arrived on the downward slope of Jimmy's property.

Dave waved him over, noticing his brother looked as if he just threw on some clothes since they didn't even match.

"How did Neil's cattle escape?" Joel asked, riding over to him.

"I don't know. I just got here. Did Tom explain it?" Dave got his lasso ready to use if necessary.

"I asked you the question, so how could I possibly know?"

He wryly grinned. "You're right."

"Oh well. I think there's twenty cattle altogether. Neil was bragging on them the other day so I remember the number."

Dave nodded. "Let's get to work." A quick assessment told him how many cattle the three men had under control, so when he spotted one that was the furthest away from the group, he prompted Jack to chase it down.

The activity took more time than Dave anticipated. He lassoed two cattle that resisted going with the rest of the group, which several of them seemed to do every ten or fifteen minutes. He was relieved when they finally put them all into the fenced area. He took his brown hat off and wiped the sweat off his brow. The early afternoon sunny weather didn't feel oppressively hot that day but exerting all that energy on the cattle wore him out.

"I'm sure you're hungry," Neil stated as he walked over to the four men as they leaned against the gate. "Would you like to grab a bite before you head on back home? It's the least I can do to thank you for your help."

The men agreed, and as anxious as Dave was to return to Mary, his growling stomach insisted he stay. They washed up at the well in Neil's front yard which stood a quarter mile from the sod house while Neil went to tell his wife to get something ready for the men to eat.

"Since when did Neil get a well?" Tom wondered as he brought up a bucket of fresh, cool water that felt like heaven on earth to Dave's hot face.

"I think it was a couple of months ago," Jimmy, the middle-aged farmer with lightly graying brown hair, replied. "He said he was tired of running down to the river all the time to get water."

"The river isn't that far," Dave responded, surprised.

Jimmy shrugged. "Maybe he did it because he figured it was time to place an ad for a wife. A woman from back east likes to have water close by."

"He got married?" Tom didn't hide his shock.

"If you went to church last Sunday, you'd have heard the announcement," Jimmy said.

Neil didn't attend their church so Dave didn't find out about it until after the fact since Neil married earlier that morning after the 8 am service.

"My girls were sick and between the two of them, it took a full two weeks for them to recover," Tom explained. "I had to stay and help Jessica. A stressed out expectant woman is no fun to be around."

"I can't believe Neil got married," Joel spoke up.

Jimmy nodded. "I was as taken aback as you are. He ran around with so many women that it didn't seem like he'd ever settle down. You can't help but feel sorry for her."

"Why do you say that?"

Jimmy took a moment to consider his words. "I've never been too impressed with him."

"Because he slept around?"

"No. Because I'm sick and tired of having to come to his aid when he neglects his duties. This isn't the first time I've had to chase down cattle for him. I only do it to keep them away from my herd. His cattle are inferior in quality. I'd hate to breed my stock with his."

Out of the corner of his eye, Dave caught sight of one of the cattle sauntering off the property. "He must have a rip in his fence. Look over there."

Tom and Joel groaned while Jimmy shook his head and muttered something about lazy people. Jimmy hopped up on his horse and immediately brought the bull back while the other men rushed over to the torn section of the fence to prevent any more cattle from escaping.

"This is going to take Neil all day to fix," Tom commented.

"If he does a good job," Dave remarked.

Jimmy sighed. "Alright. This needs repairing right away. Can I have help with this?"

The three men agreed since no one wanted to lose another full day's work running after Neil's cattle. Jimmy went to the sod house to talk to Neil.

"You know, if we refused to chase the cattle in the future, it might force Neil to take better care of his property," Tom said.

"Cattle running through town might cause a lot of damage," Dave reflected, ignoring the mooing of the animals. "That's if they head in that direction. They might wind up on my property. Then I'd have to deal with them anyway."

"Lucky for me, I'm on the other side of you."

"This is exactly why I plant crops. It can be a lot of work while planting and harvesting, but for the rest of the time, you pretty much just watch it grow."

"Dave," Joel leaned forward, "I heard you got married."

"I did. She's a great girl."

"Is she pretty?"

"I think so. Of course, if you had gone to church, you'd have seen her."

"My horse fell in a ditch last Sunday."

Tom grinned and patted Dave on the back. "You finally took my advice and posted an ad for a wife?"

"I met her from an answered ad." Granted, it was Neil's ad, but it was as close to the truth as he would tell them.

"What's her name?" Tom asked.

"Jenny said that her name is Mary," Joel told Tom. "Haven't you gone to visit Sally or Jenny?"

"Where have you been? I already said my girls were sick," Tom explained. "I don't have a lot of time to leave for town." Glancing at Dave, he asked, "Where is Mary from?"

"Maine," Joel inserted.

"I haven't lost my voice," Dave joked.

Joel grinned. "I can't let you hog all the attention."

Tom looked back at Dave. "So, when are we going to meet her?"

Dave stared at Joel to see if he would jump in again.

Joel, looking startled, asked, "How would I know? I can't read your mind."

"Just making sure it's safe to answer." Dave smiled. "I'll bring her to Pa and Ma's when we build the barn. You'll meet her next week, unless you make it to church this Sunday."

"Good for you, Dave," Tom said. "It's too bad I didn't know or I would have said hi when I was over at your place this morning."

At that moment, Jimmy returned. "Alright. Neil has some barbed wire in his shed. I'll gather what we need and we can fix this."

"Where's Neil?" Dave asked.

"He's helping his new wife cook." He chuckled and shook his head. "I have a feeling he's using that as an excuse to be with her. I got a chance to see her, and she's a good looker."

"Really?" Joel grunted. "Maybe I should advertise for a wife when I turn eighteen. Apparently, there's a good selection of women from back east."

As they worked on the fence, their conversation ranged from how their farms fared to Jimmy and Tom giving Dave advice on marriage.

Just as they completed the repair, Neil appeared. "I didn't expect you to do this but I appreciate it. Are you ready to eat?"

Dave's insistent growling stomach urged him to follow the men to the house.

"We'll have to eat out here since there's not room for all of us in the house," Neil explained.

Dave sat between Joel and Tom on the grass. Jimmy plopped down next to Tom. Dave deeply inhaled but stopped when he realized he smelled manure. He was used to that smell in his sod barn but outside of it, the sweet smell of growing clover and fresh air greeted his nostrils.

Neil sat between Jimmy and Joel. They formed a circle, making Neil in direct line of Dave's vision. Dave forced aside the urge to call the man on his rude behavior towards Mary. If it hadn't been for the fact that he wished to save Mary from others knowing what transpired at the train station between her and Neil, he would have let Neil have it. She didn't deserve the way Neil treated her, and having gotten to know her as well as he did, Dave was grateful she ended up with him instead.

"I'll be building a wooden house in that direction so Cassie doesn't have to be so close to the animals," Neil informed the group.

"Maybe you should expand your fence so your cattle have more room to roam while you're making improvements," Jimmy suggested.

"That's not a bad idea."

"Do you have the money for all of that?" Tom wondered. "I mean, you just put in this well and purchased some cattle. The lumber for building the house won't be cheap either. Even Jessica and I are staying in our sod house because it's inexpensive, though we have two children and one on the way."

"I've managed to save aside a nice amount of money over the past decade," Neil replied. Looking up, and over Dave's head, he widely smiled. "There's my beautiful bride."

Dave glanced at Cassie, blinking in surprise at her dress. The pink lace and ruffles were superfluous, and the delicate material wouldn't last long. Her long black hair was swept back with a pink bow, so her curls framed her pretty face. She was in for a rude awakening when she realized that her clothes and hairstyle had no place on the farm. Yes, she was pretty. No one could deny that, but she was too thin and didn't have the curves that Dave had become accustomed to enjoying.

"I hope you like ham and potatoes and carrots," she said in a singsong voice.

"I know I do!" Joel enthusiastically nodded as he accepted his plate.

She handed the other plate to Neil. "I'll be back with more plates."

After she slipped into the house, Joel whistled. "Neil, you lucky dog. How did you manage to marry her?"

"I told you she was good looking," Jimmy inserted.

"Good looking? She's every man's dream come true," Joel said.

"She's a pretty one alright," Tom admitted. "Though I wouldn't put her above Jessica."

"A man has to be loyal to his wife." Jimmy winked at Tom.

Neil's face glowed at their appreciation of his wife's beauty. "She's a gem alright."

Cassie returned with plates for Dave, Tom and Jimmy. "I'll be back with the coffee."

"Where did she come from?" Joel wondered.

"Pennsylvania," Neil replied.

"I'll have to advertise specifically in that state when I ask for a wife."

Dave sighed and took a bite of mashed potatoes. He fought the urge to spit the grainy and soupy slop out. He quickly glanced at the other men who also hesitated after taking their first bite.

Neil sheepishly smiled. "Mrs. Brown is teaching her how to cook. She never made anything before she came out here."

Jimmy gave a slight grimace as he swallowed his food. "Good because there's more to a woman than her looks."

"She'll get better. It's just a matter of learning what to do."

"I didn't mean anything bad by it. I'm sure she'll get much better with time."

"Who cares how she cooks?" Joel laughed. "She's worth coming home to every night. Can you imagine how great Neil's nights are?"

"Spoken like a seventeen year old," Jimmy mused. Turning to the young man, he pointed a fork in his direction. "There's more to marriage than lovemaking, though I admit a good intimate life helps."

Tom chuckled. "You're a walking contradiction."

"No, I'm not. I've been married to Doris for twenty-six years, and I've learned some things about maintaining a happy marriage."

Cassie returned with cups of coffee for Neil, Joel and Jimmy.

"Could I have water instead, please?" Dave asked her. If her cooking was an indicator of the coffee, he wanted to skip that experience. As it was, he barely managed to swallow the rubbery carrots and extremely salty ham.

She nodded and returned to the house.

"Dave, why are you so quiet?" Tom wondered. "Usually we can't get you to shut up."

"I'm tired," he blandly replied.

"Mary keeping you up all night?" Tom grinned. "I remember when I was first married. I couldn't get enough of Jessica."

Neil snorted under his breath and shook his head.

Dave's jaw clenched. He knew exactly what Neil was thinking and he didn't like it. His protective instinct kicked into high gear, and as much as he wanted to warn Neil to stop insulting Mary, he couldn't do it without hurting her. "I'm going home. Mary helped Sally and Jenny win the cooking contest last week, and I'm in the mood for some great tasting food." He forced his hands to gently set the plate on the grass so he wouldn't fling it in Neil's direction. Then he jumped up.

The other men looked stunned while Neil frowned at him.

Don't mess with me, Neil. He hoped the man read his expression loud and clear. As he turned to go to his horse, he nearly bumped into Cassie.

"Do you want the water?" she asked, raising the glass to him.

You poor woman. You're married to a snake, and you don't even know it. "No thank you, ma'am. I need to get home." He tipped his hat to her and left without a backward glance.

By the time Dave returned home, he found Mary laying out grain from the previous year to feed the horses and cow. The foal and mare looked very happy to stand side by side and eat from the same trough. As soon as Jack neighed as he rode up to the barn, she turned her attention to him. The sight of her welcoming smile warmed his heart.

He slid off his horse. He didn't realized how tired he was until he saw her concerned expression. The evening sun began to spread its brilliant pink and orange hues across the sky. Between chasing cattle, fixing a fence and fighting the urge to tell Neil exactly what he thought of him, he had gone through a rough day.

"Are you hungry?" she asked him as she walked over to him. "I can fix something right after I get Jack settled and fed."

He didn't care what Neil said or thought. Mary was the kind of woman a man was very happy to come home to. He took her in his arms and kissed her, taking in the sweet smell of the cinnamon apple pie she made earlier that day. Her flesh was soft, her curves molding into his body. She was altogether wonderful. He reluctantly ended the kiss but continued to hold her tightly to him.

"Was your day that trying?" She tried to sound playful but he noted her sympathy.

"Let's just say I'm glad it's over." He took a good look around the barn and saw that she had taken care of the animals. In the corner of the barn, he noticed a bucket of dead bugs she had pried off the corn in the field. He suddenly realized she wore her pants. "Did you do all the chores?"

She shrugged. "I had plenty of time after I finished baking. There are only so many pies a woman can make before she needs something else to do. Why don't you go to the river and take a bath? I'll take care of Jack and get supper ready. Then you can go to bed."

Despite the temptation to take her to bed right then, his aching body and growling stomach pressed him to take her advice. Once he cleaned up, he enjoyed her delicious food, which somehow tasted better than before. As he stood up from the table, she offered to rub his back and arms to ease his sore muscles. He gratefully accepted and proceeded to make love to her, taking his time to fully appreciate her. Neil had it wrong. Lovemaking with Mary was the most pleasurable experience Dave ever had, and he slept even better since he held her close to him through the night.

TWO DAYS BEFORE THEY were due to go to his parents' farm, Dave took Mary to town so she could collect a couple of items from the mercantile and check for a letter from her parents at the post office. She shrieked with delight when she saw that they had written her. While he left her to tend to his wagon, she stayed inside the small post office. She ripped the envelope open and held the letter up to the window for better lighting.

Her enthusiasm faltered as she read through the contents of the note.

We were relieved to hear that the marriage plans worked out and that your husband is a good man. We've given it considerable thought and decided you showed wise judgment when you answered that ad after all. Thankfully, decent men are in desperate need of women out there. We worried for you here since we couldn't find someone to court you because you weren't as pretty as your sisters. Now that is all in the past, and you can realize your dream of having children.

Mary's hands trembled as she debated whether or not to finish the missive. She understood that her family believed she wouldn't ever marry because of her looks, so why did the words sting? She should be used to it. She should have expected it. And yet, it no longer seemed fair that they should compare her to her sisters.

Looking out the window of the post office, she spied Dave laughing and talking to a man she didn't recognize. Did he regret marrying her? She didn't fool herself into thinking he would have married her if given the chance to marry someone more pleasing to look at. She wondered how he could act as if he enjoyed being stuck with her.

He should have sent a real ad to the paper. Did he ever wish he had? She didn't know, and she decided that she didn't want to know.

Preferring the fantasy that he honestly found her pleasant, rather than a necessity on his farm, she took a deep breath and read the rest of the note, biting her lower lip to prepare herself for whatever else her family chose to write.

Fortunately, the rest of it was full of updates regarding the people they knew. It ended with wishes of happiness. Not love, she noted, glancing at her good looking husband. The most she could hope for was that he'd be content with her. Brushing back some tears, she ripped the paper and threw the pieces into the trashcan by her feet. She didn't care to be reminded of it. Her moving to Nebraska might have been the best thing she ever did for herself.

"Are you ready to go?" Dave's voice startled her.

Aware that he stood behind her, she anxiously wiped her tears away, waiting until her emotions settled before turning to him. "Yes, I'm ready." She strode to the door he held open for her, purposely avoiding eye contact with him or the old woman who glanced in her direction.

His expression sympathetic, he said, "You must miss them."

"What?" She paused as she reached him.

"Your family. You said the letter was from them."

"Oh, the letter." She forgot she mentioned it to him. Shrugging, she commented, "They are doing fine."

"Can I read it?"

The idea of him reading what her family thought of her horrified her. He didn't need reminders that he could have done better. Neil Craftsman did a good job of that already. "Well, I...I..."

"Kind of personal?"

"Yes, you could say that." It was as close to the truth as she wanted to admit.

"Alright."

His willingness to accept her answer caused her to be grateful to him. As if there weren't many things she was grateful for when it came to Dave Larson!

She passed through the door and waited for him to help her into the wagon, thankful that she lived with him instead of her parents.

Chapter Nine

The day arrived when Dave promised his brothers that he would help them build their parents a barn. Mary's stomach did flip flops, and she couldn't blame all of it on the baby.

"You're nervous," Dave commented as they rode on the wagon, passing tall green stalks of corn that thrived from the rain that periodically blessed the landscape.

She wiped her sweaty palms on her blue dress.

He reached over and squeezed her hand. "You have nothing to worry about. You're a great woman."

"How many people will be there today?"

He tilted his head to the side as he mentally counted his siblings, their spouses, and their children. "Seventeen, if you include my parents. I reckon your family boasted of more than that." He smiled. "I can't wait to tell them we're having a baby. Of course, all the women will hover around you and tell you stories from when they were expecting."

That was good because her mother and sisters failed to mention it. She realized it was another reminder that they didn't count on her getting married.

By the time they arrived at his parents' farm, it appeared as if everyone had already arrived. He parked their wagon. The fenced area in front of them provided a resting place for the animals, and she watched as Dave unhitched Lewis and Clark so he could send them to the pasture. Taking a deep breath, she smelled the sunflowers to her right. The sound of laughter greeted her ears, so she glanced at the large group of men and women about an acre away. A quick examination of the rest of the property showed her an old sod barn, several animals, and a blue wood-framed home. Further out, the acreage alternated between corn and beans. At least she knew how Dave decided to grow the crops he did. He was used to corn and beans.

Once Dave closed the gate, he helped her down the wagon. Kissing her cheek, he said, "When the men and women separate, it won't be so intimidating."

Determined that her anxiety wouldn't show, she nodded. He took her hand and led her to the front lawn where two groups mingled. One group consisted of mostly children who surrounded a large box. The other group contained more women than men, and Dave led her to them.

"Glad to see you actually brought her out," Sally told Dave. "Is there anything new since we last saw you?"

Though she asked Mary the question, he answered. "We're expecting our first child!"

Sally and Jenny gasped and pushed him aside so they could stand next to Mary.

"How exciting!" Sally wrapped her in a warm embrace.

"My turn!" Jenny hugged her after Sally let go.

"And you wonder why I wanted her all to myself for a month." Dave shook his head before he went to the children and the box.

"Well, you had your month. Now it's our turn." Sally called after him.

Greg brought a puppy over to her.

"Can I have him, Ma?" he asked.

"Our parents' dog gave birth to seven puppies and Pa wants us to take some of them off his hands," Sally explained to Mary. "That's why the children are over there."

"There's no way my landlady will let me bring a puppy to the boarding house," Jenny said with remorse as she watched Jeremy hug a bundle of squirming brown fur before it fell out of his arms.

"He can come over and see the one Greg will pick out," Sally assured her. "You can get the benefit of a cuddly dog without the hassle of cleaning up after him."

"True."

"It looks like David might want one." Sally nudged Mary in the side and nodded towards her brother who peered into the box.

The children jumped around him to say hello, and he knelt by them to see the puppies they wanted to show him.

"Mary, you met Tom and Richard," Sally introduced, turning Mary's attention to the people around her. "This is Amanda, Richard's wife, and this is Jessica, Tom's wife. My husband, Rick, should be back soon. He's trying to avoid bringing a dog home, but once he sees Greg playing with a puppy, he'll most likely cave in and agree to it."

"We've already met Mary," Richard told Sally.

"I know but David didn't give her more than five minutes with us. The poor girl didn't have time to remember everyone."

Amanda smiled at Mary. "I heard that you won the baking contest. I bet Mrs. Brown wasn't too happy. She's not used to losing."

Mary shrugged. "She seemed to take it alright. She congratulated us."

"Us?" Sally chuckled. "You're the reason we won. I appreciate your willingness to share the spotlight, but the truth is that you were the winner that day. I can see why David gained that weight back."

Jenny yelled out to Dave, "If you have a girl and she cooks as well as Mary, then you'll be a grand old blimp."

"No. I have too much running around to do," he replied.

"I hope we have a boy this time," Tom inserted. "I could mold him into my image. Though there's nothing wrong with girls," he quickly added, glancing at his wife.

Jessica rubbed her pregnant belly. "All I do is carry them. It's up to you to determine if it's a boy or a girl."

"Up to me? You spend nine months making the baby. Can't you make one a boy?"

She glared at him.

"You've got to learn when to shut up." Richard shook his head at Tom.

Sally nodded. "I wouldn't be surprised if she clubbed you over the head with a rolling pin."

"Where's Joel?" Jenny wondered.

Tom looked relieved for the change in topic.

"He's finishing up with his chores," Richard answered. "He slept in late...again. I hope he has more sense than to go into farming. He obviously hates it."

One of the eight-year-old twin boys ran up to Richard, holding an excited puppy. "Pa, can I have this one?"

"Oh, how adorable," Amanda said, clearly won over by the creature.

"Yes. You can have one." Richard looked at Tom. "I know when it's pointless to argue." Then he followed his wife and son to the box.

"We might as well join them," Sally said, leading Mary to the box as the rest of the group joined Dave and the kids.

Mary noticed that Dave made an attempt to stand next to her, but Jenny and Sally hovered around her so he gave up and turned his attention back to the puppies.

"Have you made a decision yet?" Tom asked his daughters.

"This is a nice one." Four-year-old Nelly pointed to the brown and white mutt. "He looks like a pirate, except he has a white patch over his eye instead of a black one."

"This one," her two-year-old sister, Patricia, protested, pointing to another one.

"Those are fine puppies, but that one is the best of the litter," Dave replied.

Tom grimaced. "The runt?"

"Sure. Just look at him. He's working twice as hard as the rest of them to get our attention."

"But he's small and weak."

He shrugged. "For now. But he'll grow up to be the best dog of all his brothers and sisters. With his motivation, he'll make an excellent hunting dog."

Mary squinted in the sun so she could see his face. "Hunting?" The wind played with the strands of her hair that peeked out from under her bonnet.

"Sure. We have rabbits, squirrels, and deer on our land. They could be meat for stew or steak." His eyes lit up. "What do you say, Mary? Would you like to bring this pup home?"

Startled, she hesitated to answer. The last thing she thought she'd be doing was bringing a puppy home.

"He won't stay in the house," Dave continued. "He'll stay out in the barn, so you won't have to worry about cleaning up after him. And he'll be a good friend for our child."

Tom glanced at Richard and whispered, "Leave it to Dave to pick the worst of the bunch."

Though Dave didn't hear the sarcastic remark, she did. She frowned, realizing that she and this poor dog had something in common. He wasn't as attractive as the others in the box, but Dave wanted to take him home. *Just as he took me when no other man would have me.*

Her decision made, she nodded in Dave's direction. "I think taking him is a good idea."

Seeming pleased by her consent, he reached into the box and picked the runt out. "What do you want to name him?"

"Jasper?"

He nodded. "Jasper it is!"

"Oh, my parents! Let's say hi," Sally told Mary as she tugged on her arm.

"Who nominated you the welcoming committee?" Tom asked her.

"Sally's always been a take charge kind of girl," Richard reminded him. "She's doing a great job. She's helping Mary feel at home in a sea of unfamiliar faces."

"Thank you, Richard," she remarked.

After the usual round of greetings to her parents, the father asked, "So, how many mutts can I get off my hands today? I see Dave's claimed one."

"We'll take the patchy one," Nelly stated. She practically shoved the animal in her father's arms, ignoring her sister who cried for the other one.

"Actually, we'll take two." Jessica bent down to grab the other puppy and placed it on top of the one Tom was already trying to hold. "And if we have a boy, we might take another one. Boys require more physical activity than girls." Looking pleased with herself, she left a flabbergasted Tom so she could stand next to Mary. "I heard you make the best apple pie Ralph Lindon ever tasted. Will you make it for supper?"

Blushing at Jessica's compliment, Mary agreed.

Dave's mother smiled at Mary. "It's nice to have you here. I didn't get a chance to ask you this in church, but what motivated you to leave Maine?"

Mary briefly noted that Dave grinned at her before he set Jasper on the ground so the puppy could play with the kids. He joined the other men as they got ready to build the barn with the pile of lumber resting in the yard.

Turning back to his mother, she answered, "I wanted an adventure. I heard about the prairie but hadn't seen it." That was partly true, but she didn't feel like explaining the fact that it was her only chance of getting married.

"Dave was talking about placing an ad for a few months but said he kept forgetting to do it. I guess he remembered on one occasion when he went to town. The lack of available women out here makes it difficult for a man to marry. I'm glad he finally did it. I haven't seen him this happy in a long time."

"He didn't say anything but he was lonely," Sally added.

Mary suspected that the prospect of having a baby put the smile on his face. She had never seen a prouder smile on a man's face than when she told him she was expecting. He kept her up all night trying to pick out a suitable name for the baby. When he set his mind to something, there was no stopping him.

She felt content with the knowledge that it was her providing him with a child that gave him joy. After all, he married her for this reason, and since she fulfilled her part of the marriage, he was happy. His happiness created her own, and she loved him for his kindness towards her. He cared enough to show her affection when very few people in her life had. Being held and kissed filled her with a sense of belonging and peace that she hadn't known was missing from her life until she received it.

"She must be thinking of David again." Sally giggled, breaking Mary out of her thoughts.

Blinking, she realized that his mother had asked her something. "I'm sorry. What is it?"

The older woman smiled. "Would you like to come into the house?"

"Yes. Thank you." Mary returned her smile, enraptured that these women had indeed welcomed her into their family.

DURING THE NOON HOUR, Mary completed her two pies, salad and stew, and since she didn't relish the idea of sitting idly by when work could be done, she offered to take care of the dry linens that hung on the clothesline. The sheets and towels smelled fresh and clean, the sweet outdoor odor reminding her of the times she helped her mother with the laundry. She decided that she would assure her parents that Dave treated her well and that she was expecting her first child. Perhaps they might forget her unattractiveness as time passed. Deep down, they did love her. Didn't they?

Dave's mother wiped her hands on her apron as Mary entered the house with the basket full of clean linens. "You are a real treasure. I am very lucky that my sons have chosen such wonderful wives."

Mary blushed at her compliment. Her parents didn't place much emphasis on praise, so she didn't know how to respond. Clearing her throat, she asked, "Where would you like these?"

"I'll take the sheets and make the beds. Will you please put the towels in the scullery room?"

She nodded. Thankfully, she received a tour of the house which had more room than a sod house. Dave planned to eventually construct a wood house which would give them additional rooms as their family grew. "Now we know that you conceive right away, so we'll need the extra space in the next few years." He seemed excited by the notion of having a large family. Since she had six brothers and five sisters, he had good reason to assume they would need a bigger home.

She entered the scullery room and folded the ten towels and set them on the table in the corner of the room. Repositioning the mangle on the floor beside the table, she realized that her days of working at the restaurant left her with an unexpected habit of putting things neatly in their proper location.

"Leave it to Dave to pick the worst of the litter."

She stood up and turned, thinking that Tom entered the room, but the room remained empty, except for her. He must've been sitting on the bench under the window since she could hear him. She glanced at the open window across the small room. The thin pink curtains danced in the breeze wafting into the room.

"I can't believe he married her either," Joel remarked.

"I was talking about the dog." After a moment's pause, Tom added, "Though I guess you have a point."

"They ought to make it mandatory for a woman to warn her prospective husband that she'd be better off wearing a bag over her head."

She sighed. She overheard more of these conversations from other men who didn't realize she was in hearing distance. They were the same comments that made her parents believe she wouldn't ever marry. She wanted to leave, but her feet refused to move. A mixture of shock and dreaded curiosity held her in place.

Tom chuckled. "Joel, you're displaying an unusual mean streak today. What's gotten into you?"

"I was thinking of placing one of those ads when I turn eighteen, but I'm not sure about it anymore. I mean, Cassie Craftsman is gorgeous, but Mary... Well, when I saw her in church, I couldn't believe my eyes. What if I end up with someone like that?" He groaned. "I just don't know how I'm going to find a wife. Maybe I'll stay single."

As another breeze lifted the curtain, Mary saw Richard round the corner of the house. "What are you doing here? We're supposed to be building a barn."

"Don't get your feathers all ruffled," Tom replied. "We're taking a break."

"Yeah. It's not a crime to rest," Joel stated.

"Joel, you've already taken two breaks in the past two hours. And Tom, you're not helping by talking to him." Richard didn't sound remotely happy. "I do have houses and businesses to build in town."

"I was sent to fetch everyone," Rick stated. "I'm a judge. I don't have experience with this kind of stuff. Poor Dave and your father are the only ones who stuck with the job all morning."

"Poor Dave is right," Joel muttered.

"What is that supposed to mean?"

"It means that he got cheated out of a decent looking wife."

"You mean Mary?"

"Who else?"

"She seems like a nice woman. I think he made a good choice. He said she was the best woman out of the three replies he got."

"He needs to start making better choices," Tom remarked.

"It's too bad she didn't send a picture or he would have known how ugly she is," Joel added.

"She's not ugly, Joel," Richard argued.

"No but she's not exactly pretty either," Tom quipped. "You should see Neil's wife. Now there's a looker."

"There's more to a woman than beauty. Dave has good sense," Richard insisted.

"You can't always judge a book by its cover," Rick agreed.

Tom snorted. "I guess considering that all the women around here are either married or too young, he didn't have a choice. I mean, she came off the train to meet him and what could he do? Say no? He's not the type to turn anyone away."

From another blast of wind fluttering the curtains, she saw Richard shrug. "I don't know. Maybe he knows something we don't. That mare of his didn't look like she'd amount to anything when he bought her. She was irritable, sassy and awkward. I thought she wouldn't be trainable to ride, but she's the gentlest mare I've come across now. And to boot, she delivered a fine foal."

"Well, you can't compare Susannah to Mary. That's like comparing apples to oranges," Tom said.

"I think I'll stay single forever," Joel remarked. "It's too bad that Cassie didn't answer Dave's ad. Then she'd be his wife instead of Neil's."

Tom went "uh hum" in agreement. "No wonder Neil smiles all the time."

"Dave is happy with Mary," Richard dryly pointed out.

"Oh, our brother's always been the happy sort. He can make the best of any dire situation," Tom replied.

"You're not being fair to her."

"I have eyes. I know beauty when I see it. Maybe Dave needs a pair of glasses."

"No way," Joel argued. "He's stuck with her now. There's no sense in him realizing what a mistake he made."

Footsteps approached and Mary heard Dave ask, "Am I going to be the only one helping Pa out there?"

Tom's voice was hushed. "Dave, when you saw Mary get off the train, didn't it occur to you to pretend to be someone else?"

"Why would I do that?" Dave asked.

He grunted as if the answer should be obvious. When silence greeted him, he said, "I'm sorry I bugged you about placing an ad for a wife. Seriously, if I thought you'd end up with someone like Mary, I'd have recommended that you hold out until Becky turned sixteen."

"Becky's a lot better looking than Mary," Joel agreed.

"Take that back." She noted the tension in her husband's voice.

For a moment no one said a word.

"Let's get back to the barn," Richard finally suggested.

"Yeah. I think I hear your pa calling for us," Rick said.

"Not until I get an apology," Dave replied.

"Apology for what?" Tom asked. "Joel didn't make her ugly."

A sudden scuffle broke out and though Mary couldn't see what was happening, she knew someone had punched someone else. She sprang to action, hoping to stop Dave from doing something he'd regret. To her surprise, she wasn't the only one who noticed the brawl taking place by the side of the house.

Sally and Jessica were already outside, yelling at the men, by the time Mary made it to the crowd.

"You are acting like a bunch of idiots," Sally admonished them, her hands on her hips.

"Really," Jessica agreed, her arms crossed. "What kind of example are you being to the children? They're watching from over there!" She motioned to the patch of green grass where the boys and girls had stopped playing with the puppies so they could stare at the adults.

As soon as Dave's eyes fell on Mary, he disengaged himself from the group and stomped over to her. "We're going home." He gently took her by the elbow and led her to their wagon.

"What? Why?" She struggled to keep up with his angry pace.

"Because we don't need to waste our time with the likes of them." His tone was cold, though his touch remained soft as he helped her onto the wagon. "I'll be right back."

She watched, stunned, as he retrieved the puppy and stormed back to the wagon. His jaw was clenched and his mouth set in a firm line. He stared straight ahead, refusing to look at his family who protested his leaving. He handed her the puppy before he hopped on the wagon.

He grunted when he realized that he forgot to get Lewis and Clark, so he rushed through the task and snapped the reins so the geldings bolted forward. Her body jerked from the sudden movement so she gripped the edge of her seat to stay upright while she held Jasper securely in her free hand. He slowed the horses once they traveled far enough so they couldn't see his parents' house.

"Dave, will you tell me why you were in a hurry to get out of there?" she asked.

He stared ahead, not blinking, his frame hunched forward. She couldn't recall seeing him so agitated before. When he didn't answer, she gave up and turned her attention to the path that the horses took them down. The light green grass lining their path swayed in the breeze.

The puppy wouldn't stop wiggling in her hand so she set it by her feet.

"I'm sorry I took you out there," he finally said, breaking the uncomfortable silence.

"You did nothing wrong."

"Maybe not, but my brothers are a disappointment."

"They were nice to me."

"No, they weren't."

"They were polite."

He shook his head. "We shouldn't discuss this. I just want to get home and enjoy what's left of this day."

She frowned. She doubted that he could put aside his fight with his brothers. "Dave, maybe we should go back so you can work things out with them."

He shot her a startled look. "Why would I do that?"

"Because they are your family."

"You and our baby is my family."

"They are your brothers. You grew up with them."

He directed Lewis and Clark to turn on the grassy road to the right, leading them to their home. "I may have grown up with them, but that doesn't mean they have a prominent place in my life. The day I married you, you became the first person I look to."

"I don't want to be the reason things go sour between you and your brothers."

"You aren't."

"Yes, I am. I overheard the fight. I know they were talking about me, and you happened to stumble upon their conversation."

He groaned. "You were in the scullery room?"

She nodded.

"I'm sorry you had to hear that."

"I didn't take offense to what they said, and you shouldn't either. You can't blame someone for telling the truth. I know I'm not attractive." That was when she decided she wouldn't take offense to what her mother wrote. The experience with his brothers only confirmed that her mother had every right to write what she did.

Their sod home came into view. The tall corn stalks rustled as the warm wind pressed into them. He waited until the geldings stopped in front of the barn before he turned to her, his expression incredulous.

"I can't believe you said that."

Her eyes widened at his sharp tone. "Said what?"

"That thing you just said."

"You mean about me not being attractive?"

He nodded, his eyes a steely gray as they examined her.

She shrugged and focused on the puppy that nipped at her brown shoes. "It's the truth, Dave," she whispered. "I know I'm not pretty."

"Who told you that you're not pretty?" he demanded, his voice loud despite the wind whipping around them.

"There's a reason why I had to answer an ad for a man wanting a wife. I'm not the kind of woman who receives a gentleman's attention."

He shook his head, bewildered. "Is that what life was like for you in Maine? People told you this all the time until you believed them?"

"No one has to tell me. I can see myself in the mirror. I know what pretty looks like and I'm not it." She looked at him, jutting her jaw forward. She didn't appreciate having to spell it out for him. It was enough to know what she was without having to vocalize it.

"I can't believe my ears. I need to calm down before I say something I'll regret." He locked the brakes and jumped out of the wagon.

"Will you at least eat something before you go?" He hadn't even eaten breakfast.

"I can't eat when I'm upset." He didn't look in her direction. "I'll get to you later," he told the horses as he stormed off to the river.

Stung by her husband's strange reaction, she wiped the tears from her eyes and slowly descended from the wagon. She reached for Jasper and set him on the ground. He yipped and playfully raced around the grass to check out his new surroundings. She didn't know what to do, but driving a wedge between Dave and his brothers bothered her. Resolving to put the matter behind her until she could solve it, she let Lewis and Clark free into the gated field where Jack, Susannah, and the foal welcomed them. Securing the latch, she went to the house to get food for the puppy.

DAVE ORDERED HIMSELF to calm down. Despite the swim in the cool river, his blood boiled in his veins. Mary wasn't ugly. His initial impression of her never told him that she was ugly. He had thought she might be on the plain side, but she was never unappealing. He rested on the rock by the flowing water. He squinted but not from the sun since he sat under the shade of a large tree. Was she plain when he first saw her?

He recalled the way she stood as Neil talked to her. Her shoulders looked stiff but her face remained surprisingly neutral. She might not have been the most beautiful woman he ever saw, but she had a unique quality about her that drew him to her. No, she hadn't been plain. In fact, she was quite pretty.

Upon closer inspection, he realized her nose wasn't as big as it seemed from a distance. Perhaps the tilt of her head when Neil spoke to her gave him the impression of an awkward nose. He shook his head. It didn't matter. Her nose was as unique and endearing as the rest of her. Her lips weren't that thin either. They were rosy and curvy. He did enjoy kissing her. Her hair smelled of lilac soap when he held her, and the strands felt soft after she washed them. The adorable tight curls resisted any means of straightening them out.

The feature that most delighted him were her eyes. He never saw eyes that displayed the most amazing blend of green and blue until he met her. Depending on her mood, they changed color. They seemed to darken when she got upset or aroused. They lightened when she was calm or cheerful. They were as interesting and intriguing as she was.

Making love to her was something he anticipated. At times, the days seemed to drag on until he could caress her soft skin, seeking the womanly secrets that she carefully hid from his view. Was that why she wouldn't let him look at her bare skin? She thought she wouldn't arouse him?

She deserved to be appreciated, for she had the gentle and kind spirit of someone who would do anything for anyone in need if she was able to perform the task. He sighed. What his brothers, Neil and other men said was wrong, but sadly, she accepted their appraisal of her without questioning it. He didn't know if she would ever see herself the way he did. Perhaps she never would. Even if that happened to be the case, he had been too hard on her. Taking a deep breath, he stood up. He had to make things right.

"MARY?" THE SOFT VOICE sounded loud in the quiet house.

Mary turned from rolling the dough to face Dave who tentatively peeked around the door. She blinked.

"What is it, Dave?" Her eyebrows furrowed. Was he sorry he married her? Did he realize that his brothers had been right? Did she only confirm those suspicions? He wouldn't send her away while she was expecting his child, would he?

He shut the door on a barking Jasper and lumbered into the house, his hat in his hands. "I'm sorry for the way I talked to you."

Thrown off guard, she hesitated.

He set his hat on the end of the table and stood silent for a long moment.

She wanted to look down to make sure her trembling hands wouldn't drop the rolling pin, but something in Dave's intense stare made her focus on him. Her heart beat so fast she swore she could hear it.

He continued, "I don't like hearing other people talk badly about you. You're my wife, and when they insult you, they insult me. I guess I can't help what you think about yourself, but I don't have to listen to it from others."

Relieved, she exhaled. He wasn't going to send her away. "You didn't do anything wrong. You don't need to apologize." She smiled before she returned to the dough. "I have stew in the pot, and these biscuits should be done shortly."

He came up behind her, placed his hands on her shoulders and whispered, "I don't care what they say, Mary. I think you're pretty."

He meant those words, she realized, her shock stilling her movements. No one, not even her parents, had called her pretty.

He pressed his lips to the side of her neck and his strong hands slid down her arms. "Will you come to bed with me?"

Heat flooded to her cheeks. "It's day."

"I want to see all of you."

Despite her apprehension, she allowed him to bring her shaking hands to the water in the kitchen bucket so he could wash them with soap. He took his time, careful to remove the slightest traces of dough from her fingers. He reached for the towel and dried her hands. His hands settled on her hips before he turned her to face him. He bent forward and gave her a soft kiss. Parting his lips, he traced her lower lip with his tongue, wanting permission to interlace his tongue with hers. She opened her mouth and accepted him.

He reached the dress' top button, causing her breath to catch in her throat. He deepened their kiss each time he unfastened a button. She kept her eyes closed, unsure if she wanted to see his expression when he succeeded in viewing her without any clothing. Yet, in spite of her doubts, the fact that he called her pretty prompted something deep within her to expose herself to him, to allow herself to be vulnerable. Her pulse raced as he slid the dress off her shoulders, letting it fall softly to the floor.

"You have such a lovely body." His low voice caressed her ear. He removed her undergarments, taking his time as he allowed his hands to brush her breasts and her hips, causing her flesh to tingle with excitement.

She was going to faint. She held onto his bare arms, somehow managing to stay upright. Her eyelids flew open when she realized that he had taken off his clothes. She immediately turned her eyes to the wall.

"Look at me, Mary." His voice sounded husky. "Your eyes are darker than usual. I can see my effect on you. Now, see what you do to me." He brought her hand to his erection and wrapped her hand around it.

Stunned, she couldn't react.

"I can't control it," he told her. "It happens when I'm aroused. This is what you've done to me from the day we got married." He looked down at her breasts and cupped them in his hands. "You are very pleasing to me."

Unexpectedly excited by the throbbing member in her hand, she squeezed him, only to be rewarded with an appreciative groan.

"My body is yours," he murmured. "And your body is mine."

He slipped one arm under her knees and carried her to the bed where he gently laid her down in front of him. He took a moment to gaze upon her naked form, and she marveled that she had such a profound effect on him. Her body pleased him, and in that moment, she saw herself the way he saw her. *Pretty Mary Larson.*

He joined her on their bed. He kissed her, more passionately this time. When he ended the kiss, she thought he would kiss her on the mouth again but he didn't. He continued his descent. She gasped in surprise and pleasure as he studied her breasts with his hands and tongue. Her nipples hardened for him. Between her legs, a heated wetness began to tingle her flesh.

Holding onto his shoulders, she watched as his head went lower. Somewhere, deep within, an aching sensation held her still, in hopes he would continue his exploration. She licked her lips in anticipation as his mouth paused above the dark curls that hid her most private place. She released a sigh of satisfaction when he kissed her beneath the curls. His tongue ran across the lips sheltering her depths. When he slipped his hot tongue between the lips, she voiced her pleasure.

Her legs widened for him, eager for his entrance. The aching in her intensified, as she became aware of the need to do something, though she didn't understand what that something was. After a couple of minutes, his mouth left her sensitive flesh and traveled up the length of her body until he kissed her again. She pressed her hips against him. A part of her needed to feel him inside her, to be filled with his thickness. He accepted her unspoken invitation and slid easily into her, soothing the ache that had become unbearable to her. She hadn't experienced anything like this before, and she wasn't sure what to do about it.

"Come with me, Mary," he whispered against her ear as he began his purposeful, lazy motion, slowly stoking the fire he lit inside of her.

Where? She wanted to ask the question but was too caught up in the swell of sensations flowing through her body that she forgot to vocalize the question. His thrusting grew faster as he sought a way to get deeper into her. A rising tension made her bring her hips to help him. She intrinsically knew this was leading somewhere wonderful, but she didn't know how to encourage the journey. *This must be what he's talking about, she realized. It's what he experiences every time we do this.*

She felt him shudder as he reached the destination. He laid still on top of her for a few minutes, his heart beat gradually slowing while his body temperature returned to normal.

Part of her was disappointed. She had come close to something, but she didn't understand what it was. She wondered if she would ever figure it out. But she wasn't completely unsatisfied. He had shown her great tenderness and passion. He cared for her and desired her. He could look at her naked and be aroused. She was ecstatic by this knowledge. It wasn't love but it was more than she hoped for when she married him. No other man had treated her this well.

She wrapped her arms around him and drew him close as he dozed off. She loved him more than she thought it was possible to love another human being. Her tension dwindling down, she closed her eyes and enjoyed the realization that he really did think she was pretty, and it didn't matter if he was the only one who would ever find her pleasing to look at because his opinion was the only one that mattered.

Chapter Ten

Mary knew better than to press the issue of his brothers to Dave, so she didn't mention his brothers to him except to inform him that Rick and Richard had defended her. Sally, Jenny, Jessica and Amanda arrived to apologize to them on behalf of Tom and Joel's behavior. Dave said that he appreciated their supporting Mary but needed to hear it directly from them. Within a day, they settled back into the comfortable routine they enjoyed.

Two weeks passed without incident when Maureen Brown and Cassie arrived on their property. Mary did her best to hide her surprise. She set down the pail of milk on the ground next to the barn, walked past the jumpy puppy, and adjusted her bonnet. Shielding her eyes from the bright mid-morning sun, she looked up at the occupants of the horse-drawn buggy and waited for the older woman to pull the reins back to stop her horse.

"Good morning," Mary politely greeted. "Do you need help?"

"Good morning, Mary," Maureen nodded as she got down from the buggy and handed Mary the reins. "I need you to take care of my prized mare. She isn't used to long treks out of town."

Mary released the mare and put her out to the pasture so she could roam free with the other horses. Jasper nipped at her heels the entire time.

"Where is your husband?" Maureen asked, examining her surroundings with a critical eye.

"He's checking the corn for bugs."

Mary looked at Cassie who stood next to the older woman. Cassie didn't make eye contact with her. Instead, she seemed content to watch Mrs. Brown.

Clearing her throat, Mary said, "It's nice to see you again." Returning her attention back to the older woman, she asked, "Would you like something to drink or eat?"

"That would be lovely. Cassie and I have endured a long journey and are in need of refreshments. The weather is unbearably humid this time of year."

"If you'll follow me, I'll get coffee and brown sugar candy ready."

She picked up the pail and led the way into the house. Jasper didn't protest as she closed the door.

"I must say that these little homes are quaint, even if they are filthy." Maureen grimaced. "Though you can't blame Dave. He is doing the best he can. At least he has a better roof than old man MacPherson."

Mary tensed and got ready to defend her husband when Maureen continued, "Of course, Neil is doing much better. One can tell that from his abundance of livestock. That's where the money is, if you ask me. Cassie, you did well. When will Neil have the new house built?" Glancing at Mary, she explained, "It will be made of wood instead of dirt."

"It should be ready before winter," the raven-haired beauty sweetly replied. She adjusted her purple dress, decorated in flowers and small pearls, before she sat on a chair at the kitchen table. "I do admit, Mrs. Brown, I am anxious to be in better accommodations."

Maureen brushed off the seat of her chair and sat next to Cassie. "Neil is a man of his word. You will have better things soon enough. He's earned some money in his investments. If there's one thing Gwendolyns's son excels at, it's finances. Gwendolyn is Neil's mother," she told Mary.

Mary set the pail on the table in front of the window and reached for the coffee beans from the jar on the shelf. A quick glance out the window showed her Dave coming out of the cornfield with a bucket of dead bugs. He paused when he saw Maureen's buggy before he entered the barn.

"Ralph Linden said that you and Dave are expecting a bundle of joy," Maureen rattled on.

She turned her attention to her guests. "Yes."

While she got out the ingredients to make the brown sugar candy, the woman continued, "He said that Dave wore a grin that stretched from ear to ear. There's nothing like a child to make a man puff up with pride. In fact, Dave isn't the only one who's going to be a father next year. Cassie just discovered that she's in the family way as well."

Mary looked at Cassie and smiled at her. "Congratulations. I'm sure that Neil is pleased." To her surprise, she realized that she was actually happy for Neil. She hadn't expected to ever be happy for him after the day she met him in the train station. Relief washed over her. She hated to hold onto a grudge since doing so hurt her more than the person she didn't like.

"Oh, he is happy about it," Cassie replied. "When I read the ad he put in the paper, he specifically requested a woman who could have children."

"What a wonderful job you've done of providing that for him." Maureen nodded and patted her hand. "It's marvelous that you two are in the family way and neighbors. Why, you can experience the joys of pregnancy and birth together. Then your children can grow up side by side. There's nothing like a bond between mothers."

Mary had no desire to spend time with Cassie, though she couldn't put her finger on the reason for her hesitation. It wasn't the fact that Cassie was gorgeous. Her sister Grace, after all, had been blessed with beauty that rivaled Cassie's. Something else bothered her. Deciding not to comment, she focused on heating the brown sugar and milk on the cookstove.

"Mary," Maureen began, "I must say that you have as pristine a reputation as Cassie does. I hadn't dared suspect that you have such a lovely personality. The ladies at your church are quite impressed with you. We could use an additional member for our ladies group. Don't worry about not belonging to my church. The group is for all Christian women to get together to do good deeds in the community for those less fortunate."

"Oh." She hadn't expected this turn of events. She assumed that Maureen and Cassie simply wished to pay a social visit.

"I don't expect an answer right away. Take your time and pray about it. In the meantime, Cassie has agreed to join, and Neil was delighted to know we found her good enough to include in our group. Not everyone is welcome. We are very selective since we have an image of propriety to maintain."

Adding butter, vanilla and walnuts to the brown sugar and milk, Mary nodded.

"Do you use cow chips to get the fire going?" Cassie's voice revealed her disgust.

"Now, now, Cassie, dear," Maureen quickly spoke up. "Dave can't afford anything better than this. We need to be understanding. Remember, judge not lest ye be judged."

"Dave provides very well for me," Mary softly stated.

"Of course, he does. He does the best he can. No one is faulting him for that."

"I am glad I replied to Neil's ad," Cassie remarked. "He said he'll be able to get me a maid to do the more demanding chores in two years."

"He is going to spoil you." By the way Maureen chuckled, Mary realized that the woman was proud to be best friends with a woman whose son could afford the finer things in life.

Mary wondered how long it would take before they left.

Dave entered the house. Mary blinked. She hadn't realized he left the barn.

"Good morning, Mrs. Brown, Mrs. Craftsman. I forgot my work gloves." He smiled a greeting at Mary, so she smiled back.

"They came by for a neighborly visit," Mary told him. "I'm making some coffee and brown sugar candy. Would you like any?"

"No. I have too much work to do." He reached for the gloves on the wardrobe but one fell to the floor.

As he bent to pick it up, Cassie gave his rear end an appreciative glance. Mary's face flushed in anger, but her shock prevented her from reminding the pretty woman that not only was she married to Neil but Dave was also spoken for. Maureen hadn't noticed the exchange because she checked on the coffee.

Once Dave nodded a good-bye to them and exited the house, Mary breathed a sigh of relief. She poured the mixture into the buttered pan, thankful the candy would soon be done. The sooner she got Cassie off her property, the better off she'd be.

IT WAS LATE AT NIGHT in the middle of August when Mary woke up feeling an uncomfortable cramping sensation in her lower belly. The ache, though mild, created enough upset that it prevented her from going back to sleep. She stood up and got dressed, careful to not wake Dave, hoping that walking quietly in the dark would make her feel better. She had no idea what could be causing it. Perhaps women experienced this in pregnancy? She recalled her last discussion with Sally when she and Dave went to purchase items from the mercantile. Sally mentioned slight cramping to be normal, especially around the time she should expect her monthly flow. Deciding that was all there was to it, she relaxed and sat in the kitchen chair by the window.

She used the light from the moon to do some light sewing, though she spent a good portion of her time staring apprehensively out the window. When the sunrise displayed the beginning light blues and pinks that would soon give way to the full brilliance of the sun, she realized that the cramping had gradually gotten worse.

Maybe relieving her bladder would help ease the pressure in her abdomen. As she left the house, she noticed that the air was cool though the humidity dampened her brow. No, she wasn't sweating because of the humidity. A slight nausea caused her stomach to flip over. When did she last have a bout of morning sickness? It had been a couple of days. That was much too soon to be over considering she hadn't reached her fourth month yet.

Her mind struggled to force aside the thought that made her hands shake. Wiping the palms of her hands on her dress, she went to the outhouse to empty her bladder. When she was done, the pain seemed to get worse. Though Jasper found her, jumped around her and whined for his morning meal, her anxiety wouldn't let her tend to him. She couldn't dismiss the nagging feeling that something was wrong. She knew she had to get to the doctor but needed to get a drink of water first since her mouth felt so dry that she couldn't swallow. Her legs felt like rubber as she struggled to walk to the river. Giving up, Jasper retreated to the house. She was relieved since his movements and whining only seemed to add to her nausea.

By the time she reached the riverbank, she panted as if she had been running. Easing herself into a kneeling position, she put her hand in the water to cup enough liquid to drink when the pain gripped her with such intensity that she nearly fell face-first into the water. Tears stung her eyes. She fought to keep her body steady, but her hands sunk deeper into the sand as the water pulsed against her elbows. Her sobs came heavily while the knife twisting pain in her lower abdomen prevented her from getting out of the water. Paralyzed with fear, she tensed.

Suddenly, a pair of strong arms reached into the water and lifted her up. "Mary?"

Dave's voice and the dog's barking sounded faint against the humming in her ears. He swore, held her close to him and carried her to the house. He gently laid her on the bed. When he backed away from her, she was barely aware of the blood covering his arms and chest. She didn't have the strength to comment when he swore again and said he was getting the doctor before he ran out of the house.

DAVE PACED IN FRONT of the house, his nerves set on edge as he waited for the doctor to tell him what happened to his wife. God help him but he couldn't go in there until he knew she was going to be alright. Even the thought of changing his bloody shirt couldn't get him in there at the moment. All he could manage was to simply wash his hands. He must have looked like he needed help when he entered town. No wonder people gave him startled glances. For once, running into Sally proved to be a blessing. Now she aided the doctor in whatever Mary needed.

Mary has to be fine. She's sturdy. He chose her because of her strength, and she had withstood the harsher elements of farm life. *She has to pull through this ailment.* He shook his head. What was wrong? Yesterday, she seemed normal. But this morning, she couldn't even pull herself out of the river. He didn't have to hear her crying to know she was in pain. The tortured look on her face told him that much. And then he saw all that blood. He shivered. He couldn't recall a time in his life when he had been more terrified.

The doctor emerged from the house, his expression solemn.

"Is she going to live?" Dave anxiously asked.

"Yes," Doctor Adams assured him.

Relief flooded over him. "What happened?"

"She had a miscarriage."

The words took a moment to sink in. So it wasn't all good news. With her in pain and bleeding, he couldn't have expected the doctor to give him a glowing report.

"Miscarriages are fairly common. There isn't anything either one of you could have done to prevent it. Mary's healthy and young, and since both of you come from sizable families, chances are good that she'll carry her next pregnancy to term. For the time being, you need to abstain from marital relations until her bleeding stops to give her body time to heal. I recommend she gets plenty of rest for the next couple of days, and I set aside something for pain should she experience discomfort."

Dave nodded. He paid the doctor, thanked him, and cautiously entered the house.

Sally, who had removed Mary's dirty dress and put a clean one on her and placed new sheets on the bed, glanced up as he softly closed the door behind him. "Doctor Adams gave her something to help her sleep. I'll take the linens and her clothes to my home so I can wash them. I'll come back at supper with a meal for you two to eat. Is there anything else you need before I leave?"

He pried his eyes from Mary's sleeping but pale form so he could talk to her. "I can't think of anything."

"Did you feed the animals?"

He groaned. "No." In all the drama, they slipped his mind.

"I'll do that for you. Does the cow need milking?"

"Of course." As much as he dreaded leaving his wife, even if she slept, he turned to go to the barn.

"David!" She grabbed his arm to stop him. "I said I would take care of it. I grew up on the same farm you did. I'm familiar with feeding and milking."

"I'm not thinking straight."

"Which is why I'm going to be back later today. You should rest. After all, that was your baby too."

He recalled his excitement about holding the child. As much as the loss affected him, he realized that it had to be worse for Mary.

Sally collected the dirty laundry and patted his arm. "I'll bring supper with me, alright?"

"Thank you, Sally."

Once she left, he took off his shirt, shoes and hat so he could slip into bed with his wife. She didn't stir but remained sound asleep on her side, facing away from him. He pulled her back against his chest and wrapped his arm around her waist. Closing his eyes, he buried his face in her soft hair and inhaled the sweet scent of lilacs that he had come to associate with her. Her steady breathing calmed him down and before long, he drifted off to sleep.

MARY WOKE UP TO THE sound of people talking around her. Her eyelids fluttered open to see who spoke to Dave in hushed tones. Sally stood at the table in front of the window cutting vegetables and adding them to the large pot on the stove while Jenny sat across from him at the kitchen table.

"What will you do at harvest?" Jenny asked him. "You can't take down all this corn by yourself."

"Will you let me deal with this as I see fit?" A scowl replaced his usual easygoing smile. "I'm fully capable of handling my own farm."

"No one is arguing that." Sally sighed. "What we're saying is that Tom and Joel will need your help as much as you need theirs. You don't have to agree with what they said. You can be sure that Jessica and our parents are giving them an earful for what they said about Mary. If you don't wish to deal with Tom and Joel after harvest, then that is fine, but you shouldn't limit your profit because of ill chosen words. You work hard out here. You should enjoy the fruit of your labor."

Mary eased her stiff body into a sitting position. For some reason, she thought she should be in pain but mercifully, she wasn't. What were Sally and Jenny doing there? Why was she in bed in the middle of the day? Why wasn't Dave out working?

"You don't have to like it," Jenny told Dave. "Sometimes you do what you have to do."

He muttered something under his breath about meddling family members before he glanced at Mary. He bolted out of his chair and carefully sat next to her. "Mary doesn't need this, alright? Let's put the conversation on hold so she can have some peace." Turning to her, he gently took her hand in his and asked, "How are you?"

Sally's sympathetic expression brought the morning's events flooding into her consciousness. The doctor made sure her body expelled everything it was supposed to and Sally cleaned her up the best she could. Mary wiped the tears that slid down her cheeks. "I miscarried, didn't I?" What a stupid question. Of course, she did.

Dave took her in his arms and held her tightly against him.

Sally dumped the cut up vegetables into the pot before she and Jenny left the house so they could be alone.

"I'm sorry I lost the baby," she whispered into his shoulder.

"Mary, you didn't do anything wrong. It just happened." Rubbing her back, he kissed her on the head.

"But you were looking forward to the baby's birth."

"Yes, I was, and so were you. We'll get through this together."

The fabric of his shirt collected her tears as she mourned the loss of their baby.

NINE DAYS PASSED. On the tenth day, Jasper wouldn't stop barking, so Mary glanced out the window as she finished cleaning the kitchen table after baking a midday snack. Judging from the worried expression on Tom's face, she realized that his appearance marked an emergency. She quickly wiped her wet hands on a towel as she rushed to the front yard, ignoring the dog barking next to her.

"What's wrong?" she asked.

Tom turned the stallion from the barn and rode over to her. "Jessica's water broke and the doctor is attending to a gunshot wound. I can't find the midwife. Neil said you've delivered babies."

She nodded, her eyes squinting up at him despite the cloudy sky. Neil would know that since she wrote it to him in the letter she sent when she answered his ad. "I've helped the midwife back home. I'll be over as soon as I change into my pants."

Without waiting for a response, she ran back into the house and quickly changed. She wrote Dave a quick note telling him where she was going so he wouldn't worry about her when he returned from the mercantile with food and more cloth for her to sew into fall shirts and dresses. He had left her at home, saying she wasn't ready for a wagon ride.

She realized he wouldn't be pleased to discover she rode a horse over to his brother's property, but with Jessica needing assistance, she decided to chance the consequences of upsetting him.

Once she saddled Susannah and told Jasper good-bye, she rode over to Tom's farm where Jessica yelled at him to stay outside. "You are making me nervous! Birthing doesn't have to be the terrifying ordeal you're making it out to be. Now take the kids outside so I can have some peace and quiet!"

"But they're crying. They need their mother."

"Are you insane? I'm in labor." She shoved him out of the house and urged the two girls after him. "They're crying because you're panicking, telling them that I'm in dire straits and might not survive. Really, Tom. At least pretend to be calm for their sakes."

She slammed the door of their sod house on his face before she screamed in pain.

Mary swiftly dropped from the mare and tied her to the post. She smiled at Tom and the crying girls who clung to his legs.

"I'm sure everything will be fine," she softly told him and the girls. "I've helped the midwife back home deliver babies and each time, the mother and child were healthy."

She walked into the house and made sure to secure the door so some of Jessica's screaming would be muffled from their ears. Jessica sat on the bed, gripping her large belly, her sweaty hair pulled back into a bun. A pile of old newspapers already covered the mattress to protect it from the impending afterbirth.

"Lay back and I'll check to see how far you've progressed," Mary softly instructed.

Gritting her teeth, she laid on her back.

After Mary estimated where the baby's head was located, she gathered a bucket of fresh water, clean towels and a blanket. "It won't be long."

Jessica reached out and squeezed her hand. "Thank you for coming." She gasped.

She smiled at her. "You're welcome." As soon as she opened the door to go outside, Tom and the girls practically jumped on her.

"Is she alright?" he asked.

"Can we see Ma now?" Nelly cried, hugging her little sister.

Closing the door behind her, she bent down and said, "Your mother is doing fine. She's working hard to give you and Patricia a little brother or sister."

"But she's screaming."

"Yes. It can hurt, but it's worth it. You'll see. As soon as the baby is born, your mother will be very happy." She hugged the two girls. "I promise."

"When will the baby be here?" Tom asked, shifting his feet.

"My guess is that it'll be over in the next hour." She stood up, wondering what to do with three people who stared at her as if she had the answers to all of their problems. Taking a deep breath, she decided to give them a list of things to do around the farm to keep them busy before she returned to Jessica.

The birthing process fascinated her in the past, but she had only been an observer who aided the midwife in giving her the supplies she needed in order to perform the task. This time, she was the one who directed Jessica in when to push and caught the baby. She wrapped the child in the blanket and handed her to her mother. A certain euphoria filled her heart, making her happier than she had been since her miscarriage. Bringing a new life into the world was a humbling and beautiful honor. She felt grateful that she took part in it.

"Another girl," Jessica mused as she cradled the baby to her bosom. Her face red with exertion, her clothes sticking to her with sweat, and her weary body didn't detract from her joy. Even after the toil of labor, she looked radiant.

"She's got a patch of golden curls on her head. I have a feeling she'll be as pretty as her sisters."

"Mary, I am glad that you're my sister-in-law, and I'm sorry about what happened with..."

Mary paused as she collected the dirty towels, understanding what a woman who had just given birth was trying to tell a woman who went through a miscarriage. "Thank you, Jessica. You don't need to say anything else. Besides, it did my heart good to deliver your baby. I'm glad I was here."

"You are a beautiful person. Beauty isn't just on the surface you know. Dave did make a good choice when he married you."

Mary didn't feel beautiful on the outside, but she supposed inner beauty did count for something. She quickly finished cleaning so she could put Tom at ease. "I'll go tell Tom and the girls the good news."

Once she opened the front door, Tom nearly knocked her over as he ran up to her. "I hear the baby crying. Is everything alright?"

The girls turned their big eyes to her.

"Everyone is doing well."

Their relief came upon them so suddenly that they leaned on each other for support.

"You have another girl," Mary warned him, recalling his hope for a boy when she last saw him.

To her surprise, a big smile lit up his face. "A girl? That's just what I wanted!" He picked up the girls, ignoring the two dogs that had just returned from the fields to play with them, and ran into the house.

She shook her head but laughed. At least, he was happy about it. In fact, he told Jessica how delighted he was with her and their new baby. He also made sure his other girls felt appreciated as well. It didn't occur to her that Tom had a tender spot in his heart for those he loved, but she liked seeing that side of him.

She spent the next hour helping four-year-old Nelly give the baby a bath while two-year-old Patricia watched. Then she cooked a couple of meals to see the family through the next three days so Jessica didn't have to worry about that chore while adjusting to the new member of their house.

When she completed her work, she wished them well and walked to her horse. Again, Tom surprised her when he called after her. She paused, her hands on Susannah's reins and turned to him.

Stepping past the dogs that chased each other, he approached her, his hands in his pockets and staring at the ground. "I wanted to apologize for what I said about you. I didn't realize you heard Joel and me talking until I learned you were in the scullery room, and... Well, it doesn't matter if you overheard or not. The point is, I was wrong to even say those things to begin with. I was wondering if you'd forgive me and give me another chance to be a good brother-in-law for a change?"

"I accept the apology, Tom. We don't have to mention it again." Susannah turned her nose in her direction so she patted it.

He looked at her and grinned. "You know, you're very gracious. If Dave had to marry anyone, you'd be my first choice."

Just as she was about to thank him, she caught sight of Dave leading his wagon onto the property. She frowned. Was he mad at her?

Tom ran up to meet him.

While they talked, she slowly untied the reins. Knowing she wouldn't leave until Dave came over to her, she patiently waited for him, pretending to be intensely interested in smoothing Susannah's black mane. The sound of a couple cattle and horses met her ears but she didn't notice. She hoped he wasn't too mad. When she noticed him walking towards her, she subconsciously tightened her hold on the reins.

"How are you feeling?" he asked as soon as he reached her.

Realizing that his expression of concern meant he wasn't mad at her, she breathed a sigh of relief. "I'm fine."

"You're not in any pain?"

"No."

He pulled her close to him. "I don't want you pushing yourself too hard."

Her hands rested on his strong arms. To her pleasure, she realized that he still cared for her, even after she lost his child. Though she still mourned the loss, and knew he did too, it eased the ache in her heart to know that she hadn't suffered the closeness she and Dave had developed over the past couple of months.

"I want you to take the wagon back," he gently insisted. "I'll take Susannah. You've done enough for today."

"Alright."

He leaned forward to kiss her. "I'm proud of you for helping Jessica, even though Tom said what he did."

"He apologized for it. You don't have to worry about that any-more."

"I know. He explained things to me. Joel stopped me in town to apologize too. I won't have anyone talking badly about you if I'm around."

"So next month at harvest, we'll be helping them with their crops and they'll be helping us?"

"Yes, we'll all be getting together after all."

"I'm relieved." She really didn't want to be the cause of a family rift.

"I'll go in and see our new niece before we head home. I'll be right back." He kissed her again and went to the house.

She smiled and got ready for the trek home.

Chapter Eleven

Harvest came in September and groups of farmers joined together to help each other retrieve their crops. The wives spent their time watching the young children and cooking for the men while the older boys aided their fathers in the fields. The abundant rainfall and warm sunny days provided a good yield. Since there was no serious wind damage, the men reflected that they had a chance to make a suitable profit that year.

On their fourth day of collecting crops, the men and boys tackled Tom's cornfield. Each person took his own row and used a sickle or reaper to chop down the cornstalks. Fortunately, the August heat gave way to cooler temperatures and the breeze helped make things more bearable as they labored. Dave happened to be working between Tom and Neil, though he had made an effort to avoid Neil as much as possible. Ever since that day in the train station, Dave couldn't think of anything nice to say to the man, so he tried to ignore him.

"I heard you got another girl," Neil called out to Tom.

"Yes. I thought I'd be disappointed if I had another one, but she's the cutest thing that was ever born. It was love at first sight. Of course, my other girls are cute too."

"I bet they'll have men lining up to court them when they grow up."

Tom glanced over at him. "They will be pretty, and that's a scary prospect to a father."

Dave threw a cornstalk onto the pile he had collected in his row before he turned to the next stalk to cut down.

Neil chuckled. "Come on. You should be glad they're cute. You don't want them to have a hard time finding a husband."

"I have to make sure that they find a man who deserves them. The problem I'm going to have is weeding out all the bad apples so I can find the good ones. The bad ones will take advantage of them."

"Aren't you being a little paranoid?"

Dave threw another stalk on the pile.

Tom huffed. "You of all people should realize that young ladies have to be careful when letting a man court them. You slept with enough women in your time."

"Look, I'm not exactly proud of that, alright," Neil responded. "I thought it was fun at the time."

"That's exactly the kind of mentality I need to watch out for when it comes to their future suitors. It's a good thing you got honest and settled down." After he threw his own cornstalk on his pile, he took a good look at Neil who was busy with his own row. "You didn't get any of them in the family way, did you?"

Neil shrugged. "None of them mentioned it. Of course, I spent most of my time in the saloon with women who knew how to take measures to make sure that kind of thing didn't happen."

"If one had gotten in the family way, would you have done right and married her?"

Dave threw another stalk aside and realized that Tom had stopped working so he could focus on Neil who seemed to be oblivious to Tom's scrutiny.

"Yes, I would have," Neil replied. He glanced at Tom and sighed. "Look, I'm not completely bad."

"I never said you were, but I thought Clyde was alright too until he took advantage of Jenny. Then he abandoned her."

"If he wanted it so badly, he should have gone to the women at the saloon. Like I said, there's a place a man can responsibly take care of his needs."

"I couldn't have felt right doing that. Sex is special. I can't imagine doing it with anyone but my wife."

"What does it matter now? I married Cassie and am faithful to her."

"You better keep it that way. A woman needs to know she's the only one in your life."

Neil rolled his eyes. "Why are you lecturing me? I think the world of Cassie. I treat her like a princess."

"If she gives birth to a girl, you'll understand. Your whole perspective changes when you have a girl."

Much to Dave's relief, the supper bell rang. He chopped down the stalk he had a hold on and tossed it on the pile. He took off his hat and wiped the sweat off his forehead. He carried his reaper to the sod house while Neil and Tom continued their discussion behind him.

"So, things are going well between you and Cassie?" Tom asked.

"They're better than well. They're fantastic!"

"Spoken like a man in love."

"What can I say? She brings out the best in me."

Dave picked up his pace so he wouldn't have to listen to Neil's constant chatter. Tomorrow, he would be sure to find a row far away from Neil. All day long, Neil had been talking about Cassie and how much he was looking forward to having a child call him 'Pa.' It wouldn't have been so bad if the memory of Mary's miscarriage wasn't still fresh in his mind.

Something had changed between him and Mary that day, and he couldn't put his finger on it. Mary remained the focus of his life. She was even prettier than before, but she seemed more fragile. Losing the baby was bad enough, but he didn't want to lose her too. He learned how precious she had become to him.

The grass in front of Tom and Jessica's house had several large blankets spread out where the men sat down to eat. Dave set his reaper down in the grass and chose the spot between Jimmy and his father. In spite of the cool breeze, sweat caused his shirt to cling to his back. He used his hat to fan himself. The small children ran in and out of the house while Mildred Phillips and his mother watched them to make sure they stayed out of the way so the other women could bring out the food.

"Did Joel tell you what he's planning to do with his life?" his father asked him.

"No, he didn't." He placed the hat back on his head.

"He is going to transport goods to and from the mercantile. He decided that he's not cut out for the farm life."

"That's probably because he doesn't like to get up at dawn."

"I think he doesn't like to work with crops. If he found something he liked, he'd wake up early. Anyway, he'll get a place at the boarding house in town before winter."

Jimmy Parson glanced at Dave's father. "Charles, sometimes a boy has to leave home in order to find out who he is. I know it was that way with Leonard. Doris and I worried that he would go through life like a vagabond, but he discovered a love for dentistry and that wouldn't have happened if he stayed on the farm."

"A fine dentist he is too." Charles nodded. "I do hope Joel finds something he can enjoy and be good at."

"Are you farmers hungry?" Doris called out as she emerged from the house with two large bowls.

Tom rubbed his hands together. "Alright! No one makes stew like you do, Mrs. Parson."

"Sadly, that is true," Jessica agreed in good humor as she brought out the mashed potatoes.

One by one the women brought out a new dish and drinks for the men to feast on. When Mary brought out her pies, she handed Dave the slice he requested ahead of time.

"You're lucky you get a piece of apple pie before everyone else hogs them," Joel commented as he watched Dave smile his thanks to Mary. "I hope someone lets me have a slice today," he yelled so the men would hear him.

Dave grinned. "It's just one of the perks I get for being married to her. Go find your own wife to make you pies."

"Don't think I won't."

Mary brought Joel another slice. "I heard you didn't get a chance to have some pie yesterday and thought I'd do my part," she explained before she went back into the house.

Joel's face lit up like a boy on Christmas morning. "Apparently, it pays to be a brother-in-law too."

Dave chuckled. He was glad to see his brothers change their attitude towards his wife. In fact, over the past two weeks, it seemed that they had developed a deep respect for her.

Finally, Cassie brought out the plates and utensils.

"I was beginning to wonder if I had to eat the food directly from the bowls," Tom joked.

"Expecting a child is exhausting work," she wearily stated as she set the plates and utensils down so the men at the edge of the lawn could pass them down to the person next to him. "Forgive me, gentlemen but I must return to help the women."

As soon as she entered the house, Doris and Jessica came back out with cups and more dishes which they started handing out.

Jimmy raised his eyebrow. "I know that look on your face, Doris. Is the new girl causing you problems?"

Doris groaned and leaned close to her husband so Neil wouldn't overhear since he was sitting four spots away from Dave. "I don't even know why she bothers to come to these things," she griped.

"She's getting worse every day. At least she was making coffee and cutting up vegetables and fruits when we started. Today she said she was too tired to do much and has spent all her time sitting in a chair and staring out the window. Now I know she's in the family way and is more tired than usual, but that doesn't give her the right to boss the rest of us around like she's high society. Someone should have warned her when she married a farmer, it meant she would have to work."

He rolled his eyes. "Aren't you exaggerating?"

"Don't start that one with me. I know when someone is taking advantage of a situation."

"She is being difficult," Jessica softly stated as she poured coffee into Jimmy's cup. "I don't know why she didn't stay home if she didn't feel up to cooking."

Just as Jessica turned to give Dave some coffee, a shriek came from the house, followed by two six-year-old boys who bolted from the door and made a beeline for the barn, which was close to them.

Doris reached out and stopped them as they passed her. "What did you do?"

"Sorry, Ma, but she asked for it," one of the twins told her.

She placed her hands on her hips and glared at them. "Who are you talking about and what did you do?"

"We got tired of watching Mrs. Craftsman ordering you and the other ladies around, so we slipped a snake in the bed so when she laid down, it would mess with her."

"Benjamin," she began, obviously struggling to sound serious, "we do not do that to other people. Now, where's the snake? We can't have it slithering through Mrs. Larson's home."

"Oh. It's right here." He took his hand out of his shirt and showed his mother the snake.

The small green snake wiggled in his grasp.

"You are not to do that again, and you must apologize. Then you should release that creature into the field. Do you understand me?"

The boys looked down in shame, said yes, and turned to go back to the house.

Jimmy gave her a critical look. "I notice that you didn't tell them to release that snake before they went back in to apologize."

She shrugged. "Oops. My instructions were inadvertently out of order."

Dave stifled a chuckle while Jessica poured the steaming liquid into his cup. "Thanks," he told her.

They heard another scream before the twins raced out of the house. This time, they chose a different route so their mother couldn't stop them again.

"Doris, it's not right to laugh at another's expense," Jimmy admonished, though a smile hinted at his own lips.

She shrugged and returned to the house with Jessica.

"Maybe Cassie's not so great after all," Joel whispered before he took a bite of his pie. "I hope I get as lucky as you, Dave, and get a wife who cooks like Mary does."

Dave smiled with pride. Each day, he found another reason to adore his wife.

FOUR WEEKS LATER, MARY completed a shawl to warm her when she went out into the fall weather. Dave had already retired to bed, so she worked quietly in the kitchen area. She glanced at him. He looked content as he rested. She stood up and set the dark blue shawl in the wardrobe. After putting the knitting materials in their proper place, she decided to get ready for bed. With one blow on the candle, the flame expired. Darkness covered the inside of the dwelling.

She ignored the fierce drumming of her heart as she slowly undid the buttons on her dress. Ever since the miscarriage, she wore a nightshirt to bed, but she was healed. Harvest had been busy with little else to do but work, eat and sleep. The men finished that part of farming, so Dave would have energy to engage in other activities. She figured it would be a good time to resume their lovemaking. Though she wasn't a virgin this time, her nerves caused her fingers to tremble. She worked through the process of undressing with less finesse than she cared to admit, and thankfully, Dave couldn't see how clumsy she was, so she could at least be spared that embarrassment.

Taking a deep breath and feeling unusually hot despite the fact that she was naked, she urged her stiff feet forward and settled into bed beside her husband. She wasn't sure if he was asleep or not, but in the past, he made it a habit to wake up in the middle of the night for another round of lovemaking. She missed the closeness they shared in each other's arms and hoped to gain it back. As soon as she laid next to him, he reached for her as he did every night. His gasp of surprise when he felt her bare waist caused her unease.

"What are you doing?" he asked, bewildered.

Heat rose in her cheeks. So much for not feeling embarrassed! Forcing her voice to remain steady, she answered him. "I thought you might like to come together. You know, as man and wife...?"

He shifted away from her.

In the darkness, she couldn't tell what expression was on his face, and if she could, then she might be able to read him better, but as it was, she had no clue as to what he thought except for what he told her. She held her breath and waited for him to reply.

"I don't know," he slowly spoke. "I don't think you're ready yet."

"It's been two months since the miscarriage."

"That isn't a long time."

Her tongue ran across her dry lips. "Well, it's not, but the doctor said we could do this when I stopped bleeding, and I haven't bled since my last cycle."

"The doctor doesn't know everything. The time isn't right yet. We'll wait a little longer. Now, please put on your nightshirt so you don't get cold, alright?"

Though his tone was tender, his words pierced her heart. Biting her lower lip, she mutely got out of the bed and slipped on her nightshirt. Returning to bed, she turned away from him, unable to face him. Try as she might, the tears found their way down her cheeks as soon as he pulled her into his arms.

"I don't want to hurt you," he whispered.

You are hurting me. Despite their physical closeness, they might as well have been as far apart as Nebraska and Maine.

He sighed. "I'm sorry, Mary."

He didn't say anything else for the rest of the night.

DAVE HOOKED LEWIS AND Clark up to the wagon full of shucked stalks he planned to sell to Ralph at the mercantile. Most of the stalks remained in a cellar he had dug out two years ago when he bought the land so his horses and cow would eat well for the following year. Understanding that farming did not always guarantee a full year's food supply, Mary had preserved meats, vegetables and fruits to add to the cellar's contents. He admired her ability to plan ahead and prepare for rough times because it wasn't a question of if they would need the supplies. It was a question of when.

He stood by the wagon and waited for her to join him. He couldn't have felt worse if he tried. He knew he hurt her, and he desperately wanted to erase the damage he'd done. He hated knowing he made her cry. She didn't voice a single complaint. She simply went about that morning as if nothing transpired the night before. Her actions reminded him of that day when he saw her at the train station after Neil spoke unkindly to her. He closed his eyes and took a deep breath, willing the silent accusation that he wasn't any better than Craftsman to cease. God help him but he actually felt like he was worse.

The truth of the matter was that he desperately wanted to make love to her. Most of the time, it was all he could think about. But he caused the miscarriage. Pregnancy had seemed like such a blessing. Now it filled him with fear. He never wanted to pick up Mary and realize she bled like that ever again. Desire to be one with her, to enjoy the pleasures of her body, warred with his urge to protect her from harm.

When she emerged from the house, he appreciated her pretty face and form. She wore a light blue dress with a matching bonnet. As usual, stray strands of her brown hair refused to be properly tucked away. Her new shawl hung around her shoulders. The air was nippy but still pleasant enough to enjoy a ride into town. The cloudy sky gave them adequate shade from the sun without threatening rain.

Hoping to ease the ache he caused her, he gave her a long hug and kiss. Her soft body curved into his hard, muscular frame. Femininity flowed naturally from her, creating an awareness deep within him that it had been too long since they last came together to celebrate the marital bed. She smelled of cinnamon rolls and lilacs, and she tasted like coffee. His body responded to her, begging him to reassure her that she was still capable of arousing his sexual desire. Then the image of blood flashed through his mind.

He immediately relaxed the urgency in his kiss and embrace, realizing that, though she responded to him, her actions seemed forced. He couldn't blame her. He didn't know what he could do to fix the problem. After he helped her into the wagon, he hopped up beside her and clicked the reins. The horses moved forward.

"What color would you like your new shirts, pants and coat to be?" she asked.

He glanced at her, bewildered that she would make him clothes when she couldn't possibly feel well loved by him. "I can wear the same clothes I wore last year."

Staring at the countryside, she said, "I'm going to make myself some winter clothes and thought I'd make some for you while I was at it. Now that harvest is done, there's plenty of free time, and I like to keep busy. You'll be helping me if you let me sew you new clothes."

You should be keeping her busy in bed, came the accusing voice in his mind. Finally, he responded, "It would be nice to have something new to wear for a change. I like the colors black, brown, and blue. Thank you."

She nodded but refused to look in his direction.

Their normal easygoing conversations appeared to be slipping into awkward silences. The rift between them grew wider as guilt, fear, and regret seeped into their marriage. By the time they reached town, he spotted Jenny and Sally walking their sons in front of the bank. They stopped and waved to them.

"Would you like to talk to them for awhile?" he offered. "I have to take care of the crop, but I can meet you at the mercantile."

"Alright."

After he helped her down from the wagon and kissed her cheek, he continued on his way to the mercantile, passing five buggies and one wagon along the way. He nodded to the people and the corners of his mouth turned up when he saw a woman blanch as a horse snorted in her direction. He recalled the way Mary looked when she first rode Susannah. Sighing, for he also remembered how pleased she seemed when he kissed her back then, he directed the horses to the mercantile and applied the wagon's brake.

As he opened the door, Ralph glanced over from the three young men he talked to at the front of the store.

"I'll be with you in a minute," he told Dave.

Dave signaled for him to take his time and browsed through the items on the shelves. He caught sight of Cassie and Neil at the fabric table at the back of the store.

"But I don't know how to make clothes," she told him, sounding exasperated.

"What woman doesn't know how to make clothes?" His voice betrayed his bewilderment.

"A woman who was brought up to be a lady. I wasn't brought up for this kind of life."

He frowned. "Then why did you agree to come out here to marry me?"

"Because you said you had a farm but that it contained more animals than crops. You also assured me that you saved up a sizable sum of money so you fared better than other farmers in the area. I took that to mean that I wouldn't have to perform menial tasks like sewing. As it is, I cook. I didn't do that back home, but I've been a good sport and have learned to do it. However, I refuse to degrade myself by making clothes. I will buy my clothes."

"Making clothes is cheaper."

"But you can afford it, can't you?"

He sighed and rubbed the back of his neck as he glanced skyward.

"Dave?" Ralph called out.

Dave immediately turned on his heel and retraced his steps to the door. Waiting for Ralph to come up to him, he led him to his wagon.

"Did you remember everything this time?" the older man kindly asked as he inspected the crop.

"I did, thanks to Mary." He reached in his pants' pocket and pulled out the list she wrote for him.

"She's a real keeper alright. You couldn't have done better. She's got a sharp mind and good business sense, though she isn't much of a haggler."

He raised an eyebrow. "You don't take advantage of her generous nature, do you?" He grinned, knowing Ralph's respect for the woman wouldn't allow him to do that.

"No. She's too useful for my business. Did she tell you that she bartered some free fabrics in exchange for some towels, pot holders and blankets she made for me to sell? Last time she made some, I sold them for a great price to some old ladies. I can't keep her things in supply long enough. She made me a nice profit. Speaking of making money, I believe she intends to bring some more items in today." Grunting, he peered around the wagon. "Where is she anyway?"

"She's with my sisters, but she did ask me to load a bundle of things into the trunk back here." He jumped into the wagon and brought out the long wooden box. "I don't think I've ever seen a woman who sews as much as she does. Besides cooking, it's her favorite past-time."

"She certainly has a knack for both. I was one of the judges for the cooking contest. My mouth still waters when I think of that pie. You're a lucky man."

"Tell me something I don't know." Dave grinned.

It took both of them to bring in the pile of items from the trunk to the back room. The older man gave an appreciative whistle as he sorted through them. "These are better than the last batch."

"I hope you find my crop as much to your liking."

"We have enough people needing feed for their horses and livestock, so I'm sure I can give you a decent price."

After Ralph inspected the dried shucked stalks, they worked on a good price for the crop. Since Ralph enjoyed the haggling process, he intentionally started his price low. Dave obliged him and stated a higher price than he knew the man would accept. Once they agreed on an amount that made both of them happy, he helped him unload the livestock food and put it into his storage shed for safe keeping.

Dave wondered if he would have to track Mary down at one of his sister's residences when he emerged from the back of the store and heard his wife's familiar soothing voice.

"I don't mind," she said from the section of the store that included the fabrics from which she made clothes and blankets. "I enjoy sewing. Dave said there won't be much else to do except take care of the animals during the winter, so I have plenty of time."

"You are an angel," came Cassie's response.

He gritted his teeth in aggravation. Though the woman's tone dripped with sickening sweetness, her voice reminded him of nails down the blackboard. He shook off the shudder that involuntarily slid across his back so he could approach them with a smile on his face.

"Good afternoon, Mrs. Craftsman." He greeted her with a tip of his hat. "How are you doing, sweetheart?" he asked his wife when he reached her side.

"I'm fine." Mary held a bundle of various fabrics in her arms. "I was just looking for a basket. I found some wool over on that counter. I thought it might provide warmth for a coat."

"Over here?" He motioned to the various shades of wool.

She nodded.

Glancing at Cassie, he asked, "Would you excuse us for a minute?"

Cassie smiled. "Oh, I don't mind."

He gently urged Mary to the wool. "I think this color matches my best pants the best, don't you?" In a quieter voice, he said, "You know, you don't have to do anything you don't want to."

"But I do want to make you warm clothes for the winter. I've seen your old things, and they're ready to fall apart."

"No. I was talking about Cassie. You can tell her no."

She shrugged. "She's never learned how to sew. I offered to teach her but she's been worn out, so I thought I would help out."

"I'm afraid she's taking advantage of you."

She took a moment before responding. "I'm not a fool. I understand what's going on. Really, I'm fine with it."

His eyebrows furrowed. "Do you mind if I ask why?"

"Sometimes it's best to do what one can to keep the peace."

"You mean that you don't want to argue with her?"

"I mean that I don't want her to argue with her husband."

His eyes lit up with understanding. "You came in and found them arguing about clothes. But their problems aren't yours."

"I know but they are married, and I will do my part to help them if I can."

"What if she starts using you?"

"I don't see her often enough for that to happen. Besides, I can say no."

He wondered if that was true but kept his doubts to himself. Finding a basket, he placed the materials into it and held it for her. His annoyance gave way to full blown anger when Cassie ran off a list of instructions on what she wanted on her dresses. By the time he was ready to yell at her, she giggled and said she had to make a mad dash to Mrs. Brown's before the woman worried about her.

Mary turned back to the counter and selected some things that she wanted. He recalled Doris' complaints about Cassie trying to pawn the work off on the other women during the harvest. Even Jessica, who notoriously saw the good in everyone, made an unkind observation regarding Cassie's unwillingness to help them. It seemed that all the women complained at some point. All of them except for Mary. He hadn't thought of it until that moment, but it suddenly occurred to him that Mary never complained about anything. She accepted whatever life handed her, which explained why she didn't question the miscarriage. Unlike her, he questioned it often. If there was ever a woman who was made to be a mother, it was her. Her patience, calm, and generous nature were wonderful maternal attributes. It didn't seem fair that she was denied the chance to enjoy motherhood.

"Are you ready?" Mary asked.

Focusing on her, he noticed that she had added more fabrics, buttons, and decorations to a second basket. He agreed and followed her to the front of the store, carrying both baskets for her.

Chapter Twelve

Three days later, Mary sat on the bed, sewing a dress for Cassie. The sunlight pouring through the window gave her ample light. The smell from the cooling apple pie should have given her the calm it usually did, but she wondered if it would please Dave enough so he'd be happy with her.

She pulled the thread through the soft purple fabric and paused. Cassie was beautiful. She didn't need a fashionable dress to look good. Men had no trouble praising her. Neil certainly enjoyed being married to her. Maybe Dave wished he married her as well.

Brushing the tears from her eyes, she added a button to the waistline and pulled the thread through the small hole. What could a woman do when men judge by the outward appearance? If Dave had married Cassie and she suffered the miscarriage, Dave would still want to make love to her. *I was only attractive when I was expecting. It was the child he wanted. Not me. Why can't I have one thing uniquely my own to endear my husband to me?*

The door swung open. She bolted off the bed, dropping the dress to the floor. Bending down to pick it up, she didn't see who entered the house. The familiar voices caused her heart to race. Excited, she ran to greet Sally, Jenny, and her nephews.

A few moments later, Dave entered the house. "I thought I recognized that buggy out there."

"We came by for a visit," Sally replied. A twinkle in her eye, she continued, "I hope you don't mind that we're intruding on your time with your wife."

"I'm sure I can manage," he said. "I'll take Greg and Jeremy outside so you three can talk." He gave Mary a quick kiss on the cheek before he put Jeremy on his shoulders and headed for the door.

"I want a ride," Greg pouted.

"You'll get your turn," he assured the boy and waited for him to leave the house before closing the door.

Mary frowned. Children made him happy, and she couldn't give him one.

Sally set a bowl of salad on the table before she sat in a chair. "We thought we should come bearing gifts."

"Oh, you didn't have to do that. You are always welcome here." Mary smiled. "I'll get the coffee brewing." She put the dress on the mattress and went to the shelf by the kitchen window.

"I didn't know you like lace," Jenny noted, standing by the bed and glancing at the pile of the frilly material that rested in a heap on the side of the bed.

Sewing the lace around the edges of the garments proved tedious and time consuming work, but she promised Cassie she would add it since she seemed to like it so much.

"It's not for me. It's for Cassie." She took out the coffee pot and can of coffee beans.

Sally's eyes widened. "You're making Cassie Craftsman's clothes?"

"Yes."

"I suppose that Neil has enough money to pay someone to make his wife's wardrobe."

"Well, I volunteered to do it." She finished her task so she wouldn't have to see the same dumbfounded expression on their faces that she saw on Dave's face whenever he watched her sewing the dresses.

Sally was the first to speak, which didn't surprise Mary since she was more vocal than her sister. "I don't like being the one to point this out, but I think Cassie is taking advantage of you."

"I know she is."

Now Sally appeared confused. "Why are you letting her?"

"Dave and I shared this conversation a couple days ago. He doesn't like the fact that I'm doing this either."

"Good for him, but you still didn't answer my question."

She shrugged. "I thought it would help her and Neil. I didn't catch the details but he expressed his concern about the cost of a seamstress, so I offered to ease the burden."

"And Neil let you?"

"No. He was already gone by the time I talked to her."

Jenny interrupted Sally before she could say anything else. "Mary's free to do it if she wants. Making clothes is not the worst thing she could do."

"True," her sister relented. "I heard about Cassie though. She has a habit of handing over her duties to other people. I just don't want this to become a pattern for you."

"It won't," Mary assured her. "I only offered to do it since I enjoy sewing anyway." She sat on the bed and picked up the violet dress. She picked up a black button and sewed it into the waistline.

"You already have three buttons. Why are you adding another one?"

"Since she's in the family way, her waistline will expand, and as it does, these buttons will accommodate her."

Jenny nodded and sat next to her. "Very clever. I'll need to do the same thing for my customers."

Sally groaned, her arms crossed. "I just hope Cassie appreciates it, especially since you had a miscarriage. If you ask me, and I know you didn't, it's thoughtless to ask a woman who miscarried to sew clothes for an expectant woman."

"Speaking of the miscarriage, how are you doing?" Jenny handed her another button.

"I'm doing fine," Mary replied. "It was a shock, but life goes on and it does no good to dwell on the past or what might have been. I've grieved it but can't do anything to change it. So I focus on the present."

"Hopefully, you'll carry your next pregnancy to term."

Deciding not to comment, she pulled the thread through the small holes on the next button.

Unfortunately, Sally picked up on her mood. She stood up and sat on the other side of Mary. Placing a gentle hand on her arm, she asked, "Are things between you and Dave alright?"

Her face flushed with humiliation. She did wish to talk to someone she could trust but didn't know if it would be appropriate.

"What's wrong?" Jenny softly pressed.

Gripping the dress in her hands, she uneasily exhaled. "I'm not attractive."

Sally frowned. "Is this because of what Tom and Joel said?"

"No, but I can't fault them. They were only speaking the truth."

"We don't think that."

She smiled at them. "You're women. You see things differently than men do. The reason I answered a wife wanted ad in the paper was because the men back in Maine wouldn't court me. I figured that agreeing to marry a man out west was the only chance I had of getting married and having children."

Sally wrapped her arm around Mary's shoulders. "David isn't one to talk about his feelings, but we can tell that he adores you."

"Maybe he did, but I failed him."

Jenny frowned. "How so?"

Mary subconsciously pressed her nails into the palms of her hands. "I couldn't give him the child he wanted."

"The miscarriage wasn't your fault. No one can prevent something like that from happening," Sally responded. "Besides, the doctor said that most women who miscarry go on to have a baby."

"That doesn't matter. Dave isn't interested in coming together. All he does is kiss and hug me."

"Maybe he thinks that you aren't ready for it yet. After all, your body did go through a shock."

Embarrassment washed through her. "I went to bed naked and offered myself to him. He said that I wasn't ready, but I knew he was lying. He's repulsed by me."

"What if he honestly thinks you're not ready?"

"It's been two months since I lost the baby."

"Oh. Well, that does seem like enough time. Have you had any complications?"

Mary shook her head. "I healed nicely." The pain in her palms intensified. "I should be grateful that he was even able to consummate the marriage. Other men have told me that they wouldn't consider sleeping with me."

"You're making that up," Jenny insisted.

"No, I'm not." So Mary's sad confession poured forth. "I originally answered Neil's ad."

"Neil?" Sally's eyes widened. "Neil Craftsman?"

"Yes." Disgrace tore at her heart as she continued. "I came out here to marry him, but he took one look at me and told me that he couldn't get drunk enough to get me with child. Dave overheard and married me out of pity. I was ready to search the want ads in the paper for a job when he proposed to me."

For a moment, neither woman spoke, as if they couldn't believe their ears.

Slowly, Sally shook her head. "David said he married you because he felt sorry for you?"

"No. He was very noble about it. He said he needed a wife and that I would be doing him a favor if I married him. He didn't want to go through the trouble of posting an ad and waiting for a response."

"Well, you're better off without Neil anyway. You wouldn't believe the number of women he slept with."

Mary had heard rumors concerning his loose living. Many times she found herself feeling grateful that he rejected her. "You won't let anyone know how Dave and I met, will you? It's not exactly a story I want to recall."

"I like this version better than the one David told us. It's much more romantic, but we'll keep our lips sealed, right Jenny?"

Jenny nodded. "Of course."

Relieved, Mary admitted, "I am lucky that Dave saved me from a life of spinsterhood. I hope you don't think I'm complaining about him. He is a wonderful man."

"He praises you to the family. He's obviously proud to be your husband." After a moment of silence, she asked, "Was he hesitant to be intimate with you before?"

"No," Mary cautiously replied, feeling uneasy about describing their private life. "We did it often before the miscarriage."

"It stands to reason that he's afraid to be intimate with you," Sally decided. "Maybe he thinks he'll hurt you. Are you tender down there? After Greg was born, I was sore for months."

"No. I feel fine."

"You need to talk to him. Men can't be expected to know these things."

Mary didn't feel comfortable following Sally's advice. What if he revealed that the thought of touching her did, in fact, repulse him? What if he only performed his husbandly duty in order to have a child, and now that he knew it didn't work, he felt no need to do it? It truly was a kindness on Dave's part to try to make her feel attractive. He even convinced her of it before the miscarriage, but actions spoke louder than words.

"Well, we happen to think that you are a lovely woman," Jenny told her. "Dave must have seen something in you that he liked in order to marry you. He's not one to settle for anything out of pity. He does have a gift for detecting beauty where others don't."

"It certainly seems that he thinks you're pretty when he looks at you," Sally added. She gently squeezed Mary's shoulder. "Just so you know, we are glad he married you. You have made him happy."

Mary considered their words. Perhaps Dave didn't see her as romantically appealing, but then again, she hardly expected love when she married him. Maybe he did value her for her companionship. They seemed to be good friends. It was enough. She could be content with that. But even as the thoughts echoed through her mind, her heart ached. Since when did she yearn for his love? She had been content without it before, but now it didn't seem to be enough.

MARY COLLECTED THE clothes she made for Cassie so she could deliver them to her. Dave insisted on helping her into the wagon after he hitched Lewis and Clark to it. She wasn't particularly looking forward to seeing the beauty, but she wished to get the meeting over with so that she could go back to sewing clothes for her and Dave for the upcoming winter. The end of October was upon them, and the red, orange, and yellow fallen leaves dotted the light green landscape as if someone haphazardly threw together patches for a quilt. Fall in Maine did seem more spectacular, but she wouldn't trade her new home for the endless supply of pretty leaves there. She enjoyed her new world, or at least, parts of it. Refusing to utter a complaint for how things might have been if she was still in the family way, she pulled the shawl tightly around her shoulders and turned her attention to the rolling hills in the distance.

"Penny for your thoughts."

Startled, she glanced at Dave who had reluctantly agreed to take her to the Craftsman farm. "Oh, I was just marveling at the pretty scenery."

He smiled at her. "You go well with it."

Uncertain as to his meaning, she shrugged. "I do like it here." She clenched the shawl in her hands and returned her gaze to the hills in the distance.

"That's good because if you went to Maine, I'd have to find you and bring you home. I wouldn't want to spend the rest of my life without you."

His words offered her a glimmer of hope. Maybe her worth extended beyond her ability to give him children. She might have proven herself valuable for the other things she could provide him, such as cooking and sewing. Feeling better, she relaxed her rigid posture. "I wouldn't dream of leaving you, Dave."

His tender slate-gray eyes met hers. "Will you come closer?"

She obeyed, keeping one hand on the seat so she wouldn't trip since the ride bumped her around. He put his arm around her waist, encouraging her to lean against him.

"Promise me you won't let Cassie talk you into doing anything else for her." His warm breath brushed her ear.

"I won't."

"Good because I don't want anyone using you."

She closed her eyes, settled her head on his shoulder, and enjoyed the way his strong arm supported her. The morning sun shined on her, warming her despite the cool air, and the breeze carried the sweet smell of autumn. However, she hardly noticed her surroundings. A sense of their former closeness settled between them. She still loved him, even if he didn't love her. Resolving to be the best wife she could possibly be for him, she rested her hand on his thigh. The simple action spoke of familiarity and intimacy, and since she had often done it in the past, she did it out of habit.

When they reached their destination, she reluctantly sat up straight so she could grab the clothes from behind their seat. He used the reins to lead the geldings to the front of the sod house.

She noticed that Neil told six men where to unload five wagons full of lumber.

Beside her, Dave grumbled.

Reaching for his arm before he hopped to the ground, she asked, "What's wrong?"

Sighing, he pulled the brake on the wagon wheels before turning back to her. "Neil's building a wood house. I reckon that the neighbors will have to help build it."

"Does Neil ever help anyone build anything?" she whispered, not wishing for anyone to overhear them.

He leaned closer to her than necessary, his breath tickling her ear. "He usually finds a reason to be busy." His hand stroked her lower back and his lips lingered close to her cheek. When she turned to face him, he lightly kissed her. "Mary, there's something I've been meaning to tell you." His tone was tender, assuring her that whatever he wanted to say, it wouldn't be bad.

"What is it, Dave?" she whispered, her heart thumping loudly in her ears.

Cassie called out to them before he got a chance to continue.

Mary noticed his slight frown before he smiled at the raven-haired beauty. "Good morning, Mrs. Craftsman."

"Good morning, Mr. Larson," she sweetly replied, her hands folded in front of her chest, reminding Mary of a praying angel.

Dave hopped out of the wagon, sauntered to Mary's side and reached around her waist to help her down. He pulled her against his solid frame and pressed his lips gently to hers. "I can carry those for you."

"I'm fine. They aren't heavy."

"Alright. I'll go talk to Neil while you talk to her."

She nodded and approached Cassie.

"Oh, Mary, are those for me?" Cassie's delighted squeal revealed her pleasure at seeing her new clothes.

"Yes." Her hands shook as she sorted through them. Being next to Cassie made her feel inferior as a woman. "Two dresses. I sewed buttons that you can use to adjust the waistline as your belly gets bigger."

Her nose wrinkled as her smooth, slender hands ran over the soft fabric. "There's no silk."

Clearing her throat, she explained, "Silk isn't practical on a farm."

"What a shame. Silk is luxurious against the skin. I wish I understood what farming entailed before I answered Neil's ad. I admit that I didn't anticipate how different life is here." She touched her arm. "Tell me, did your husband warn you about living here?"

She shrugged. "I did some reading on Nebraska after I answered the ad. I knew the general aspects of farming but didn't realize how much work it is."

"You came from Maine?"

"Yes."

"Hmm... I came from Pennsylvania. Well, I guess I should have found out what I was getting myself into." She sighed. "At least I talked Neil into building a reasonable house. I never feel clean surrounded by dirt. Being the wives of farmers isn't easy for us."

"I don't mind it. A home is more than a structure. It's who you're with."

She giggled. "You're precious. How wonderful that harsh living hasn't unsettled you. Anyway, thank you for the clothes. You are a gem!"

Mary doubted the woman's sincerity but smiled as if she believed her.

"Would you like to come inside and get a cup of coffee?"

No, I wouldn't. But instead of voicing her true feelings, she joined Cassie.

Cassie hung the clothes in the wardrobe. "Would you believe that I'm still exhausted? I had no idea that carrying a child could wipe a woman out! I'm tired all the time and I feel sick. Why, just the smell of certain foods cause me to vomit." She patted the small mound that sheltered her child.

"You'll reap the benefits of being pregnant in a short time." For a brief moment, Mary grieved the fact that she didn't experience the 'great sufferings' Cassie complained about.

"The men will expect coffee, but I can't even smell coffee without getting nauseous. Would you please be a dear and brew a pot for them?" She shot Mary a pleading look.

Biting a cutting remark because she realized that Cassie led her into the house for this reason, she glanced out the window. Her husband and six men emptied the wagons of lumber and stacked them into piles. A hot drink should satisfy their thirst. Despite her better judgment, she brewed the coffee while Cassie laid down on the mattress and closed her eyes to rest.

As Mary poured coffee into the mugs, Neil entered the place. He stopped when he noticed her. "Good morning, Mrs. Larson."

"Good morning, Mr. Craftsman." She didn't take her eyes off the hot brown liquid as it flowed into the last cup.

He glanced at Cassie. His jaw clenched but he didn't say anything to his wife. Instead, he walked over to Mary. "You don't have to make coffee. It's my house, and I can do it."

"Your wife is tired. You and the men are working hard out there. Coffee is easy. Here. Have a cup. I'll call the other men over to take their cups."

Picking up four hot cups by the handles, she headed for the door. "I'll get that." He ran in front of her and turned the doorknob.

"Thank you." Feeling awkward, she stepped through the doorway.

Once he shut the door behind him and followed her, he whispered, "I'm sorry you had to make coffee and make my wife clothes."

"Don't worry about it."

"I wish I didn't have to."

They brought the men their mugs. On her way back to the house to get the last two mugs, Dave joined her. "Is anyone giving you a hard time?"

"No."

"Did Cassie help you?"

"I don't wish to argue with you, Dave," she softly spoke, realizing the truth would upset him. Her hands clenched the folds of her skirt. "When everyone is done unloading the wagons, we'll go home." She understood that he had to stay and help out.

"I don't like this." His face darkened. "You deserve better treatment."

An uneasy tension knotted in her stomach as they stopped three feet from the door. She turned to face him, barely noting the men who drank their coffee and laughed. "You treat me well. That's what matters."

By the expression on his face, she knew that he wasn't pleased, though he didn't protest when she went inside the house to retrieve more coffee for the men. She wondered if she displeased him.

A half hour later, Maureen Brown brought two other women to the farm. Brewing another pot of coffee and cooking lunch, Mary glanced at the door as the three giggling women walked into the house as if they owned the place. Cassie, who had fallen asleep on the bed, immediately woke up and grinned at them.

"Oh my dear, you are exhausted," Maureen cooed, rushing over to her and patting her hand. "And isn't it wonderful that Mrs. Larson has come to your aid?"

"Yes, I've been sick again," Cassie chirped. "I can barely stand to eat, let alone cook."

"What we women go through to give our husbands children." Maureen placed her hand over her heart and turned to the overweight brunette. "Gwendolyn, isn't it wonderful that your daughter-in-law is going to bless you with a grandchild?"

"I am blessed." Gwendolyn offered Cassie a warm smile and sat next to her on the bed. "Is there anything I can get for you?"

"Actually, I could use a cup of water," Cassie reported, appearing grateful for the assistance.

"I'll get it right away," Maureen volunteered. "You two need to sit together and do some mother-daughter bonding. What a pity that you lost your parents at such a tender age."

"Yes, the accident was a horrible ordeal. I am fortunate to have married Neil so I have a new mother." She gave Gwendolyn an adoring gaze.

Mary stirred the pot of chili, feeling ill from the exchange which seemed too good to be true. *Cassie doesn't have a sincere bone in her body.* Startled, she paused. Why did she have such a mean-spirited thought? She got along wonderfully with Dave's mother. In fact, his entire family had been kind to her. Was she jealous of Cassie's pregnancy? Running her tongue nervously across her lower lip, she stirred the beans.

"Mary," Maureen began as she made her way over to her, "I commend you on your good deeds." She motioned for the redhead to come near them. "Connie, this is Mary Larson. I told you about her. She's a marvelous cook. Why, she's the one who beat me in the baking contest! Mary, this is Mrs. James. Mrs. James is the head of the church ladies group I told you about."

Mary greeted the fifty-year-old woman with a polite smile. "I've heard you sing at my church. You have a lovely voice."

"Oh, thank you." Connie blushed, apparently flattered. "Do you need any help?"

"I was planning to make frying pan bread."

"Say no more," Maureen interrupted Connie before she could respond. "I can bake that so well that your mouth will water. Cassie, sweetheart, do you mind if I cook?"

"I'd appreciate it very much," Cassie replied.

Neil's mother put her arm around her shoulders. "Well, you must try to eat something for the baby's sake, even if it's only a bite."

"Yes. I will do my best."

Connie's eyes fell on the open wardrobe. "What a beautiful dress! Did you make this?" she asked Cassie as she ran her fingers over the cotton and lace that Mary sewed together.

"Mary made it," Maureen inserted.

"I recall Neil saying that Mary offered to make his bride some clothes since she is in the family way," his mother added.

"Mary, you have a way with a needle and an eye for style," Connie complimented.

Cassie frowned. "I've been too tired to do much. I fear that you must find me lazy."

"Nonsense," Gwendolyn immediately assured her. "You have the most important job a woman can do."

Her body relaxed as she accepted more of the woman's compliments.

Maureen shook her head and turned her attention to Mary while she mixed together the flour, baking powder, salt and water. "There's nothing like loyalty between a mother and daughter-in-law. Speaking of which, Dave's mother praises you to everyone in town. She certainly has lucked out. All of her daughters-in-law are excellent examples of what it means to be a lady." She laid the cake on the pre-heated skillet that Mary greased for her. "I don't suppose you've reconsidered joining the ladies group?"

Mary wiped her hands on the flour sack towel. "No. I'm too busy helping Dave at the farm."

"But winter is fast approaching. Farmers don't do much during that time, do they?"

"There's always work to be done. I do appreciate the offer though."

"Well, it still stands."

Connie went over to her. "I hate to inconvenience you, Mary, but I wondered if you'd be kind enough to teach me how you sewed the lace into the dress? I rather fancy that design and would like to duplicate it."

"I'd be happy to oblige you."

"Wonderful! Can you come to my house tomorrow at noon? I'll have lunch prepared."

"I can do that."

"What a great honor for you," Maureen told Mary. "Connie only allows those she deems worthy to pay her a visit. You are quite popular."

"Since you mentioned houses," Cassie spoke up, "Neil is going to make me a gorgeous wood-framed home. It will have two floors."

"And it's about time." Maureen nodded. "People shouldn't be subjected to these substandard living conditions." A cringe crossed her features. "Just look at this floor. It's made of dirt!"

"Neil is a terrific husband," Cassie gushed. "He treats me like a princess."

Mrs. Craftsman's face shone. "A mother likes to hear when her son is doing right."

"You have every right to be proud of him."

The rest of the morning passed with similar talk until it was time to eat. Then the men took a break for their meal.

At one point, Neil's mother told him, "Cassie wanted to help but the poor girl's too worn out, so we insisted she get some rest."

Mary thought she saw Neil roll his eyes but later figured that she imagined it. After all, Neil adored his wife, didn't he?

Chapter Thirteen

The next day, Dave took Mary to Connie James' residence so she could help the older woman improve her sewing. He didn't need to wear his jacket since it was unusually warm, and the lack of a breeze and bright sunlight added to the higher temperature. To his surprise, Maureen and Connie waited for Mary on the front porch of the green house.

"You sure are winning the hearts of many people," he noted. He knew that Maureen and Connie selected their company with great care.

Sitting by him, Mary shrugged. "I'm helping her with her sewing. It's not a big deal."

He raised an eyebrow. "Jenny sews too but she'd never get an invite to Mrs. James' house." Getting down from the wagon, he helped her step down and saw her to the porch.

Tipping his hat to the two women, he said a quick greeting and left. He brought more shucked stalks and some corn ears to the mercantile. As he finished doing business with Ralph, Jenny strolled in, holding Jeremy's hand.

"Usually I run into Sally," he said. Grinning, he knelt in front of his nephew. "I reckon I owe you some candy."

"If you insist on treats, then you can't give him anything sticky," his sister said. "I don't like having to wash up everything he touches."

"Are you giving your mother a hard time?" He tickled the boy who rewarded him with laughter.

Several people glanced over at them and smiled.

"Candy please, Uncle Dave."

"You got it, squirt." Standing up, he asked her, "What can I buy him?"

"A mint or licorice will do fine."

"Which do you want?" He looked at the two year old.

"Mint."

He chuckled. "I'll take him to the counter up front while you shop."

Jenny thanked him and headed for the sewing supplies. He knew that she managed to support herself and her son by making clothes, novelty pillows and towels, and coats, but he worried about her so he slipped Ralph some money to add to her account so she wouldn't have to pay for the purchase or future purchases for awhile.

After Jeremy ate his candy, Jenny finished her shopping.

"Can I talk to you? In private?" she requested as he took the items for her.

He opened the door for her and Jeremy and followed her outside. "Do you want to go to the boarding house? We could talk and I could drop these off for you."

She agreed.

When they arrived at the house, she asked her landlady to watch her son. "My room is up the stairs."

"I know where it is," he reminded her as they climbed the wooden steps. Wondering if he wanted to hear what she had to say, he entered her modest room that contained her bed and a small bed for Jeremy. He placed her purchases on the old dresser and turned to face her. Taking his hat off, he prepared himself for her answer. "Is Jeremy sick?"

"No. He's fine." She paced in front of the window, wringing her hands.

"Are you sick?"

"No. I'm fine too."

The hairs on the back of his neck stood on end. "Is Clyde back? Because if he is, don't you dare marry him. I don't care if he is Jeremy's father. I'll run him out of town before he uses you again."

"No, Clyde hasn't returned."

He relaxed. "Good. As much as I believe a man ought to do right for mistreating a woman, I don't want you to suffer in a marriage with him. You're better off alone."

She sighed. "I agree. A day doesn't go by that I don't regret what I did with him. But I don't want to talk about my past. I wanted to talk about you and Mary."

"Why?"

"I'm concerned about you two."

"There's nothing wrong. We're alright."

"No, you're not."

Irritated, he shifted the balance from one leg to the other and crossed his arms, his hat still in his hand. "What are you saying?"

"Before you get the wrong idea, I want you to understand that Mary didn't want me or Sally to mention it to anyone else, including you. But on her behalf, I'm going to risk upsetting her."

He frowned. A heavy weight seemed to sink into the pit of his stomach. If there was a problem, his wife needed to come to him with it instead of going to other people, even if those other people happened to be his sisters. He waited for her to speak, aware of the landlady's cooing over Jeremy in the parlor in the lower level of the house.

Jenny nodded to herself before standing still and turning to look him in the eye. "Mary said that ever since the miscarriage, the two of you haven't been together...as man and wife."

He stared at her, not getting her meaning.

She took a deep breath and blurted out, "You need to go to bed with your wife."

His jaw dropped and his eyes nearly popped out of his head. "What?"

"I'm pretty sure you heard me the first time."

"Mary told you and Sally about our private life?" My goodness! Was nothing sacred?

"Now before you get upset with Mary, hear me out. A woman longs to be desired by her husband. She wants to be the focus of his life."

"Mary is the focus of my life."

"Dave, you're interrupting." She groaned and stamped her foot on the wood floor. "Come on. Don't give me that look. I'm trying to help you." She straightened her back and met his shocked gaze. "For a woman to feel valued, she has to be sexually appealing. You can't separate lovemaking from the marital relationship. The two go hand in hand. When you aren't being intimate with her, she begins to doubt you love her."

He shook his head, hoping to clear it. "I can't believe I'm hearing this!"

"Do you want to be intimate with her?"

Of course, he wanted to be intimate with her, but he didn't feel comfortable telling his sister that! "Why are we having this conversation? This should be between me and my wife." He gritted his teeth.

"She might be your wife but she's my best friend. She thinks that you find her repulsive."

"That's ridiculous."

"Is it? What would you think if she didn't want to make love to you?"

"This has nothing to do with what I want or don't want."

"Doesn't it?"

"No!" His face flushed from a mixture of irritation and embarrassment. "It's about her health. I don't want her to go through another miscarriage."

Jenny's expression softened. "Dave, there are many things that can go wrong, but you can't let the fear of the unknown prevent you from enjoying life. Would you refuse to let your horses pull a plow because they might get hurt?"

"That's completely different."

"Is it?"

"Lewis and Clark are horses. They can be replaced. I can't replace Mary."

"Which is exactly why you need to show her that she matters to you. When you withhold your body from her, you are denying her the love and affection that should be a part of your life together."

He sighed and rubbed his eyes. "You don't understand, Jenny. I'm the one who found her at the river. That's not an image I can forget."

"I'm not telling you to forget it. I'm asking you to move beyond it. The best way both of you can heal is to renew your intimate life. If she gets in the family way, then she gets in the family way. And she might give birth to a healthy baby next time."

"I didn't think something as natural as pregnancy could be risky."

"Life is all about risks. You didn't know what you were getting when you advertised for a wife, but she came off the train and she's made you very happy. You know what Pa says, 'The bigger the risk, the greater the reward.'"

All the fight departed from him. Jenny was right. And he couldn't fault Mary for talking to her and Sally. When Mary came to him that night without any clothes on, he told her to get dressed without explaining why he turned her away. He felt like a contemptible person. If what Jenny said was true, then Mary must have assumed that he saw her the way Neil did. He winced at the thought. No wonder Mary cried. Why didn't he get it? He knew he upset her, but he assumed it was because she wanted to get pregnant right away and he wished to wait, to give her body and heart time to recover.

"Is there anything else?" he softly asked his sister.

"No."

He unfolded his arms and put his hat back on his head. "I promised Mary that I'd pick her up."

"Are you mad at her?"

"No." In the future, he would pay better attention to what Mary said and did so she wouldn't feel the need to go to his sisters for comfort. "And I'm not mad at you either."

Looking relieved, she ran over and hugged him. "You're a good husband, Dave."

He returned her hug and went to Connie's house. He vowed that he wouldn't let the sun go down that day until he made things right with his wife.

ON THE WAY HOME, DAVE drew Mary close to him on their wagon ride home. He noticed that Lewis favored his left rear foot. When Dave stopped the wagon by the barn, he helped her down. He welcomed Jasper with a pat on the head.

"I have to check on Lewis' horseshoe," he told her.

"Do you need help?" She turned to inspect Lewis' foot.

Touched by her willingness to assist him, he lightly touched her arm to stop her. "I got it. Why don't you rest?"

She blinked. "I got plenty of rest at Mrs. James' house."

"Then do something for yourself for a change."

Seeming to consider her options, she finally nodded. "I could use a bath. Alright. When I return from the river, I'll cook supper."

At least he knew where to find her later. As she left, he went to investigate what was troubling his horse. After he cleaned out Lewis' horseshoes, he put his horses in the pasture. He took a deep breath, knowing this would be the right time to approach her so he could settle her doubts. Handing Jasper a bone from the root cellar so the dog would leave him alone with his wife, he gathered his bathing supplies and strode to the river.

The sight of his wife naked, standing with a bar of soap in her hand, lured him to her. What a welcoming view this was compared to the one he found that morning in August when she had the miscarriage. He stood by a tree, unashamedly staring, hoping that this image would forever replace the one that haunted his memory. The gentle current reached her waist, hiding enough of her to whet his appetite for more. She was the very image of sensuality. Her hands massaged her wet and soapy hair that she had piled on top of her head, causing her breasts to stand out as if inviting him to wash them.

His body prompted him forward. Pulse racing, he quickly removed his clothing, eager for the freedom to enjoy her the way he used to in their first months of marriage. *Don't think about it. Just do it.* He knew that if he allowed his instincts to take over, then he could get over his apprehension. Jenny was right. He couldn't let his fear of what might happen ruin the joy of the moments he did have with his wife, and he did want that joy back.

He slowly approached her. She was humming a tune under her breath, and though she misplaced a couple of notes, he found it endearing all the same. As soon as she noticed him, she paused, her hands still in her soapy hair. Her cheeks grew a pretty shade of pink and she began to dip into the water to cover herself from him.

"Don't. Please." His request came out tenderly, as if asking more than telling.

She hesitated but resumed her standing position. Bringing her hands down, she washed them in the water. "I thought you were checking on Lewis," she said, looking down at her hands.

"I finished. I thought I'd take one last swim before winter creeps in."

Despite the heat of the day, the water remained cool from the previous chilly days. His passion for her boiled in his veins so his body temperature hardly decreased as he submersed himself into the river. Swiftly, he made his way over to her. She looked magnificent standing before him.

"May I help you wash up?" His husky voice sounded strange to his ears, but she didn't seem to notice.

Nodding, she handed him the bar of soap.

He took it from her and worked up a lilac scented lather. "I'll start with your back."

She turned around. Since her hair was still on top of her head, he got a good view of her neck, shoulders and back. He idly rubbed her neck and shoulders, easing the tension in her muscles as she did for him every night of the harvest when his body ached.

"Thank you for making me clothes," he whispered, suddenly awestruck that she did so much for him.

"Hopefully, they will last for many years. Once I make your coat, I want to make you a leather belt and gloves to go with your boots."

"Why do you do so much for me?"

She shrugged. "Why not? You are my husband."

He sighed, gently cleaning her soft back. "I'm not a good husband to you."

She turned to face him, starling him. "Why did you say that?"

"Because I've been keeping you at a distance." He couldn't look her in the eyes as he made his confession. She drew him to her like a magnet, and heaven help him but he couldn't take his eyes off of her lovely breasts which were mere inches from his chest. His soapy hands caressed them.

"You're not keeping your distance now." There was a hint of amusement in her tone.

Smiling wryly, he admitted, "I'm tired of fighting my desire for you."

"Why have you been fighting it?"

He stroked the underside of her breasts, cupping them in the palms of his hands. "I found you here and took you back to the house that morning you miscarried. I saw the blood and didn't realize what was going on. I thought I was going to lose you. You're the most important person in my life. It was painful to lose the baby, but losing you would have been worse."

"I thought you were disappointed in me," she whispered.

He looked in her eyes then and saw the unshed tears in them. "No. I was never disappointed in you. I'm sorry I gave you that impression."

"I miss being close to you."

"I miss it too."

She ran her tongue along her lips, an action he now recognized as the nervous energy that she carefully hid. Whenever he saw her do that simple and innocent action, he longed to kiss her so he could taste her. His heart beat anxiously against his chest as he cupped her face in his hands. Her eyes widened. He detected the blue darkening them, hinting her desire. Closing his eyes, he leaned forward and caressed her lips with his. Her lips, still moist from having licked them, felt soft and warm against his. She slightly parted her mouth. Giving a low, thankful groan, he accepted her unspoken invitation and slid his tongue into her waiting mouth.

He pulled her to him. Her softness pressed into his hard flesh, his arousal throbbing in anticipation. For a moment, the image of blood flashed through his mind. He pulled away from her. His eyes flew open, reassured when he saw her in front of him, looking lovelier than she had at any other moment since he'd known her.

"It's going to take awhile before I stop seeing you in pain," he explained.

"Do you want to stop?" Her hands traced his shoulders and glided across his chest. Though she asked the question, her hands continued their southward descent.

Intrigued, because she hadn't been forward in their lovemaking before, he waited to see what she would do next as the disturbing memory of that August morning slipped from his mind. He sharply inhaled when she wrapped her warm hands around his aching member. He immediately picked her up and led her to a shallow area where he sat down and straddled her on top of him. He hungrily kissed her breasts, focusing on her pink buds that seemed to beg for his attention.

"I'm not going to last long," he warned her, already aware that his body was primed for release.

"Maybe not this time, but we can do it again."

She allowed him access into the warmth of her body. He groaned in pleasure, wondering why he resisted this for two months. It truly was the best feeling in the world.

She kissed the top of his head and held him close to her. Her movements had just begun when he reached his climax. Somehow, it seemed more intense than the ones he experienced before. Perhaps that stemmed from the fact that it had been too long since they came together or maybe it was the fact that she instigated part of it. Then he wondered if it was because he never felt closer to her until he told her how important she was to him. Whatever the reason, he didn't want to avoid their intimacy anymore.

When he tilted his head to look up at her, he realized she was crying. He frowned. "It was too quick."

"No, it's not that. I'm crying because I'm happy you still want me."

He moved from under her so that she sat next to him. Hugging her to him, he softly kissed her. "I do want you, Mary. I always did. I'll try to do a better job of showing you that in the future."

"I want to make you happy." Her eyes had changed from the dark of blue to the light of green with bluish specks surrounding the pupils.

"You do make me happy. You've made me happy ever since you agreed to marry me. I couldn't have asked for a better wife. And I must add that you have the most beautiful eyes I've ever seen. You really are a pretty woman." Then he mischievously grinned. "Your figure doesn't hurt either."

Though she blushed, he noted the thrilling effect his words had on her.

"Do you know how to swim?" he asked.

She looked startled by the change in topic. "Actually, I don't."

"Would you like to learn?"

"Alright."

"We should rinse out your hair first."

"Oh, I forgot about that." She touched the soapy strands.

"That's a change. Usually, I'm the one who forgets things."

Once he finished cleaning her hair, she accepted his hand as he led her to the deeper section of the river. The current flowed smoothly around them. It turned out that she was a quick learner, for she gracefully moved in the water in a matter of minutes. She mastered the activity within a half hour.

"What do you think? Do you like swimming?" He swam over to her.

"I do. It's invigorating."

"You do it well." He glanced at the sky. The clouds seemed to be gathering, giving the impression that the warm weather would soon revert back to the cool days they had been experiencing. He hated to end their carefree swim. "I reckon it's time to head back. I should clean myself up." He shot her a sly look. "I never did finish bathing you. Interested?"

She giggled and agreed.

Chapter Fourteen

Six weeks later when Mary woke up, she saw Dave watching her. She was curled up on her side, and he laid on his side next to her, facing her.

He smiled at her and caressed her cheek. "Good morning."

She glanced up at the window, noting that streaks of light blue had begun to light up the sky. The longer nights hinting to winter made it too easy to sleep in. Returning his smile, she whispered, "Is it time to get up already?"

"Unfortunately."

For a month and a half, she had joined the women while he and the other farmers in the neighboring area helped Neil build his small three bedroom two-story home.

"Do you think it'll be completed this week?" she asked.

"I hope so. It's already December. We're lucky snow hasn't fallen yet."

"You're a good man, Dave. I know that it's not easy to work twelve hour days in the cold weather."

"Do you think we'll ever be done doing things for Cassie?"

She looked sympathetically at him. "Is it that bad?"

He raised an eyebrow. "You tell me. You made her clothes, even redoing one that wasn't up to her standards," he rolled his eyes, "and then you and the women spend all your time fussing over her."

"We don't fuss over her."

"No? That's news to me. Children have a tendency to tell us men what's going on in that house."

She shrugged. "Cassie thought life would be similar to the one she experienced back east. I don't think she's adjusting to it very well."

"Or she could be used to using people to get what she wants."

"You don't usually speak ill of people. She must really bother you."

"Let's just say that I'm grateful I ended up with you. I was ready to write an ad for a wife, and if you hadn't shown up when you did, she might have answered my ad instead of Neil's." He wiggled closer to her so that their bare bodies touched beneath the warm blanket. "I knew you were special the first moment I saw you."

"You do make me feel special."

"Good." He softly kissed her. "You're not pushing yourself too hard over there, are you?"

"You don't need to worry about me. I can handle cooking and watching the children. Besides, ever since Doris, Jessica, and your mother found out that I'm expecting again, they've been forcing me to sit down often."

He closed his eyes and brought his forehead to hers. "Promise me that if you feel any pain or start bleeding, you'll tell me right away."

"I promise you every day. Do you think I'll forget?"

"No, but I worry about you."

She snuggled into his arms and pressed her cheek to his shoulder. Inhaling the strong masculine scent she'd come to associate with him, she enjoyed his warm embrace. "If it makes you feel better, I've been slightly sick to my stomach and more tired for the past two weeks."

"Why would that make me feel better?"

"Because as long as I feel this way, it means the baby is alright. My sickness stopped right before the miscarriage."

"It seems like a double-edged sword to be glad you're not feeling well."

His kisses worked their way from the top of her head, down the side of her face and to her mouth where it deepened. Then he made love to her. For a reason she couldn't explain, the pleasure she received from it intensified the more they came together, and she loved the affection he showered on her. She couldn't recall a time in her life when she felt as wanted or needed as he made her feel. Her love for him grew stronger each day.

Afterwards, she reluctantly joined him in getting dressed and made breakfast while he brought her fresh water. When they finished eating, she milked the cow while he fed the animals. Then he hooked Lewis and Clark to the wagon.

She brought out a pair of leather gloves and a knitted scarf to him. "I finished these last night." She wrapped the dark green scarf around his neck and tucked it into the neckline of his coat.

He leaned forward to kiss her. "You take good care of me. Thank you."

Blushing from his compliment, she took his hand so he could help her onto the wagon. She watched him as he walked to the other side. The leather gloves matched his leather belt and boots. She didn't make the boots but had ordered them through Ralph as a birthday gift when he turned twenty-three in November.

Sitting close to her, he snapped the reins to urge the geldings forward and told Jasper to watch the farm during their absence. As if the dog understood his mission, he barked.

Dave smiled at her. "You know, that pink shirt you're wearing brings out the color in your cheeks. You look good in pink."

"I haven't worn pink before, so I thought I'd try something new."

Wrapping his arm around her waist, he pulled her against him. "I like it."

She adjusted her thick, long beige skirt, glad she succeeded in pleasing him.

He peered up at the gray sky. "The wind seems to be picking up. I hope it doesn't snow."

Resting her hand on his thigh, she smiled and enjoyed the ride.

When they arrived at Neil's farm, she commented, "The house is finished on the outside. What are you doing today?"

"We'll work on the bedrooms." He locked the wagon wheels and jumped out to help her down.

She saw Tom, Jimmy, Zachary, Roger Sloane and Dave's father, and Neil conversing in the front yard. Roger was a widower with sons who were seventeen and nineteen years old, so they helped with the house too. Jimmy's and Zachary's sons, who were old enough, helped as well. With the thirteen males constructing the house, she figured they should easily have it completed before Christmas.

"I'll miss you." Dave took her hand and gave it a gentle squeeze.

"I'll be nearby," she whispered, grinning. "I'll save you a slice of pie."

"Only if you feel up to making it. Don't strain yourself." He kissed her and walked her to the sod house filled with three women and Jessica's baby girl, Erin. The rest of the children ran around in the yard.

After greeting the women, he leaned over and whispered in her ear, "When this project is done, I intend to spend as much time in bed with you as possible."

In spite of the biting chill in the air, he had her blushing so much that she sweated under her coat. Too shocked to respond, she stared at him as he went over to the other men and started talking to Tom and his father.

Doris chuckled. "Young love. It makes a woman forget everything but her husband."

Breaking out of her trance, Mary quickly closed the front door so the cold air wouldn't cool down the house. She removed her coat and set it next to the others on the chair by the door.

Jessica giggled as she nursed her baby. "You and Dave make a good couple. We do hope that you'll be nursing your own little one this summer. When are you due?"

"August." She glanced at the women and realized Dave's mother and Zachary's wife weren't there. "Where are Mrs. Larson and Mrs. Phillips?"

"Mrs. Larson had to go into town to help Joel get settled in. Mrs. Phillips didn't feel well enough to come out."

Mary nodded. She suspected Mildred's reason for not feeling well had something to do with her arguments with Cassie over the past few days.

"We'll certainly be keeping you in our thoughts and prayers," Doris told Mary.

"My baby's kicking all over the place," Cassie interrupted, her feet plopped up on the bed. She adjusted the bow in her hair and straightened the dress that Mary made for her. "I wish I had my energy, but this little one hasn't let me get it back yet, and I'm already halfway through this pregnancy."

"You might be tired because you don't work." Doris made no qualms about hiding her irritation at the way Cassie had been lying around for the past five weeks. "In fact, I heard the doctor say that if someone gets up and moves around, it improves their ability to be beneficial. I know it seems like a contradiction, but I've found that the more I do, the more energy I have."

"Cassie," Jessica kindly began, "why don't you make the coffee today? All you need to do is boil water, so you won't get too worn out."

Cassie stuck out her lower lip and crossed her arms. "You two have been on my case ever since I married Neil. I think you're jealous."

Doris scoffed. "I can assure you, I'm not jealous. I'm sick of hearing you complain about how tired you are all the time."

"Well, maybe Neil won't let me sleep at night. I am hard for men to resist."

"Oh please! I know how men are. They do it and then they fall right to sleep, especially after a long day of building a house."

"Neil is virile."

"Honey," Doris turned from the pot on the stove, setting her hands on her hips, "if Neil were spending the night amorously involved with you, he wouldn't be wide awake this morning."

Her face flushed with anger. "What are you saying?"

"I'm saying that you're lying. You're not tired, and I've had enough of your excuses. It's time for you to earn your keep. Our men are building you a larger house. The least you can do is make them something to eat and drink."

Cassie jumped off the bed, her nostrils flaring in anger. "I don't need to put up with this in my own home!"

"Are you ordering me to leave?" The woman crossed her arms, as if challenging her.

"I don't need you around if you insist on putting undue stress upon my person. I do have my child's health to think about."

Doris threw the washcloth on the table. "Then I will take Jimmy and my children and get out of here." She quickly said good-bye to Jessica and Mary before she grabbed her coat and stormed out of the house. She yelled to her kids to join her and made a beeline for her husband who looked shocked to see her.

Mary cautiously turned from the window to see what Cassie would do.

Setting her hand on her round stomach, Cassie sighed. "I handled that miserably, didn't I?"

Glancing at Jessica who seemed as if she didn't want to say anything, Mary stammered, "Maybe you should apologize."

Cassie gasped. "You think I was wrong?"

She smoothed her hands on her skirt, gathering the strength for a possible confrontation. "I think that everyone is eager to get the house built so we can go home and rest. It's been a long five weeks, and we've been together almost every day for twelve hours. Given those circumstances, an argument was bound to occur. If you apologize, it can help smooth things over."

Though she opened her mouth, she decided to shut it. After an awkward minute of silence that hung in the air, she relented. "You're right. I suppose I can make coffee."

When she left the house, Mary stirred the rabbit stew and nearly gagged on the smell.

"Morning sickness getting to you?" Jessica kindly grinned.

"It strikes here and there."

"A trick that works for me is to frequently snack during the day. It doesn't matter what you eat as long as it's something you can stand to swallow."

Mary caught sight of the jonnycakes that she made the previous day. She could probably eat one without difficulty. She took a plate and sat at the table, confident that Cassie and Doris would work things out on their own. Taking a small bite, she poured herself a cup of water.

"I also recommend sipping the water instead of gulping it down," Jessica added. She put her baby over her shoulder and patted her back until she burped. "Are you nervous about the baby?"

"To be honest, I've been so busy that I haven't had time to worry, which is good. I don't like to dwell on what might be."

"Good. I have to agree with Cassie that the less stress you're under, the better it is for you and the baby." She smiled. "I'll set Erin down for a nap."

As she set her child on the bed, tucking her in with her shawl, Mary managed to finish the jonnycake, already feeling her stomach settle. "What do you want to make today?"

"This stew is for dinner. Neil seemed to collect a lot of jerky when he was single, so we can make pemmican with that."

"Dave had a box full of jerky when he married me." She chuckled. "Maybe it's a single man's meal."

"It's easy to prepare. You just bite off a piece and go." Jessica got the can of jerky, container of lard, and sugar that rested on the shelf next to the window. "Pemmican is ideal for energy, and it fills the men up for a long time, which is what they need on days like this."

Mary got up from the chair. Deciding she could stir the stew without getting queasy, she lifted the lid on the large pot and inserted a long ladle into it.

"How did you and Tom meet?" She had wanted to ask the question before but wished to do so when no one else was around.

"We met at a barn dance."

"What attracted you to him?" She already knew what attracted Tom to Jessica. Jessica was beautiful.

A smile crossed her lips. "His dancing was awful. The other young ladies refused to dance with him, but I felt sorry for him so when he asked, I said yes." She cocked her head in Mary's direction. "He was so nervous around me. He'd keep stammering and tripping over his feet. I thought it was adorable that someone would put forth that much effort to try to please me. So I ended my engagement to another man and let Tom court me instead."

"I didn't realize you were engaged. Do I know him?"

"He was Peter James."

"Connie James' son?"

"The same." She ground the jerky into a bowl. "He got married and has two children now, so it all worked out. I don't regret choosing Tom. He may stick his foot in his mouth, but deep down, he has a good heart."

"Well, he's certainly proud of you and the three girls."

Jessica looked out the window and frowned.

Curious, Mary ventured a peek through the lacy pink curtains. Apparently, Doris had talked her husband and children into leaving, so that left Cassie crying to the men and children.

"I wonder if they'll believe Doris or Cassie," Jessica murmured.

Mary sighed. "I think they understand that Cassie's made things difficult for Doris. Dave doesn't like her. He says that she takes advantage of me."

A mischievous grin crossed her face. She skipped to the door and opened it a crack so they could hear the conversation outside. Though Mary didn't make it a habit to eavesdrop, she wanted to know what was transpiring in the front yard, so she joined her sister-in-law.

"I don't know why you're being so hysterical," Tom told Cassie as he struggled to hold onto his five and three-year-old daughters who insisted on climbing on him. "I mean, we all heard Doris bellyaching for the past month about how lazy you are. Didn't you see this coming?"

"Leave it to Tom to speak his mind regardless of the consequences." Jessica stifled a giggle so they could hear more of the conversation.

"That is not fair," Cassie protested, her voice shaking. "I'm in the family way. I need my rest."

"My wife needs rest too," Dave snapped.

Mary's eyes widened in surprise, pleased that he spoke up on her behalf.

Tom huffed. "Rest? Just wait until that baby comes out. Babies scream their lungs out all night long. Even when they finally sleep through the night, they follow you all over the place." He motioned to his daughters who tugged on his clothes. "You can kiss your peace and quiet days good-bye."

"It's not a good idea to scare her," Neil argued.

"Scare her? I'm giving her a dose of reality. Why, Doris has nine kids. They range from six to twenty-four. She spent many months in the family way during harvest time and cooked. Jessica is the hardest working woman I know. She juggled two kids, maintained the house, and cared for me when she was expecting Erin. If they can do it, you can too."

"You can't compare me to them." She looked appalled. "I grew up in a city back east. This world is unfamiliar to me."

"Pa," the three year old said.

"Not now, sweetie," he gently warned. "Your pa has a point to make. You remember what I said about interrupting adults." Looking back at Cassie, he continued, "Fine. So you come from back east. My sisters, brothers and I came from there too. My mother worked hard for all of us, just like Doris and Jessica do. Even Mary's managed to adjust to farm life. Why did you come to Nebraska if you couldn't handle it?"

Cassie shot a look at Neil. "Are you going to let him talk to me like this?"

Neil shook his head in irritation. "This discussion isn't necessary. We need to get back to work. Go join the women."

"I can't believe you're defending him."

"I'm not defending anyone. It's already December, and I'd like to get this house finished before it gets too cold to be outside all day. As it is, my feet get numb if I stay in one spot for long."

"Well, I'm sorry I'm inconveniencing you!" Anger dripped from her voice.

"We're building this house for you." He motioned to the almost completed structure.

"I will stay with Mrs. Brown until it's done. I won't spend another night in that dirt box." She pointed to the sod house.

Jessica quickly shut the door. Mary followed her to the kitchen and returned to their work. A few seconds later, Cassie stomped into the house, Jessica's girls at her heels. The girls ran to Jessica while Cassie grabbed her floral traveling bag and shoved her clothes into it.

"I need someone to take me to Mrs. Brown's residence," she ordered once she finished packing. Her back stiff, she stared expectantly at them.

"Uh...I have to ask Dave if I can drive the wagon," Mary reluctantly volunteered since Jessica had to watch her children.

"I'll wait."

Mary didn't realize that convincing Dave to let her take Cassie to town would prove a daunting task, but after five anxious minutes, he agreed and grabbed the geldings from the gated pasture so he could hook them to the wagon. She was secretly relieved to see Cassie stay in town for the next two weeks. Doris, Mildred, and Dave's mother returned, so the remaining time was pleasant.

Chapter Fifteen

It was a sunny cool morning in the middle of March when Mary joined Dave in going to town. She pulled the shawl around her shoulders and enjoyed the wagon ride as he brought her closer to him. Giggling as he sprinkled kisses on her cheek and neck, she hardly noticed the scenery.

When they reached the mercantile, he asked, "Are you going to do any visiting?"

"I would like to see Jenny and Sally."

"I think I'll go check on Joel and see how he's doing." He jumped out of the wagon and jogged to her side.

She accepted his hand as he helped her down. Joel worked for Ralph at the mercantile. She did wonder what he thought of transporting goods to and from the store. She hoped he liked it more than farming.

Dave held her for a moment, seeming to be oblivious to the fact that other people walked by them. "I could give you a ride to Sally's or Jenny's." His breath caressed her ear.

The corners of her mouth turned up. "I can walk there."

"Then can I walk with you?"

"If you want. They live nearby."

He kissed her, making her blush.

"Dave, people are staring," she whispered, though she enjoyed his affection too much to care.

"Oh, then I better stop." He winked. Resting his hand on the small of her back, he guided her to the boardwalk along the street. "I might as well say hi to Sally and Jenny. They are my sisters, after all. Where to?"

"Ever since Sally got the dog, Jenny's been taking Jeremy to her house, so I'd like to go there."

He nodded.

"I'm looking forward to watching the plowing and planting process," she told him as he directed her steps away from a puddle as they crossed the street. "Does everyone get together to help with that?"

"No. I do that on my own. I'll grow some corn and beans this year."

"I'll help you anyway I can."

"I reckon you would do that, but I can handle it." They stepped on the sidewalk, out of the way of the many horses and riders who trafficked the busy street. He glanced at her and smiled. "However, I would love it if you made some of your cookies and pies."

"Don't I do that already?"

"I meant for the main course."

She laughed. "Why, Dave, you are positively evil. I can't neglect making you a proper meal. But I will slip in a couple of snacks for you while you're in the field."

They reached Sally's house and saw Greg and Jeremy playing with the big dog in the backyard.

"You called it," he said. "Everyone is at Sally's." Once they reached the wood fence, he called out to them.

Sally and Jenny immediately stopped talking and ran over to them.

"Mary, it's wonderful to see you!" Sally greeted as she opened the gate. She took her hand and led her in.

"How are you feeling?" Jenny wondered.

"Very well." Mary answered.

Dave cleared his throat. "I'm still your brother."

Sally and Jenny jerked their heads in his direction, as if just noticing him.

"We didn't forget you, David," Sally assured him. "We just wanted to make sure Mary's alright."

He didn't look convinced but grinned at Mary. "And you wonder why I keep saying they're trying to steal you away from me."

"We don't see her as much as you do," Jenny argued. "You get her all to yourself on the farm."

"I've noticed you come by for several visits."

Sally sighed. "You should be happy that we get along with her as well as we do. Some family members don't like each other. Marcia Brock's sister-in-law spreads false rumors about her."

"Poor Marcia. She's a nice woman too," Jenny added.

"Oh, we should see Amanda while you're in town," Sally told Mary. "She has the day off from helping Richard with the customer orders."

Amanda did the paperwork for her husband's business, so she spent most of her time working while her children were in school.

"Mary, I'll be by to pick you up in two hours." Dave paused and asked his sisters, "Is that enough time?"

"Yes. We'll have her ready for you to take back so you can have her all to yourself again," Sally promised.

The women and children went to Amanda's residence, and upon entering the cozy home, Mary caught sight of herself in the mirror. She didn't make it a habit of looking at her reflection. In fact, she did everything she could to avoid it. But today, she noticed something different about her face. It was odd, really. She knew that she hadn't changed, and yet, she had. For some reason, she actually looked...pleasant.

"Mary, are you going to join us?" Sally asked, interrupting her thoughts.

Mary blinked and turned to her friend. "Oh, of course." She nodded and followed her to the parlor where she sat next to Jenny, ate cookies, drank coffee and watched the children play with the set of toys that Amanda's children had outgrown.

When it was close to two hours, Sally announced that they better leave before her brother went crazy searching for his wife. Though she teased Mary about it, Mary sensed that his sister was happy that her brother enjoyed a good marriage.

On their way to Sally's house, a familiar voice called out, "Yoo hoo! Mary! May we have a moment of your time, dear?"

Mary turned her attention to Maureen Brown who waved her hand in a friendly gesture. She sat with Connie, Cassie, and Neil's mother on the front porch of Connie's house.

Mary hesitated to reply since they made it a point to snub Jenny anytime they saw her.

"We'll take the children to the grass over there and let them run around," Jenny assured her, pointing to the park across the street.

"I won't be long," Mary replied before she climbed the steps of the porch.

Cassie and Neil's mother, Gwendolyn, chatted while Maureen and Connie smiled at her.

"Good morning, ladies," Mary greeted.

"How are you doing, Mary?" Connie inquired as she stood up from the rocker. "I trust this pregnancy is progressing well?"

Appreciating the woman's concern, she nodded. "I am fine. Thank you."

"Do you need to sit?" Connie motioned to the empty rocker.

"No thank you."

"You must be having an easier time of it than me," Cassie wearily commented. "I feel like I am ready to pop." She rubbed her large belly.

"We are very excited about the little one," Gwendolyn said and patted Cassie's hand.

"Does someone need something?" Mary looked at Maureen since she had been the one who called her over.

"Oh yes," Maureen said, as if recalling what was on her mind. "There is a banquet to honor women at the church, and I wished to invite you. I was going to come out to your place later today but since you're in town, I figured I might as well ask you now."

Mary shifted uncomfortably from one foot to the other, taking note of Sally and Jenny who inspected the bugs that the boys had picked up to show them. Turning back to Maureen, she replied, "Will they be invited?"

"Well, Sally would be welcome to attend, of course."

"And Jenny?" Despite her best effort, she realized her voice slightly shook, for she knew the question would result in a confrontation.

"Jenny isn't...one of us." The woman's tone remained gentle but firm.

Taking a deep breath and ignoring the pounding of her heart, she countered, "Why not?" She knew the answer but she couldn't bear to see her best friend shunned any longer.

"Do I really need to say it?"

Here goes. She strengthened her resolve and blurted out, "Have you ever done something you regret?"

Maureen appeared surprised by her question. She shrugged. "I suppose I have."

"And I have too. We have all done or said something that we regret. It's just that what we've done didn't result in an out-of-wedlock birth. Unfortunately, we can't change the past, so we are stuck with the consequences of our actions, just as Jenny is." She took another deep breath. "I think that if we are granted grace and mercy in spite of those things, it makes our lives better. I care very much for Jenny, and I know she regrets what she did with Clyde. What else can she do but give Jeremy the best home she can? What good will it do to constantly bring up the past?"

Connie cleared her throat and softly added, "She has lived a respectable life since then."

Maureen's harsh expression changed into a thoughtful one. "I suppose everyone deserves a second chance."

Mary breathed a sigh of relief. She feared they would turn on her and shun her the same way they had shunned Jenny.

The two women looked at each other and nodded a silent agreement that Mary didn't understand until they walked over to Jenny and Sally.

Cassie giggled. "Oh, I just felt the baby kick."

Gwendolyn smiled adoringly at her daughter-in-law. "May I feel him?"

"Certainly."

She chuckled. "He's a strong one alright, just like my son."

"Neil will make a fine father, Mrs. Craftsman. I can't wait to see him holding his baby. Why, it's only two months away before he makes his entrance into the world!"

"What a thrilling experience! I am blessed."

Again, something in the exchange bothered Mary, though she still couldn't figure out why.

"Would you like to feel the baby kick so you know what to expect?" Cassie asked her.

Startled that the young woman even bothered to talk to her, Mary agreed and timidly rested her hand on Cassie's belly. The resulting bump beneath her hand sent a shiver of delight through her. She marveled that she would soon feel her own child move within her. Though she wasn't even showing yet, she knew all was well. She hadn't experienced that certainty with her first pregnancy.

"That's amazing," she whispered, pulling her hand away and subconsciously touching her belly. She couldn't imagine what she would look like when she came close to giving birth. "So, have you and Neil picked out any names?"

"Well, we'll name the baby Neil Jr. if we have a boy and Gwenda, after Gwendolyn," she sweetly smiled at her mother-in-law, "if we have a girl."

"I am honored," Gwendolyn inserted.

"I think that's wonderful," Mary replied.

"Have you and Dave picked any names?" the older woman wondered.

"Not yet. We're waiting until we get closer to the birth."

"I hope all continues to go well for you."

"Yes. Motherhood is a lovely experience," Cassie quickly said. Then she gave a slight pout. "I do worry that the clothes I am sewing for the baby won't turn out right. I fear that I am a miserable failure, and the baby isn't even born yet." She glanced at Mary.

A wave of dread washed over Mary. She knew what Cassie wanted. Had Maureen and Connie stuck around, then Cassie might never had gotten the chance to talk her into making her baby's clothes.

"Oh my dear. That is a problem." Gwendolyn brought her hand to her cheek and shook her head. "Of course, I can buy some blankets and clothes and cloth diapers, but there's nothing like a homemade garment. I wish I could sew something, but my arthritis flares up at the worst times."

Dave would be upset if she agreed to this. Mary anxiously licked her lips. "I hear that Jenny makes beautiful clothes," she quickly inserted before they could ask her to do it.

"That is true. However," Mary's gut clenched as Cassie's pleading eyes met hers, "I do so admire your handiwork. Why the buttons you sewed to expand the waistline as my baby grew was a stroke of genius."

If only Cassie was as easy to deal with as Maureen and Connie were! "Perhaps if I explained to Jenny what you like, then it will be acceptable?" She swallowed the nervous lump in her throat.

"Oh. I...I guess." Her countenance fell as she glanced at her belly and rubbed it.

"Well, I don't wish to intrude," Gwendolyn spoke up, "but Mary, you live closer than Jenny does and it would be neighborly of you to help out. I'd be willing to pay you."

Mary felt like shrinking under the woman's intense stare. She considered her options. She realized that she had every right to say no. Dave spent so much time with her that it wouldn't be easy to sew the clothes without him noticing it, and when he found out, he was bound to be furious. He couldn't stand Cassie, and Mary wasn't particularly fond of her either. But how could she say no when the grandmother of the baby offered to pay her?

Stiffly, she nodded her consent, and as soon as she did, Cassie gave her a detailed description of what she wanted. As she dutifully listened, she could almost hear Dave griping about Cassie using her. And he would be right.

DAVE STOOD OUTSIDE the mercantile with Joel. Leaning against the wooden structure with his hands in his pockets, he waited for the time when he could go to Sally's house. She would be upset if he went to get his wife before the full two hours were up. People strolled past them as they went in and out of the store. Presently, his brother animatedly described his morning of delivering medicine to the doctor.

"The boy dislocated his shoulder while playing a game," Joel stated. "I showed up just as the doctor put it back in place. You should have been there. It was amazing."

He inwardly grimaced. The thought of witnessing that event held little appeal, but he noticed that his brother seemed thrilled by it. "Doesn't Doctor Adams need an assistant?"

"I did see a help wanted sign on his office window."

Nudging him in the arm, he pressed, "Why don't you offer your services?"

"I don't have any experience in the medical field."

"Well, the way I figure it, we all got to start somewhere. Wouldn't you like to accompany him on his errands?"

"I would. That would be more fun that picking up and delivering supplies all day." He rubbed his chin.

"Apply for the position. The worst that can happen is he'll hire someone else."

"Maybe I should." He nodded, staring off into space.

Dave glanced at the clock on the bank across the street. He had fifteen minutes left before he could pick Mary up.

Ralph exited the mercantile and approached them as soon as he saw them. "Joel, I need you to deliver a barrel of pickles to the restaurant."

Joel sighed but politely said, "Right away, Mr. Lindon."

Dave realized, at that moment, that Joel didn't care much for his job. Working with the doctor might suit him better.

Ralph turned to Dave. "That wife of yours is popular with the women. I can't hold onto the potholders, towels, and blankets that she makes. I'm glad you brought more in today. Here's the credit amount due to you and her for making me a nice profit."

Dave took the piece of paper, his eyes widening in surprise.

Joel leaned forward and whistled. "Wow, Dave. Mary is a keeper alright. I never imagined a woman could be as kind and talented as she is. She's kind of pretty too. I hope I get a wife like her someday." He took off his hat and scratched his head. "I can't recall why I thought Cassie was all that great. Mary's much better than her." He placed his hat on his head and looked at his boss. "I'll get the stuff delivered." Tipping his hat to them, he opened the door for an elderly couple before entering the store.

Dave's heart swelled with pride at the fact that people thought so well of his wife. He knew she was special, but it warmed his heart to know others saw it too.

Ralph peered through the window. "I better get back into the store. I see that a couple of people are ready to make a purchase. Saturday is my busiest day."

"Mary and I will be in shortly."

He knew it was pointless to shop until she accompanied him or gave him a list since he usually forgot something they needed. Even though he had ten minutes to spare, he decided to go to his sister's residence. He hadn't taken three steps when he saw Mary appear from the next street. A grin formed on his lips as he picked up the pace.

When he reached her, he gave her a light kiss on the cheek and took her by the arm to lead her to the mercantile. "Did you have a good visit with my sisters?"

"I did."

"I can't believe they let you leave earlier than agreed."

She shrugged. "Mrs. Brown and Mrs. James wished to spend some time with them."

He shot her a curious look, almost tripping on the edge of the boardwalk. "Mrs. Brown and Mrs. James?"

"Yes. They decided to invite them to the women's banquet coming up next weekend. I've been invited as well."

"Mrs. Brown and Mrs. James?" He had to repeat the names to make sure he heard right.

"Yes." She smiled at him. "Are you shocked?"

"Actually...I am."

They waved to Joel as his brother passed them, his face red from the effort of lifting the heavy barrel of pickles. He grunted his own greeting.

"Anyone can have a change of heart," she told Dave once they turned their attention from him.

He began to shake his head when a thought occurred to him. "Did you have something to do with this 'change of heart'?"

Focusing on the ground to avoid stepping into a puddle, she admitted, "I might have said a few words but it was up to them to act on it."

They reached the mercantile entrance, so he held the door open for her.

She stopped in the doorway and glanced back at him. "Do you have something you need to do?"

"No. I already took care of repairing the wagon and making my rounds to the city folk. I'm all yours. Just throw whatever you want to buy into the basket and I'll tug it along."

A worried frown momentarily crossed her face before she shrugged and turned her attention to the inside of the store. He wondered about it, and just as he got ready to ask what bothered her, another customer brushed passed them, in a hurry to get out of the store.

Dave immediately apologized, picked up a basket and followed her while she selected the ingredients she planned to use to make her delicious meals. His mouth watered when he realized she intended to make brown sugar candy.

"Will you and Jasper hunt for meat?" she asked as she selected a meaty soup bone and placed it in the basket. "The stew tastes better with deer or rabbit meat in it."

"I can take him hunting. When do you plan to make the stew?"

"Monday."

"That should give me plenty of time to kill something and get it ready to eat. I'll save any leftovers in the root cellar. We should get salt to preserve it." He grabbed the bag of salt and put it next to the flour.

As they approached the fabrics section in the back of the store, he noticed that her steps became hesitant. Turning to him, she asked, "Would you buy these items and put them in the wagon while I see if I missed anything?"

He thought that was an odd request since she hadn't asked him to do that before but did as requested. By the time he returned, he found her kneeling in front of the buttons.

"I thought you were done making clothes." He knelt beside her and saw that she had a basket full of materials. He smiled, his heart growing warm at the sight of the patterns that suited a baby. "I thought you wanted to wait until you felt the baby kick before making clothes and blankets."

She appeared startled.

Didn't she notice me?

"Oh. Uh...I thought I would keep busy." Her cheeks flushed red and her hands slightly shook as she threw several buttons on the pile of clothing supplies. "Well, that should do it. Let's go." She grabbed the basket and bolted up.

Something wasn't right. He quickly stood up and reached for her elbow to stop her. "You are making clothes and blankets for our baby, aren't you?" His voice remained low so the four customers wouldn't overhear them.

The fact that she didn't answer right away notified him of her intention. Her eyes darted to the two women near them at the stationary display.

"Who else did you run into today?" he softly demanded.

She closed her eyes and exhaled. "Please, Dave, can we discuss this on the way home?"

He gritted his teeth. "No. I won't have her using you again." He forced himself to remain calm despite the anger surging through him. "Put them back."

Licking her lips, she opened her eyes and looked at him. "I don't really have a choice. Mrs. Craftsman was there when Cassie asked and they backed me into a corner. Besides, Mrs. Craftsman offered to pay me."

"You let me deal with them. Give me that basket." He held his hands out, waiting for her to comply.

The moment spanned into what felt like an eternity before she finally gave it to him. He noticed that she dug her fingernails into the palms of her hands while he neatly put the items back to where they belonged. He couldn't believe the nerve of Cassie. As if she hadn't given Mary enough orders! Though Mary insisted she could say no, he didn't see this event happening. He would do it for her.

Standing up and facing her, he realized that she fought back her tears. The anger drained out of him. He took her in his arms and held her against him. "You don't have to do anything you don't want to do. I'll support you, Mary."

She clung to him and buried her face in his shoulder. "I don't like to upset people."

"I know. But you can't please everyone all the time. In the end, you have to do what's right for you." Ignoring the curious stares from the women, he gently kissed her forehead. "Do you want to make the baby clothes?"

"No."

He breathed a sigh of relief. At least he hadn't overstepped his bounds. "I'm your husband. It's my job to make sure people don't take advantage of you. Will you let me do that for you?"

She nodded.

"Where is Cassie?"

"She's at Mrs. James' house."

Wrapping his arm around her waist, he led her outside. Once she sat in the wagon, he told her to wait for him. She assured him that she would, so he left for Connie James' residence.

By the time he stomped to Connie's, he relaxed enough so that he wouldn't yell at Cassie who, predictably, was sitting in a chair. Mrs. Brown, Mrs. James and Mrs. Craftsman surrounded her on the porch. They seemed to adore her. What the attraction to Cassie was, he didn't know, nor did he care to find out. Without waiting for an invitation, he climbed the steps and waited for the young woman to acknowledge him.

Obviously surprised, Cassie and the other women turned their attention to him.

He took their sudden silence as his cue to speak. "Mary won't be making clothes for your baby."

He didn't think it was possible, but Cassie's eyes grew even wider. "I didn't press her to do it. She offered."

Untouched by Cassie's show of sincerity, he continued in a firm voice, "I told her to put everything back. I'm her husband and I'm putting my foot down."

"I must say it is not very neighborly of you to do this," Mrs. Craftsman argued.

"With all due respect, ma'am, it's not neighborly to guilt-trip another woman into making clothes. Mary's already made your daughter-in-law plenty of clothes. She won't be making any more."

"I said I would pay her. Certainly, it is not a crime for a woman to make clothes."

"I made my decision. As her husband, I have the final say."

"Jenny does make some lovely clothes," Mrs. James told Mrs. Craftsman and Cassie. "I'm sure she could use the money."

"She made the banner for the church on Douglas Street," Mrs. Brown added, nodding in agreement. "We'll talk to her about it."

Mrs. James and Mrs. Brown began talking about possible designs for the baby clothes. Mrs. Craftsman reluctantly agreed while Cassie openly cried about how Dave was being mean to her. Rolling his eyes, he spun on his heels and left as the women comforted her. On his way down the front walkway, he bumped into Neil.

Neil paused in mid-step as soon as he saw Dave glaring at him. "Is something wrong?"

"Yes, there is. Mary is not Cassie's personal dressmaker. I caught my wife collecting materials to make your baby some clothes, and it was apparent that she was guilt-tripped into doing it. I refused to let her buy them. Mary's days of doing things for your wife are over. I recommend you have a talk to your wife about not using people. There are people in town who choose to make clothes for a living. Cassie is welcome to their services."

He sighed, his shoulders slumped. "I know what Cassie is doing and I have talked to her."

Neil's contrite response surprised him. "Well, maybe she'll pay attention since I told her too." Dave tipped his hat to him and proceeded down the walkway so he could return to Mary.

Chapter Sixteen

During the second week in April, Joel rode up to the house. Since Mary made it a habit to glance out the window while she cooked, she saw him as soon as he arrived. By the anxious look on his face, she knew that this visit constituted an emergency. She set aside her flour, baking powder and salt so she could rush outside to meet him.

Dave came out of the barn to join her. "What's wrong?" he asked, his eyebrows furrowed with concern.

"Doctor Adams isn't available and Cassie went into labor," Joel anxiously replied. "I've never delivered a baby before. And you delivered Jessica and Tom's girl." He looked with pleading eyes at Mary.

"I'll be right there," she consented and ran to the house.

To her surprise, Dave followed her. Surely, he wasn't going to prevent her from aiding Doctor Adam's new assistant! Joel had much to learn about bringing babies into the world, and she understood the task.

She found her pants from the hanger in the wardrobe.

"I can take you in the wagon," Dave insisted. "You shouldn't be riding a horse in your condition."

Taking her dress off, she hastily slipped her shirt and pants on. "The horse is quicker. Something has to be wrong. She shouldn't be giving birth for another month." She tried to button her pants but her stomach had expanded, making them too tight. She grabbed one of Dave's belts to use to hold them up.

"I don't know." By the tone in his voice, she realized that he worried about the early birth too.

"I'll be fine. You taught me to ride and said I do well on Susannah." She secured the belt so her pants would stay in place.

"What if you fall?"

She glanced at him and smiled. "Or what if Susannah bucks me off?"

His cheeks grew red. "Oh, you figured out what that means."

"It took awhile but the meaning became clear after overhearing some conversations." She took off her shoes so she could put on durable boots and tied the laces.

"Promise me you'll be careful."

Touched by his concern, she kissed him. "I will. I handled the ride to Jessica's when she gave birth. I'll handle this one too."

"Do you need anything?" He looked around the small dwelling.

"No. Cassie has more stuff than we do. I'll use her things. I might stay to clean up. This might be a long process. I can't guarantee when I'll be back."

"I understand that. I reckon Joel can get you anything you need. The doctor should be out soon."

She nodded. "I'll see you when everything settles down. I hope I'll bring good news."

"Don't push yourself too hard."

"I won't."

After another kiss, he saddled Susannah and handed her a leather bag of food.

When she and Joel arrived at the Craftsman residence, he said he'd tie up the horses so she quickly jumped off and ran into the house. She flew up the stairs and found Cassie lying on her bed, twisting in the sheets and groaning. Running over to her, she felt her forehead, reassured that it was cool to the touch despite the perspiration on her brow. Mary hoped the strong chilly wind blowing through the open window would offer some comfort to the laboring woman.

"Cassie," she began, "it's Mary. I'm going to help you through this, alright?"

"Just get it out of me!"

Though Mary hadn't gone through labor, she noticed that women in labor tended to be irritated, so she didn't take offense to the woman's sharp tone. She patted Cassie on the shoulder. "I'll do everything I can to ensure a safe delivery."

Joel bounded up the steps.

Mary hastened out of the room. "Where's Neil?"

He shrugged. "I don't know."

"Have you looked for him?"

"Of course, but it's like he disappeared after he came into town to tell me she was in labor." He looked green when he heard Cassie screaming again. Swallowing hard as he shifted his eyes from Cassie to Mary, he asked, "What do you want me to do?"

She ran off a list of supplies she needed. He nodded and nearly slid down the banister to get them. As she turned to the closet to see if a fresh supply of towels were on hand, she glanced at another bedroom and noticed that Neil slept in a separate room. The baby furniture decorated another room. Was it normal for married couples to sleep in different rooms if they had the room to do so? She thought back to her parents. They had slept in the same room, even when her siblings left to get married. Shrugging, she turned her attention to the closet and sighed with relief as she retrieved a couple of clean towels.

The next two hours tested Mary's patience. Not only did Cassie scream so loud that Mary had to cover her ears, but she found reasons to order Mary around. She would yell out, "Close the window. I'm cold. Open it. I'm hot. The pillow needs fluffing. Get rid of the pillow. It's lumpy. Put it back. I need back support. This cloth is too warm. Get me a cool one to press on my forehead."

During the third hour, Mary urged Cassie to stand and move, supporting the wobbly woman who leaned against her. The exertion of rushing around caused her to feel weary and hot, but she determined to proceed as if Cassie wasn't the most difficult woman she'd ever helped give birth.

"You expect me to walk? I'm in pain," Cassie snapped another hour later, her feet scuffing across the wood floor.

"But the walking will help speed up the process." She quietly grunted in case Cassie complained about that too. Despite the woman's thin frame, it took most of Mary's strength to hold her up. What was taking the doctor so long?

"I don't know how much longer I can bear this," Cassie gasped, clenching her teeth and banging her stomach. "Get out already!"

Startled, Mary held her hands to stop her and brought her back to the bed. "Maybe you should try squatting."

"I'm never having children again. This is it! A baby just isn't worth all this pain!"

She gently urged the groaning woman to squat by the bed and rubbed her lower back. Sometimes rubbing the lower back helped other women in labor, so she hoped it would ease Cassie's discomfort too.

Joel appeared, looking as ragged as Mary felt. "Is there anything else?" He leaned his hands on his knees and gulped for air.

"Is the doctor here yet?" Mary silently begged him to say yes.

"No, not yet. I wish he'd get here. This waiting is driving me insane."

She knew how he felt. Taking a deep breath to settle her nerves, she simply nodded. "Joel, why don't you go outside for awhile and get some fresh air? You can eat some of the pemmican I brought along. We need to keep up our strength."

"Don't you need a break?" He stood up and stretched his back.

She knew he was in no shape to tend to Cassie, so she replied, "Maybe later." She paused before asking, "Did you find Neil?"

"No. But I haven't had much time to look for him with all the things I've been gathering for Cassie."

Understanding that looking for Neil had turned into a lost cause, she didn't ask him to try again. So the father of the baby decided to abandon his wife and child when they needed him. He was even worse than she thought. Keeping her comments to herself, she applied pressure to Cassie's back.

"That does feel better," Cassie admitted between gasps and groans.

Relieved, Mary continued her work.

A half hour later, Doctor Adams climbed the stairs. Mary couldn't recall a time when she was as glad to see someone as she was to see him.

"She's getting close," she reported as he set down his black bag and took off his hat. She continued to knead the muscles in Cassie's back, her hands numb from their efforts to soothe the screaming woman.

"I heard you were good at this kind of thing. Apparently, the tale holds true. Thank you." He turned to Cassie and urged her to lay back in bed, lifted her gown and checked her progress. "She's ready to push."

After Mary propped the pillows behind Cassie so she'd have an easier time pushing, she motioned to the doctor for a moment of privacy with him. He obeyed and followed her out of the room, ignoring Cassie's loud protests.

"Tell me the truth," Mary said. "Is she in danger?" She never assisted in a birth when the woman delivered early, so she needed to be emotionally prepared in case something went wrong.

"No. Everything is going as it should."

His answer did little to assure her. The hesitant look in his eyes alerted her that something wasn't quite right, though there seemed to be no concern to the health of the mother or child.

Reluctant, she followed him back in while Joel resumed his role of fetching things. The next twenty minutes, filled with piercing cries and pushing, came to an abrupt end when the baby came out, crying and kicking.

Mary nearly collapsed with relief.

Cassie limply rested on the bed, murmuring, "It's over. It's over. It's finally over." When the doctor went to hand the baby to her, Cassie shook her head. "I'm too weak to hold her right now. Mary, will you be a dear and hold her for me?"

Stunned, Mary mutely accepted the baby and gave her a quick bath while the doctor tended to the afterbirth. What just happened? Didn't Cassie want to hold her child? Tears formed in Mary's eyes as she swallowed the bitter lump in her throat. Each birth she tended to in the past was filled with glowing faces from new mothers who eagerly held their babies close to their bosoms and showered love on them. It was as if they got their second wind once they heard their babies cry. Even Susannah wanted to bond with her foal.

After she put a cloth diaper on the girl, she wrapped her tightly in a soft yellow blanket. Standing in the room, she didn't know what to do for the sleeping child. The doctor had left so he could discard the newspapers that contained the afterbirth. Biting her lower lip, Mary ventured, "Would you like to see her?"

Cassie kept her eyes closed, as if she hadn't heard Mary's question.

The doctor strode into the room. "Cassie, you did a good job. You and the baby are healthy." He turned to Mary. "I'll take the baby to her father."

Nodding, she handed the baby to him. She cleaned Cassie up and put a new garment on her. The process proved to be a struggle since the woman kept muttering that she felt exhausted. She laid Cassie on the bed and covered her with a clean blanket.

"You have a beautiful child. She has your dark hair. She also has curls." Forcing a laugh, she added, "She looks like a doll."

"I'll see her later. I need to sleep for a moment." Cassie yawned. "Giving birth wears a woman out. I'm glad it's over."

"But it's worth it, isn't it?"

"I'm not having another one, that's for sure." She swept her hair up so the nape of her neck settled on the pillow.

"You're tired, Cassie. You don't mean that." Mary hoped to have a house full of children, just as Dave's parents and her parents had.

"Mary, would you close the window? I'm cold." She closed her eyes and settled into the bed, ready to sleep.

Stunned, it took her a good five seconds before she obeyed the request. Despite the fact that her sweaty clothes stuck to her from her day's efforts, a shiver crawled up her spine. An image of Cassie flashed in her mind, and she didn't see any beauty in it. Quietly making her way down the staircase, she wanted nothing more than to return home and make love to Dave. When they came together, she felt safe and loved, things she desperately needed at the moment.

As Joel got ready to hand her the reins of the horse, she overheard the doctor and Neil arguing over the baby.

"I'll be right back," she told Joel.

She entered the barn. Neil's slurred speech testified to his drunken state, and the bottle of whiskey in his hand only condemned him further.

"I'm not holding it," Neil spat at the doctor. "I don't want any part of it."

Furious, she stormed up to Neil and slapped him. The bottle fell out of his hand and shattered on the ground. He brought his hand up to his face, appearing mortified.

"Hold your daughter!" She stared at him, daring him to argue with her.

Yelling and swearing, she expected, but his bitter laughter confounded her. He flung his arms out and replied in words she could barely decipher, "That's not my child." He pointed to the baby and laughed again. "The doctor can vouch for me on that."

Doctor Adams sadly nodded, still holding the infant in his arms.

Neil put his hands on his head. "Guess when I found out? Last month. Cassie told me she married me because she was expecting and needed to save her reputation. So there you have it. My perfect marriage, my perfect wife, my perfect life... They're all lies. Deception! And I'm stuck until I die."

She glanced at the rosy-cheeked child who did look big for being born early. "Do you think his mother will suspect the baby's bigger than she should be?" she asked the doctor. The last thing the child needed was to be shunned because she was conceived out of wedlock.

"No," the doctor said. "It's been years since Gwendolyn's been near a newborn." His expression revealed his solemn sentiment over the events that transpired before their eyes.

Taking a deep breath, she looked at Neil who seemed coherent enough to understand her. "You listen to me," she ordered in a firm tone she wasn't accustomed to using. "That baby needs someone to love her. She didn't ask to come into this world, but now that she's here, you have a responsibility to her, regardless of whether or not you were tricked into marrying her mother. This child did nothing wrong." She took a deep breath to steady her emotions. "Cassie just turned her back on her, Neil. Don't you do that too. Be a man and be this child's father because, like it or not, you are the only one she's got." Her voice cracked and tears filled her eyes. She anxiously blinked, making them slide down her cheeks. She continued, "She needs someone who's going to take care of her! She deserves that much." Her sobs prevented her from saying anything else.

What she said that changed Neil's mind, she didn't know, but his face softened before he turned to the doctor. "I'll take her."

"I'll make you a pot of coffee so you can clear your head." Mary, still crying but glad he listened to her, passed Joel on her way out of the barn and returned to the house to perform the task.

Within the next hour, the coffee sobered Neil so he could adequately care for the child. His mother arrived shortly after that, ecstatic, and held the baby, already filling in as the loving grandmother. Mary was secretly relieved. At least someone would love the girl.

Assured that they weren't needed anymore, the doctor, Mary and Joel rode off the property on their horses. Finding no solace in the horrific experience, they spent the ride to her farm in silence.

Dave stepped out of the barn when they approached the building. "Did the mother and child make it?"

The doctor nodded. "They are doing well."

Dave didn't look convinced as he helped Mary down from Susannah. His face held the unspoken question that she knew she would have to answer, but for the moment, she needed him so she wrapped her arms around him and softly cried on his shoulder.

"We better head back," Doctor Adams told Joel before he nodded to Dave and turned his horse to ride off the property.

Joel quietly followed his employer.

Chapter Seventeen

Mary determined to put the painful experience behind her. Upon visiting her after a stop at the Craftsman farm in the first week of May, Maureen and Connie notified her that Neil had become an attentive father, which Mary was glad to hear. Mary did express her surprise when Maureen told her that Neil named the girl Emily, for she recalled that Cassie intended to name her after Neil's mother. Maureen just shrugged. "He decided that he liked the name Emily more." Mary nodded and went about her business in serving them coffee. To her surprise, she found that she enjoyed meeting with them. Maureen, as it turned out, wasn't so bad after all.

The next week, Mary rested in her chair making a dress to better accommodate her expanding belly. Being in her fifth month of pregnancy, she became accustomed to feeling the baby kick, but it seemed that as soon as she went to get Dave, the baby stopped being active. She waited for a minute and the baby continued its relentless assault on her belly. She decided to press her luck.

Excited, she jumped out of her chair, accidentally knocking it over. Letting it lay on the floor, she ran to the door and flung it open just as Dave was about to enter the house.

"Oh!" she gasped in surprise, setting her hand over her heart.

"Is something wrong? Should I get the doctor?" he asked, looking concerned.

"No, I'm fine," she immediately assured him. "The baby's kicking! It's amazing, Dave. Here." She took his hands and placed them over the bulge in her lower abdomen.

He patiently waited for the child to move. When it did, a wide smile spread across his face. "That's really something, isn't it?" His eyes met hers. "Is it uncomfortable?"

"No. It's strange but in a wonderful way. I don't think I can adequately describe it."

"It must be one of those things you have to experience."

She nodded and the baby kicked again.

He laughed. "He's pretty active in there." He pulled her against him. Bending his head, he kissed her, his joy causing her heart to race.

How wonderful it is to be happy with the impending birth of a baby, she thought, her mind unwillingly shifting to Emily's birth. Forcing aside the stab of sorrow, she wrapped her arms around Dave's neck and returned his passion with her own.

When their kiss ended, he continued to hold her, seeming to enjoy their embrace as much as she did. The door, still open, gave her a view of Jasper as he barked at the squirrel which darted across the grass in front of the fenced pasture where the horses ate grass. She sighed and clung to her husband. His body, strong and solid, could also be tender and warm. So much like his personality.

He eased from her and seemed to be ready to speak but stopped. He took a long look at her, as if he were seeing her for the first time. "You know, Mary, you're the most beautiful woman I've ever seen."

She started to correct him since she knew that, though she might have some pretty features, she couldn't possibly be beautiful, but there was something in the way he smiled at her that caused her to consider his viewpoint. And in doing so, she realized that he was telling her the truth. When he looked at her, he saw a beautiful woman. Beautiful Mary Larson. For the first time in her life, she believed it. His love made her beautiful.

His fingers brushed her cheek. "I love you, Mary," he softly confessed.

"I love you too, Dave." Her heart swelled with joy. Not only did he find her desirable but he loved her. It was more than she dared hope for when she came to Nebraska, and here she was with a remarkable man who treated her better than anyone else ever had in her life.

Cupping her face in his hands, he kissed her again, this time deepening it.

Wishing to act on her powerful emotions, she asked, "Do you have to go back to the field right now?"

"I can hold off for a little while. Do you need me for something?"

She licked her lips. The last time she initiated lovemaking, he told her to put on a nightshirt. Of course, that was different. She didn't go through a miscarriage this time. Forcing aside her nervousness, she decided to kiss him, hoping he would correctly interpret her invitation.

As it turned out, he didn't require further motivation. He shut the door and threw his hat aside. He reached for her and drew her back to him. She couldn't think of a better way to solidify their love than to come together in the most intimate way possible, for she truly felt closer to him than before.

Once they shed their clothes, he whispered, "Wait." He stepped back from her. "Let's not rush it. It seems that you don't get to enjoy this as much as I do."

"I enjoy it," she argued, her hands resting on his strong biceps.

"I know you find it pleasant but there's greater satisfaction to be had. I'm not sure how to get you there, so you'll have to guide me."

She realized what he was talking about. He wished for her to 'come with him' and often asked her what he could do to make it happen. "I've already told you that I don't know what to do."

"Let's take the time to learn, together." He led her to the bed and asked her to lay on the mattress.

She did as he requested. Without prompting, she widened her legs enough so that he could kneel between them. Her heart fluttered when she looked up and noted the adoration in his eyes. A quick glance at his arousal revealed how much he desired her. No longer feeling insecure when she was naked before him, she obeyed his request when he asked her to close her eyes.

"I'm going to start from the top and work my way down," he whispered as his hands progressed from her feet, up her legs, over her hips, across her arms and to her shoulders. "I want you to tell me what you like, and if you like it a little or a lot. Alright?"

She nodded. Subconsciously holding her breath, she waited for him. She jerked when he brought his warm lips to hers.

He lightly chuckled. "I thought you didn't scare easily." He didn't wait for her response. Instead, he kissed her again, lingering at her mouth.

Her body relaxed against the bed. Her breasts pressed lightly against the muscles in his chest, his fine hairs slightly ticklish. He smelled of the earth and hay, though he was clean. The time spent outdoors made him seem powerful, and she savored the taste of him on her tongue. Deepening the kiss, he allowed his hand to travel down her jawbone and down her neck.

"Do you like this?" His breath caressed her ear.

"Yes."

She sharply inhaled as his mouth followed his hand, causing her breasts to press firmly against him.

"You feel so good," he told her.

Her body trembled as he slowly cupped her right breast with one hand. His mouth moistened her left breast, his tongue teasing the rose bud that seemed more sensitive than it had any of the other times he did this. She reasoned that closing her eyes heightened her other senses, touch being one of them. She shivered beneath him.

"Are you chilly? I could get the blanket."

She ran her tongue along her dry lower lip. "No. It's what you're doing. It feels nice."

"Do you want me to continue?"

"Yes." She almost felt embarrassed to even request for him to gratify her since she was used to considering his needs rather than hers.

Without protest, he obeyed, switching breasts so both could receive his care. She groaned as she became aware of the familiar ache between her thighs. She was no stranger to the sensation, but she hadn't been able to satisfy it in the past. Perhaps that would soon change. After a time, the mattress shifted under her, notifying her that he changed positions. He had been laying partially on top of her before, but now he sat between her bent knees.

"You're lovely to gaze upon," he said, his voice hinting at his wonder of her naked form.

His words eased her inhibitions to enjoy what he was doing to her, and she desperately wanted to enjoy it. As he gently stroked down her belly, he paused for a moment over the new mound their baby created with its growing presence. A feathery kiss touched it, and she smiled at his love for his child.

"Isn't it amazing that our coming together to share one of life's most beautiful moments can result in this?" he asked in wonder.

"It is." Her voice came low. She doubted he heard her. This was how it should be when a child was created. There should be joy, laughter, and anticipation.

When he massaged her thighs, the ache deep within her increased. She shifted her hips upward, silently encouraging him to touch her in her most sensitive region. Her flesh craved his attention. Centering on the tender lips beneath the triangle of brown curly hair, he caressed her with his fingers.

She gasped. "I like that."

Her breathing suddenly seemed irregular though she gave it no more thought as his fingers played with her entrance. She groaned again, louder this time, and wiggled closer to him. To her surprise, he stopped. Ready to see what stopped him, her question didn't even make it to her lips when she felt him shift so that his mouth could kiss her where his fingers had been.

She shuddered in excitement, her heart pounding frantically in her chest. "Yes. Do that." She moaned, wrapping her legs around his shoulders.

He began his sweet torment with kisses. A swell of desire coursed through her body, suspending her in a dreamlike state of urgent need.

"You're beautiful, Mary," he told her.

Then he proceeded to taste her wetness. Her ragged breathing made it difficult to tell him how much she was enjoying it, but he seemed to understand since he didn't budge from his position. His fingers worked their way around his mouth and when he found the center of her desire, she grabbed his biceps and said, "There. Touch me there. And I do like it when your fingers are in me."

Returning to his sitting position, he slid one finger into her. Murmuring his appreciation for her inviting wet warmth, he slid another finger in and stroked her. He pressed his thumb to her anxious bud. "You like this?"

"Yes," she replied in astonishment. He hadn't handled her this way before, so she was shocked that it felt intensely pleasurable. "Yes. Oh Dave, yes." She grabbed the blanket beneath her, clenching it in her fists as she became aware that the sensations pouring from her core was quickly building towards something even more wonderful.

"That's it." He sounded excited as he rubbed his thumb faster over her. "Come to me, Mary."

Beyond caring about anything but how remarkable he was making her feel, she whimpered his name, her back arching and hips pressing closer to him. When her climax came, she felt as if her core shattered in a million pieces, her narrow channel clenching fast and hard around his fingers. Suspended in the moment, she didn't understand what happened when he moved his fingers out of her, knelt over her and guided himself into her. Her muscles renewed their strength, squeezing him as he slowly moved inside her. His thrusting only served to prolong her release.

His hands clasped hers as he kissed her, his tongue intimately tasting hers. Breathing hard, he broke the kiss and promised, "It's going to be like this every time we come together from now on."

She knew he would make sure that happened. Marveling that he loved her enough to give her the gift of sexual fulfillment, she tightened her hold on his hands to signal her gratitude. Her legs firmly gripped his waist and her body hummed with satisfaction as he found his release.

Afterwards, sated and in each other's arms, they expressed their love for one another and discussed possible names for their baby.

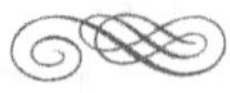

THE END OF MAY BROUGHT sunny and bright weather. The wind gusts cooled the air so that Dave could spend time preparing the fields for planting his corn and beans. He looked forward to the day when he could teach his child about farming. A son would learn more than a girl, of course, but he planned to give her the basics in case she married a farmer.

He whistled a happy tune as he hooked Lewis and Clark to the wagon. When Mary emerged in her light blue dress with small white flowers on it, he couldn't help but smile. There was something primitively satisfying in seeing her belly filled with his child. He sauntered up to her and took the pile of baby clothes, bibs and towels that she made for Neil and Cassie's daughter.

Once he heard what happened on the day of Emily's birth, he didn't argue with Mary when she said she wanted to make the girl some clothes. He realized that if she didn't make the baby clothes, then the child most likely wouldn't have anything to wear since Neil's finances suffered after hail damaged most of his livestock. Dave knew it would take time before Neil got ahead.

"You have a good heart," he softly told her as he placed the neatly folded bundle of items on the seat. Turning to her, he took her hand and helped her onto the wagon. "You move well for an expectant woman."

"My stomach isn't that big yet," she replied.

He hopped up next to her. When she placed the clothes and blankets on her lap, he eased her close to him. Something changed in their relationship after he told her he loved her and realized she loved him too. Their bond strengthened. He hadn't thought such a thing was possible but it was. Her face glowed, and he suspected it had more to do with their love than with the impending birth of their child. *She is beautiful. I don't know why I only thought she was pretty a few months ago.* Shrugging, he realized that it didn't matter now.

He picked up the reins when Jasper ran over to them and barked. Grinning, he gave her a knowing look. "I reckon he wants to tag along."

She giggled as the dog bounced around the wagon wheels. "He did run down a rabbit and deer the other day. He deserves a reward for his hard work."

Unable to argue with her logic, he waved the dog up. Jasper didn't need further prompting. He leapt onto the wagon and rested beside Mary's feet. She reached over and patted him behind the ears. The contented whimpering and wagging tail notified Dave that the dog couldn't be happier if he had gotten a bone to bury in the yard.

Chuckling, he urged the geldings forward. They spent their time during the ride to town engaging in easy conversation, though the dog was too engrossed in the changing scenery to pay them any mind.

"Are you sure Cassie will be at Mrs. Brown's?"

Mary nodded. "When Jenny and Sally came over yesterday, they said that Maureen and Connie invited Jenny, Cassie and Gwendolyn to Maureen's house to discuss what songs to sing at the fair."

"You did Jenny a lot of good. I'm glad you stood up for her like you did."

"How did you find out?" She turned to him in interest.

He grinned wickedly. "I have my sources." Actually, Sally bragged about it to him.

"Well, Jenny will be singing a solo. I heard her and she does have an angelic voice. I can see why the preacher was anxious to have her join the choir."

"You've got quite the reputation in town. Everyone praises you wherever I go."

Her cheeks flushed a pretty shade of red. She reached for his hand and squeezed it.

Once they arrived at Mrs. Brown's residence, he asked her if she wanted anything from the mercantile.

"Jerky," she replied.

His eyebrows furrowed. "Didn't we just get a whole box of that last month?"

"I know but we're out."

"What do you do? Inhale it?" he joked.

She shrugged. "I can't explain it."

"I understand. It's one of those cravings women get when they're expecting." He gave her a quick kiss. "I'll be sure to pick some up."

"You won't forget?"

"No. I promise."

How could he forget? He'd seen more jerky in their house for the past two months than he could recall seeing in his entire life. To her credit, she continued to make him her delicious meals so he didn't have to eat it, which was good because if he had to eat another piece of the tough meat, he'd gag on it.

Running to her side of the wagon, he assisted her down from it. He halted the dog when it attempted to jump down to go with her.

"Let him join me," Mary protested, placing her hand on his arm. "He brightens Connie's face. She's been through a rough time since her husband's death."

"Are you sure? I didn't think Mrs. Brown cared for animals."

"She changed her mind once Connie laughed at some of the antics he and her grandchildren pulled last time he came out, and Connie is watching her grandsons today."

He nodded. "It's your call. Jasper," he told the dog, "you got lucky this time."

The dog panted his agreement as he anxiously jumped down and stood by Mary's side.

Dave chuckled. "I've never seen a more loyal dog."

She told him good-bye and kissed his cheek before turning to the house where Maureen waved her in.

He went to the mercantile, making sure to add a box of jerky to the list, and visited Joel at the doctor's office, pleased to know his younger brother was enjoying his job.

"I'm going to post an ad for a wife next year," Joel said as he organized the new shipment of medicine in the doctor's office. "What was it you asked for to get Mary out here? I know Neil requested someone pretty. He didn't specify anything else."

"I asked for a woman between the ages of seventeen and twenty-two who could cook, sew and clean. I also said I wanted someone who wasn't afraid of doing chores on the farm, such as milking a cow." It was what he told Mary when he pretended to write an ad, so it was just as good as the truth.

"Oh, I'm not a farmer, so I should ask for all the things you did, except instead of farm chores, I'll have to request someone who understands that I'll be busy with the doctor, no matter what time or day it is."

He grinned and patted him on the shoulder. "Sounds good." He glanced at the clock on the wall. "I reckon I should get over to Mrs. Brown's. I'll see you around."

Joel waved his good-bye while Dave exited the small building.

As he stopped the wagon in front of Maureen's house, Jenny ran over to him, Jasper loudly barking at her heels. "Dave! Thank goodness, you're here!"

He tensed, already not liking the way this conversation was going. "What's wrong? Did Mary…?" He couldn't bring himself to finish the sentence. *Please, don't say she lost the baby.*

"She's missing." Jenny grabbed his hand and practically dragged him off the wagon. "Cassie wasn't feeling well, so she and her mother-in-law took Emily back to Mrs. Craftsman's house. About ten minutes passed and Mary realized Cassie left Emily's clothes behind, so she went to take them to her. Jasper tagged along, but when he came back, Mary wasn't with him and he wouldn't stop barking. We've been to Mrs. Craftsman's house, but she says that Mary never showed up. Dave, I'm afraid! Where would she go without telling anyone?"

He forced his mind off the dog's insistent barking so he could fully comprehend everything his sister was telling him. A different type of panic washed over him. "Didn't anyone see her in town?"

"We've been looking everywhere from here to Mrs. Craftsman's place, and the only thing we've come up with is that she passed by the firehouse. It's as if she disappeared into thin air." She clenched her hands together and winced.

He racked his mind over the possible places Mary might go but his mind came up blank. When the dog's barking rattled his nerves, he shouted, "What?"

Satisfied, the dog turned in the direction where the businesses were.

"That's the way to Mrs. Craftsman's," Jenny noted.

Dave stared at the dog for a long moment. Did Jasper know what happened?

As if to answer his unspoken question, the dog barked.

"Alright," he said. "Where did she go?" He figured he didn't have anything to lose in asking the animal for help.

Jasper quickly turned his attention to the road in front of him and ran down the street. Unhooking Clark, Dave got on the horse and followed him to the train station. Why would she come here? As far as he could tell, she didn't have a reason to enter this place again.

Jumping off the horse, he hastily tied him to the post before running after Jasper into the building. Despite people's protests that a dog shouldn't be allowed loose there, he joined Jasper who anxiously barked at him.

A quick look around the establishment notified him that Mary wasn't anywhere in sight. In fact, the place seemed deserted, except for a dozen patrons who lingered about, watching him and shaking their heads. Ignoring them, he looked at the dog. "What are you trying to tell me?" *As if the dog can talk!* With a wave of his hand in the animal's direction, he approached the ticket counter.

Surprisingly, this simple action caused the dog to stop his insistent barking. The only indication that something was wrong was his whining.

Forcing aside the knot in his gut, he patiently waited for the agent to take care of the two passengers in front of him. When his turn came, he asked the old man if a woman meeting Mary's description bought a ticket. *But why would she do that? She didn't say any-thing about leaving.*

The man shook his head. "I'm sorry, sir, but no one I sold tickets to today matches that description."

Shooting an anxious look at Jasper, he realized the dog honestly believed Mary boarded a train. The animal wasn't capable of making that up.

"Are you sure?" Dave pressed, unwilling to leave his spot.

A man grumbled behind him but he didn't care. *This is my wife we're talking about!*

"I haven't dealt with any expectant women today," the man behind the counter insisted. "I assure you, sir, that she hasn't been here."

"But my dog wouldn't lie."

Jasper's barking resumed, and this time, he bounded towards one of the station managers.

Without thinking, Dave followed him.

The middle-aged bearded man turned to the dog. "Sir, we don't allow dogs in the train station," he grimly told Dave, his hands behind his back.

"I apologize. He's helping me find my wife."

The man raised an eyebrow. "Well, he found me instead."

Pushing aside his agitation for the man's sarcasm, he asked, "Have you seen a woman with long brown hair, greenish blue eyes, and a fair complexion? She's also in the family way."

Dave briefly noted that Jenny and Sally hurriedly made their way over to him as soon as they entered the station.

"I see a lot of women with brown hair and white skin," the man responded. "Can you tell me what she wore?"

Of all the details that could slip his mind, it would be her clothes. "A dress."

The man frowned.

"I don't know. I don't pay attention to what she wears."

Jenny quickly stood between them. "Mary is wearing a light blue dress with a matching bonnet. The dress has a white floral design on it."

"The white flowers are small so they might look like dots," Sally added.

"Oh, her." The man's eyes lit up with understanding. "She wasn't feeling well."

Dave felt as if the wind got knocked out of him. Did something happen to the baby? Did they have to take her to the doctor?

"So you've seen her," Sally prompted.

"Yes. Her husband said she fell asleep because she wasn't feeling well. He paid for their tickets and took her on the train. I helped him with their travel bag and even brought him a glass of water to give her when she is well enough to drink something."

"I'm her husband!" Dave didn't mean to shout but the fact that another man pretended to be him infuriated him.

Jenny rested her hand on his arm to silence him. "Are you saying that she was unconscious?"

"That's exactly what I'm saying. He carried her on the train." The man eyed Dave warily, as if expecting another outburst from him.

None came.

"Can you describe him?" Sally asked. "What did this man look like?"

"He was about six feet tall. He wore a dark suit with a gold pocket watch. He had dark brown hair, was clean shaven, looked strong. He was obviously a farmer."

"Neil Craftsman." Dave gritted his teeth. Why would Neil kidnap his wife?

The man shrugged. "I didn't concern myself with his name."

"Can you tell us where they went?" Sally persisted.

"The ticket agent can do that for you. We have a record of all our purchased tickets." He pointed to the ticket counter.

"Thank you," Sally said, smiling.

Dave turned to stomp over to the counter when the manager cleared his throat. "What?" he snapped, not in the mood for small talk. He had to find his wife, for goodness' sakes!

"That dog has to go," the man dryly replied.

"I'll take him out," Jenny offered. "You two find out where Neil took Mary."

He didn't wait for further instructions. He directed his attention to the ticket counter, determined that he would find Mary and bring her home. *If Neil hurts her, I'll...* His first thought was to kill him. His second thought was to arrest him. He shook his head. He could deal with Neil later. Right now, he had to get Mary.

Chapter Eighteen

Mary slowly came to consciousness, aware that she was lying on her side on something that moved. Caught between sleeping and being awake, her mind processed her surroundings. Did she hear people talking? No, there wasn't anyone nearby making any sounds, nor was it completely silent either. The familiar chugging of a train greeted her ears. How did she get on a train?

Her eyelids fluttered and she cleared her throat to rid the lump in it. For some reason, her body hovered in her dreamlike state, unwilling to cooperate with her mind's command to sit up. She struggled to open her eyes so she could see what happened to her. Certainly, she slept on a bench instead of the seats. The fact that she remained out of sight of other passengers gave her enough strength to open her eyes.

She gasped when she saw Neil sitting across from her, calmly reading a newspaper as if they made it a habit of riding together, in a sleeping car no less! The blood rushed through her like wildfire, her pounding heart momentarily blocking out the sounds of the train.

Neil casually lowered the paper and peered at her. "Oh good. You're up." He folded the paper, set it on the seat beside him, and went over to her.

Too weak to stop him, she let him help her sit up. A feeling of dread came over her. He could do anything he wanted to her and she couldn't stop him! Shifting away from him, her side hit the wall, trapping her in. Shooting a quick glance at the door, she knew that her tired body wouldn't make it out in time. Her slow movements hindered her from any immediate action.

"What are you doing?" she finally asked. If only she could remember how she ended up here!

"I've seen the error of my ways, Mary." His excited expression scared her. He clasped one of her hands in his. "When you came to Nebraska, you came for me. You didn't come for Dave Larson. You answered my ad, and I was too stupid to realize what I was giving up. But that's all changed now. Things can go back to the way they were meant to be. We can be together. It'll be like the past year never happened."

Despite the fact that she shook her head no, he continued in a boyish manner, "I know I was a fool, but I'll make up for it. You'll see. I'll treat you like you were made to be treated. You don't have to worry about Cassie. I don't love her. I love you."

"No, Neil. You can't do this."

"I can. It's so easy!"

"But I'm married and you're married." For emphasis, she added, "We're married to different people."

"That doesn't matter. We'll have to leave Omaha, but we can start a new life somewhere else. We'll just tell people that we're married. If you want, we can find a judge to make it official."

"That's against the law."

"No one has to know. We'll find a remote area so no one will discover the truth. Out west, it's easy to hide."

Struggling to process the nightmare she found herself trapped in, she tried to recall what led her to this moment. She carried clothes. She thought she heard a sound from an alley, so she turned and the next thing she knew, Jasper barked and someone covered her mouth. She recalled the sweet smell on the cloth. Was it chloroform? That would explain her exhaustion.

"How did you get me on the train?" she demanded. Didn't anyone notice him carrying her on board?

"I covered you in a large coat and claimed you were my sick wife. The train employee didn't recognize you when I showed him your face, so it worked out."

Her strength began to return. She placed her free hand protectively over the movement in her belly. Despite her dry throat, she said, "I'm carrying Dave's child."

To her dismay, he smiled. "I already know that, and I'm prepared to raise that child as my own. You have nothing to worry about. We'll just tell people that your husband died and we married to give your baby a good home."

"What about...?" She almost said 'your daughter' but stopped.

"Emily is right over there." He pointed to the baby that slept in a bassinet. "I couldn't leave her with Cassie. She doesn't care if Emily fares well or not. You'll care for her much more."

"But..." She felt overwhelmed.

"You want to know how I managed to get Emily here without my mother knowing about it? I told her that I meant to take Emily for a walk. I took her to this train and settled her in this car. I paid a nice old woman to watch her while I went to get you."

Glancing out the window, she felt her apprehension grow with each mile the train traveled west. "Neil, I love Dave. I don't want to leave him."

"Give it time. You'll love me too. It will work out, Mary. You just wait. I'll work hard and make a good home for you and the children. I will do right by you. You don't have to worry about anything. I have the details all taken care of."

Mary knew arguing with him at that point wouldn't do her any good. He had too many regrets to listen to reason. As he sat by her, excitedly explaining his plan, she made her own plans to get back to Dave as soon as possible.

When Emily woke up, Mary helped him take care of her. She sadly noted that he had a supply of bottles and goat's milk. Cassie wouldn't even breastfeed her own child? Though Mary wished she could detest Neil for abducting her, she felt sorry for him instead.

After Emily ate, he said, "Come on. Let's get something to eat. You need to keep up your strength, especially since you're eating for two."

Realizing that she might find an opportunity to escape, she nodded and followed him to the dining car. He held Emily during their meal. Mary barely tasted her food. In fact, she could only manage a couple of bites. She kept staring out the window at the rolling landscape, hardly aware of the people chatting at their own tables. Her mind raced with possible ways she could get off the train without him noticing her.

Neil carried on the conversation, either not aware of her silence or talking because of it. "I could only pack one traveling bag. We'll worry about clothes for us when we reach our destination. It'll be rough at first but I can work as a farmhand out west. I heard that help is sorely needed in Washington. Fortunately, I have experience taking care of cattle."

With each minute that passed, her heart squeezed tighter. She had to think! How could she get away from him?

"We're going to be happy." He smiled at her, rocking Emily in his arms. "I know you'll have to adjust to our new life together, so I'll be patient."

Taking a deep breath, she ventured, "If you wish to find another woman, surely, you can find one better suited for you. I am plain to look at." She hoped the reminder would bring him back to his senses.

"It's funny but I can't remember why I ever thought that. You're actually pretty."

She sighed. She spent her entire life praying someone might find her attractive, and now that she succeeded, she wanted him to find her as repulsive as he had when they first met. Her fingernails dug into the palms of her hands, a subtle action she carefully hid under the table.

Think. Think. Think!

She decided to reason with him. Tracing her lower lip with her tongue, she nervously began, "Neil, think carefully about what you want to do. There are people in Omaha who will miss us. Your mother loves you and Emily."

"I know. She's a good woman. It won't be easy to leave her, especially after my father's death."

Grasping onto that straw, she added, "You're her only child, and Emily is her only grandchild. Granted, she's not related to her by blood, but your mother doesn't know that, and there's no reason that she should ever know it. And no one has to know about this either. If you're afraid I'll embarrass you by telling others what happened, I won't. I can keep a secret, and there won't be any ill feelings between us. I will still help out with Emily when I can."

Softly smiling at her, he replied, "Your heart is what endears people to you. You're worth leaving all of the people and things behind. I didn't know your value before, but I do now. I won't ever forget."

Don't panic. Think! Glancing at the uneaten food in front of her, she asked, "What about Dave? You were devastated to learn that Emily isn't your child. Wouldn't it be wise to let Dave know his baby?" When he hesitated, she continued. "We can't do anything about the past. Things have turned out the way they did for a reason. It's not up to us to know why, but I do believe if we do what is right, then good will come from it."

He shook his head. "You and I being together is the right thing to do. That's why you answered my ad. I'm the one who messed things up. I readily admit my guilt. I am sorry for my mother and Dave, but we should have done this to begin with."

Clenching her dress in her sweaty hands, she forced her expression to remain calm. "It won't do anyone any good to dwell on regrets. The best thing we can do is focus on the future."

"Which is what we're here to do."

Talking sense into him wasn't working, so she needed to pray and act. Patting her belly, mindful of her baby's kicks, she asked, "May I be excused to take care of a personal need?"

"Of course."

To her dismay, he placed money on the table to pay for their bill and accompanied her to the group of lavatories at the end of the car. She reluctantly went to the restroom before she joined him in returning to their sleeping car. Her plan to find the conductor and ask for help had failed. Did Neil intend to follow her for the duration of their trip?

How could she get away from Neil?

She spent the rest of the day sitting stiffly beside him on the bench that could be pulled out to a bed. He maintained his distance, which she silently thanked him for. The only man she wanted to touch her was her husband.

When nightfall arrived, she helped him settle Emily down to sleep. She knew that the girl would wake up in the middle of the night for another bottle, but Emily might sleep long enough to give her a chance to escape. Neil slept on the berth above her fold-out bed. Once everyone settled and Neil's snores assured her that he was unconscious, she slid out of her bed, grateful the chugging of the train muted her movements.

Just as she reached the door, Neil stirred.

"Mary, are you up?"

Realizing he couldn't fully see her in the dark, she immediately stepped towards the bassinet. Clearing her throat, she answered, "I thought I heard Emily whimper."

To her surprise, he leapt out of his bed and stood next to her, checking on the baby. Resting his hand on the child's head, he breathed a sigh of relief. "I worried that this trip would upset her, but she seems to be handling it well."

She nodded. "I must have imagined I heard her." Quietly, she returned to her small bed and forced her agitation aside.

The farther west they traveled, the more anxious she grew. Closing her eyes, she pretended to fall back to sleep, hoping Neil would resume his snoring soon. After what seemed like hours, he finally slept.

Slowly getting out of bed, she tiptoed to the door. Pausing with her hand on the handle, she nearly jumped out of her skin when someone knocked on the door. Emily immediately woke up and began to cry. Out of instinct, she rushed to the child and held her close.

Neil stopped her on the way to the door. "I got it. You should keep quiet and stay out of sight." He took the crying baby from her.

Shocked, she immediately stepped into a corner so whoever was on the other side wouldn't see her.

Neil opened it. "May I help you?"

Emily had settled down, though her eyes inspected her surroundings.

The man on the other side of the door, said, "My wife and I are in the car next to yours and she has a bit of motion sickness. Do you have anything that may settle her stomach?"

Mary noted Neil's shoulders relax. She walked up to the two men and said, "I know some ingredients you can mix into a drink to help her." An idea sparked in her mind. "I'll need to find an employee to get them and I'll mix the drink if you'd like."

"I would be very much relieved if you would, ma'am," he readily agreed.

Neil put his hand on her arm before she could race down the corridor. "Actually, it might be best if he gets the ingredients."

"I don't mind doing that." The man waited for her to speak.

Her hope fading, she gave him the list of ingredients and he ran off to gather them.

"I better calm his wife." She quickly braided her hair which had become disheveled while she had lain in bed.

Neil grabbed a bottle, filled it with goat's milk, and followed her to the next car.

She did feel disheartened that she lost her chance of escaping for the rest of the night since it would soon be dawn.

Neil sat on the bench across from the woman who laid down, moaning and holding her stomach.

Sympathetic, Mary grabbed the cool washcloth beside the ill woman and put it on her forehead, hoping it would ease the symptoms. "Your husband said you're experiencing motion sickness. I do know how to rid you of it. As soon as he returns, I'll make you a drink and you must drink all of it. I know it'll be difficult but I promise you'll feel better in ten minutes."

The middle-aged woman nodded. "I'll do anything you want."

Neil quietly sat, feeding Emily, while Mary made small talk with the woman, hoping to take her mind off the severity of the pain.

As soon as the man returned, she made the drink. The woman grimaced with each gulp she took. Mary smiled encouragingly to help her finish it. Just as she predicted, the woman felt like her normal self in a matter of minutes.

"I don't know how to thank you," her husband said, relief written across his face. "Poor Lois has never been on the rails before, so we didn't know this would happen."

"Gary worries about me." She offered him a warm smile. "We'll be married for twenty-five years in three weeks."

"I'm more in love with her today than when we first met." His lips curled upward. "I don't know what I'd do without her."

"We see that you have a little one." Her eyes darted to Emily. "But you are expecting?" She looked at Mary, not hiding her wonder.

"Her husband passed away, so we recently married. My wife died as well," Neil quickly lied.

"How sad. Fortunately, you have each other to get you through it. Gary and I have seven children and nine grandchildren. We feel very blessed. I'm sure when you're our age, you'll feel that way too."

Mary tried to speak but with Neil carefully watching her, she realized it wasn't the time to do so. Instead, she politely smiled and listened as Lois and Gary told them about their marriage, sadly wondering if she would ever see Dave again.

Don't think like that! Of course, I'll see Dave again. I'll escape. I just have to wait for the right time. Patience.

MARY DIDN'T SLEEP AT all that night. Despite that, she anxiously waited for the chance to escape. During a late lunch, she found that opportunity. Neil decided to leave her alone in the dining car so he could change Emily's diaper.

As soon as he was out of sight, she jumped out of her chair and raced through the exit of the dining car. She hurriedly made her way through the aisles, ignoring people who she accidently bumped into as she approached the conductor.

"Sir!" she called out before he had a chance to turn from her.

His eyebrows raised, he waited for her to reach him.

"I need to get off the train at the next stop. Can you help me?"

He took a good look at her and examined the piece of paper he held in his hands. Glancing back up, he asked, "Are you Mary Larson?"

"Yes." She gave a brief look behind her, relieved that Neil remained busy with Emily.

"Your husband, Dave Larson, has been looking for you." He hesitated before continuing, "Did you intend to run away from him? He hasn't been mistreating you, has he?"

"Oh no. Dave is most kind to me. I want to go back."

"So a man by the name of Neil Craftsman abducted you?"

"Yes. I don't wish to be here."

"I've been looking all over for you. When I went to check Mr. Craftsman's sleeping car, no one was there."

"He took me to the dining car."

"That explains it. The station manager notified my supervisor that Dave is on a train following us. I just got this message a short while ago, so I didn't even know about this yesterday." He slipped the paper into the breast pocket of his uniform. "I will escort you off this train at the next station and we'll get you two back together. We'll have to apprehend Mr. Craftsman too. I'm going to tell my supervisor I found you. I'll be back. Just sit tight."

Grateful, she sat in the empty seat he offered her. Her heart raced with the knowledge that she would be returning home to Dave. Overwhelmed with the swell of emotions coursing through her, she focused on taking deep breaths so she wouldn't burst into happy tears. Instead, she stared out the window at the mountains, eagerly waiting for sight of the next train station.

As businesses and houses began to pop up along the way, her anticipation caused her to fidget in her seat. All she wanted to do was get off the train and feel Dave's arms around her, keeping her safe.

A sudden movement next to her made her gasp. Directing her attention to the distraction, she nearly cried with alarm when Neil sat next to her. Surely, the conductor would return soon and keep her from continuing on the train with the man beside her.

Neil held a sleeping Emily in his arms and sighed in despair. "You must love him."

Knowing he talked of Dave, she held her tongue.

"We'll arrive at Salt Lake City, Utah within the half hour. I'll see you off the train and pay for your ticket home."

Shocked, she could only manage a weak response. "You're letting me go?"

He nodded. Giving her a repentant look, he explained, "The couple we talked to last night have the kind of love that you and Dave share. If Cassie loved me as well as you love Dave, I'd want her to return to me. And if the roles were reversed...if you had married me and Dave took you away from me, I'd want him to come to his senses and let you come back." He shrugged, apparently finding his words hard to say. "I was selfish. I've been selfish my entire life. It's time I owned up to my actions and accepted responsibility for them. I deserve what I got when I married Cassie. Dave's a better man than I am. I can't think of anyone who deserves you more than him. You two do well together. I'm sorry, Mary. Do you think you can forgive me?"

She smiled sympathetically at him. "Yes. Of course, I forgive you. And thank you for letting me go back."

He sadly smiled in return. "I'll always regret not being as smart as Dave was on that day you arrived in Omaha. But I do have Emily. Maybe that is worth being married to Cassie. And there is my mother to consider. I am all she has in her old age."

"I'm glad you have them. Your mother speaks well of you. As for Emily, she's in good hands with you. There's more to being a father than getting a woman in the family way."

The conductor returned, ready to speak to Neil. Mary knew he meant to be harsh with her captor, so she quickly intervened and informed him that they resolved the matter and she would wait for Dave's arrival.

"Nonetheless, I will remain with you until you are reunited with your husband." He shot Neil a wary look before sitting in the row in front of them.

"I will gather the traveling bag," Neil told her. "I'm going to face the consequences of my actions, no matter how unpleasant."

Once they disembarked, the station manager stayed by her side the entire time. "Do you want to notify the police about this?" he asked while Neil stood at the ticket counter to buy tickets back to Omaha.

She shook her head as she watched him hand the ticket agent some money. An overweight man following two young chatty women momentarily obscured her view of him, but the slump in his shoulders spoke volumes of how much the past year changed him. He was no longer the arrogant, self-seeking man who took one look at her and told her that her coming to Omaha had been a wasted trip. If only Cassie had been the woman he assumed she would be. If only he had fathered her child. If only Cassie cared that she had a child. There were too many if only's, and despite everything he did to her over the past year, Mary mourned for him.

Later that afternoon, as she sat with the station manager, the train pulled in and she jumped up, gripping the skirt of her dress. Passengers filed out of the doors. A young couple with two young rambunctious children looked relieved to be at the station. "I'm not doing that again," the man grumbled as they passed her. A young woman squealed with delight and raced by her so she could hug her mother. The station quickly filled with patrons who hustled about their business, making Mary reminiscent of the day she met Dave.

As soon as she saw him, she rushed to him. She knew he was coming for her but seeing him there spoke of his love more than his words ever could. He looked at her in time to open his arms and wrap her in a big, warm hug. His passionate kiss revealed how much he missed her.

"Oh Mary," he whispered in her ear, still holding her tightly to him. "I didn't think I was ever going to see you again. I-" His voice choked, preventing him from speaking further. He buried his face in her neck.

She felt moisture on her skin and realized that the thought of losing her made him cry. Closing her eyes, she held onto him, oblivious to the activity around them.

A minute passed before he asked, "Did Neil hurt you?"

Noting the sudden anger in his voice, she hurried to assure him, "No. I'm fine. He realized that I wanted to be with you and agreed to let me go."

"I need to have a few words with him, and it won't be talk meant for a lady. Will you stay here and wait for me?"

Her eyes darted to Neil who sat on a bench, cradling Emily. "Don't be too hard on him. He did come to his senses in the end."

He didn't respond. Turning from her, he approached Neil and with all the people laughing and talking around her, she couldn't make out what he said. *It's just as well. I don't really want to know.* After a couple minutes, Dave returned to her and took her hand. She couldn't tell how he felt since his face was unusually expressionless.

"He won't be bothering you anymore," he said, serious but relieved. He squeezed her hand. "Let's get something to eat and then board the next train home."

She nodded. After the long ordeal, she leaned against him as they walked to the restaurant.

IN MID-AUGUST, MARY gave birth to Isaac, saying that his name meant laughter, and since marrying Dave, she had a reason to laugh because she not only loved her husband but he loved her too. Dave agreed to the name as he held his son with a deep sense of love and pride.

In late September, while they ate breakfast, she finally showed him a letter her parents wrote. Though she showed him the ones her sister Grace sent, she didn't show him any from her parents. He let the matter go, figuring she had a good reason. In this particular letter, her parents congratulated them on their son and expressed their hope to visit them before Thanksgiving. She gasped in surprise when she read their statement saying their new grandson had to be "adorable" because she was pretty.

"They never called me pretty before," she said, glancing up at him from the vanilla stationary.

"Well, we'll have to correct them on their thinking," he replied after he swallowed his coffee. "You're not pretty. You're beautiful."

On this day, they went to his parents' farm to help with the harvest. After Mary and Isaac joined the women, he joined the men and boys who were old enough to chop corn. He picked the row between Tom and Jimmy and got to work cutting down the stalks with his reaper.

"It feels strange without Neil pitching in at the harvest," Tom commented.

"What made you think of him?" Dave wondered.

The last person he cared to dwell on was Neil Craftsman. He forgave the man but didn't want to have anything else to do with him. Neil stopped planting crops and focused on bettering the quality of his livestock, so he didn't join in the harvest, which was fine with Dave.

Tom shrugged as he threw his stalk on the pile in his row. "I don't know. I guess I recalled this time last year when we were out in the fields and he and I had that conversation about having daughters. I bet he's come around to seeing things my way now that he has Emily to look after."

"Neil's done a lot of changing," Jimmy replied. "And growing up too. I haven't caught a stray animal on my property in months."

Dave had to admit it was nice to no longer rope cattle and horses for the man.

"Dave," Tom began as Dave chopped down a stalk, "how did you luck out with a boy?"

Dave shrugged. "Because I was meant to have a boy. You have girls because you were meant to have them."

"What's your fascination with having a boy anyway?" Jimmy wondered.

Tom loudly sighed. "I want a boy who can protect my girls. I can't be there all the time to watch over them. If they had a strong brother, men will think twice before taking advantage of them."

Dave threw his stalk on his pile and shook his head. "Aren't you forgetting Richard's nine-year-old boys, Mark and Anthony? There's also Greg, Jeremy, and my son. Your girls have five male cousins to rush to their defense."

Suddenly, Tom's mood brightened. "You know, I never thought of it that way. Their cousins will want to protect them. And Richard's boys are older than my girls. What a relief!"

Jimmy chuckled. "I'm sure your wife will agree."

They continued their work until Doris chimed the supper bell.

Rather than sitting on the ground as he usually did with the other men, Dave slipped into the house where the women scrambled around the children to bring portions of the meal to the men.

Grinning when he noticed that Mary was alone in the kitchen cutting an apple pie, he wrapped his arms around her and kissed her neck.

She gave a startled shriek before she burst out laughing. "Dave, that's not fair. You scared me!"

He softly laughed. "Will you save me a slice?"

"Don't I always?"

"You do. I'm just hoping you won't forget."

"You're the one with the memory problem, not me." She turned to him and gave him a peck on the cheek.

Realizing they had the moment to themselves, he pulled her against him and deeply kissed her, taking in the mouth-watering scent of apples and cinnamon. She felt wonderful, and he found himself anticipating nightfall.

"I do love you, Mary," he whispered in her ear.

"I love you too." Her arms tightened around him.

He reluctantly released her when he heard the voices of his mother and Jessica as they entered the house.

"So that's where my son disappeared to," he said.

His mother cradled the baby in her arms. "You can't deny a grandmother the joy of holding her grandchildren. Little Erin is already walking away from me." She pouted and looked at Isaac. "Babies don't wait long before they run off."

Mary giggled and turned back to the pie resting on the table in front of her.

Dave ruffled his son's fine blond hair and kissed the top of his head.

Isaac cooed at his father.

"I love you too, little one." Standing up straight and glancing Mary's way, he said, "I reckon I better get out there so I can eat that piece of pie."

"I'll bring it right out," she promised.

Once he settled between Tom and his father, the men commented on how lucky he was to be guaranteed a slice of Mary's pie as she brought it out to him. There never seemed to be enough slices for everyone.

"What can I say? I got lucky when I married her," he innocently told them before taking his first bite.

Watching her return to the house, he considered that he was, perhaps, the luckiest man in the world to have married someone with the inner and outer beauty of Mary Peters.

Don't miss out!

Visit the website below and you can sign up to receive emails whenever Ruth Ann Nordin publishes a new book. There's no charge and no obligation.

https://books2read.com/r/B-A-MDLI-CTEHC

BOOKS 2 READ

Connecting independent readers to independent writers.

Did you love *Eye of the Beholder*? Then you should read *A Bride for Tom* by Ruth Ann Nordin!

Tom Larson is having trouble finding a wife, and Jessica Reynolds decides to help him overcome his awkward and clumsy manners so he can attract women.

Read more at https://ruthannnordinauthorblog.com/.

Also by Ruth Ann Nordin

Husbands for the Larson Sisters Series
Suitable for Marriage
Daisy's Prince Charming

Marriage by Arrangement Series
His Wicked Lady
Her Devilish Marquess
The Earl's Wallflower Bride

Marriage by Bargain Series
The Viscount's Runaway Bride
The Rake's Vow
Taming the Viscountess
If It Takes a Scandal

Marriage by Deceit Series
The Earl's Secret Bargain
Love Lessons With the Duke

Ruined by the Earl
The Earl's Stolen Bride

Marriage by Design Series
Breaking the Rules
Nobody's Fool

Marriage by Fairytale Series
The Marriage Contract
One Enchanted Evening
The Wedding Pact
Fairest of Them All
The Duke's Secluded Bride

Marriage by Fate Series
The Reclusive Earl
Married In Haste
Make Believe Bride
The Perfect Duke
Kidnapping the Viscount

Marriage by Necessity Series
A Perilous Marriage
The Cursed Earl

Marriage by Obligation Series
Secret Admirer

Marriage by Scandal Series
The Earl's Inconvenient Wife

Nebraska Prairie Series
Interview for a Wife

Nebraska Series
Her Heart's Desire
A Bride for Tom
A Husband for Margaret
Eye of the Beholder

Pioneer Series
Wagon Trail Bride
The Marriage Agreement
Groom for Hire
Forced Into Marriage

Wyoming Series
The Outlaw's Bride

The Rancher's Bride
The Fugitive's Bride
The Loner's Bride

Standalone
A Deceptive Wager
An Earl In Time
Her Counterfeit Husband

Watch for more at https://ruthannnordinauthorblog.com/.

About the Author

Ruth Ann Nordin has written over 100 books, most of them being Regencies and historical western romances. As fun as writing is, she has also learned that time with family and friends is just as important. She has also learned that writing for passion is the best reason to write since it is what sustains an author's work for the long haul. That's why she's been able to keep writing for as long as she had. It's hard to believe she started out in ebooks back in 2009. How time flies.

Read more at https://ruthannnordinauthorblog.com/.